DEPRAVED

THE DEVIL'S DUE (BOOK 1)

EVA CHARLES

QUARRY ROAD PUBLISHING

- Murphy Rae, Cover Designer
- Dawn Alexander, Evident Ink, Content Editor
- Nancy Smay, Evident Ink, Copy and Line Editor
- Virginia Tesi Carey, Proofreader
- Lisa LaPaglia, Evident Ink, Proofreader
- Faith Williams, The Atwater Group, Proofreader

For more information, contact eva@evacharles.com

Created with Vellum

For Veronica, who believed I could write something different, and gently nudged me to do it. Your insight, unflappable demeanor, and friendship are the beacons in my little corner of the literary world. The light is dim without you.

He was her dark fairy tale and she was his twisted fantasy and together they made magic.

— F. Scott Fitzgerald

A NOTE FROM EVA

Dear Readers and Friends,

Welcome to a new chapter in my writing career! If you have read and loved The New American Royals, please be aware that you are no longer in Meadows Shore. In fact, you have veered far, far, off the path. Depraved is as sinful as those are sweet.

JD, the anti-hero, is complicated and flawed, perhaps irreparably flawed. I'll leave that for you to decide. You will either love him, or hate him, but he will not leave you untouched.

Depraved is romantic suspense that ventures into the shadows, places where real evil lurks. Those who are sensitive to dark storylines, please proceed cautiously.

Now that I've warned you away, I'll share a secret. Of all the characters I've written, JD is my hands-down favorite. I hope you love him, too!

xoxo

Eva

PROLOGUE

My name is JD Wilder, and tonight my father will be elected president of the United States. Satan himself will occupy the Oval Office for the next four years. There have been others, all compelling imposters, but Damien Wilder is the real deal.

As for me?

I'm the devil's spawn.

1

Gabrielle

"Ughhhh!" I whack the edge of the frozen laptop. "Why won't you behave tonight?"

"Can't beat those things into submission. I've tried."

An ominous chill raises gooseflesh, as I struggle to make sense of the voice. *It can't be. It just can't be.*

Can it?

Curling my fingers into the leather blotter, I lift only my eyes, peeking carefully over my lashes. A tremor builds as the animal filling my doorway comes into focus. Long and lean, a broad shoulder braced against the wooden frame, his right hand buried deep in the trouser pocket of a trim navy suit.

My heart bangs furiously on my chest wall, as though fighting to escape. Like the rest of me, it wants to run and hide. But this is *my* office. *My* hotel. And I will not be cowed by JD Wilder.

Ever again.

I try to summon some anger so my voice won't wobble. My

lips part to speak, but my mouth is dry, my tongue rough and heavy, and the words don't come.

"The hotel is stunning," he drawls, in that seductive baritone he uses to charm and cajole. "The photo layout in *Charleston Monthly* doesn't do it justice. You've done a hell of a job with the restoration."

His tone rankles me. Arrogant? Condescending? I'm not sure. But the annoyance stiffens my backbone, and allows the words to flow freely.

"How did you get in here?"

He says nothing.

"I'm sure you didn't come by after all these years to admire the hotel. Especially tonight. I'm surprised you're not at Wildwood Plantation, celebrating. Or commiserating."

With two long strides, he eats up the space between us, bringing the dark, musky scent of sin with him. When I dare to blink, my eyes flit to the starched white collar grazing his neck. It makes a sharp contrast to a jaw that hasn't seen a razor in days.

We peer at each other across the desk. It's awkward and uncomfortable. And dammit, my heart hurts. Just a little.

"It's been too long," he murmurs.

I lower my eyes to ease the discomfort, but his hands are there. Large and forbidding, splayed on my desk with both thumbs hooked under the carved lip. Skillful hands that probed and teased, wakening my flesh with a practiced touch. Luring me into dark, dreamy corners where there was only pleasure—until there wasn't.

I look away, my eyes searching desperately for a place to land. Somewhere safe that won't dredge up painful memories. But there's no eluding him. No escaping the flood of emotion that took hold of me when he entered the room.

When I glance up, his jaw is set and his eyes dilated, as though they haven't grown accustomed to the dim light in the room. Or maybe he's remembering the white-hot nights, too.

The heat creeps up my neck, and I push the salacious thoughts away, focusing instead on how out of place his callused fingers look against the polished mahogany. But there is little reprieve for me.

"Gabrielle." My name glides off his tongue, as though he speaks it all too often.

I don't give him the satisfaction of looking up. I will not do it. He had my rapt attention once, and I'll be damned if he gets it again. Without even a cursory glance in his direction, I lift the stack of papers in front of me and bounce the edges off the desktop, again and again, until I'm satisfied each sheet has fallen into line.

"I have a business proposition for you."

A business proposition? After all this time? I don't buy it. Not for a single second. "I'm not interested."

"You will be."

"Not a chance."

How did he get in here? Georgina locked the door to the suite when she left for the day. I heard the lock catch. I know I did. "I'm still wondering how you obtained access to a private area in my hotel. Breaking and entering might be business as usual for you, but security is no small matter for me."

He steps back and lowers himself into a chair directly in front of the desk. The rich wool fabric stretches taut over his thighs, hugging the thick muscle like a second skin. I feel a small unwelcome pang between my legs. The barest of sensations. But *God help me,* it's there.

For a fleeting moment, I consider calling security. I want him gone, right now, before—

"Hear me out."

"You can't possibly have time for this tonight." I roll back the chair and stand to signal the discussion is over, but he doesn't budge, not even when I start around the desk to see him out.

Anyone else would take the hint. But not JD. Yes, he knows I want him to leave. He just doesn't give a damn.

"I need you to go."

He doesn't blink, but his eyes travel over me in an all-too-familiar manner, before settling on mine. His gaze is steely. I suppose it's meant to make me heel. If so, he'll be disappointed. I'm not the love-struck teenager he coaxed into doing *anything* and *everything* he wanted. She's long gone.

"It wasn't a suggestion, Gabrielle. I might have phrased it politely, leaving you to believe there's a choice other than to listen, but it's not at all what I meant. You *will* hear me out. Sit."

Sit? The hell I will. "I am not a dog. And I prefer to stand, thank you."

"*Sit* down."

I'm torn. There's a small part of me that's curious, and a larger, saner part that wants to throw him out of my office before he utters another word. But above all else, what I want is to lash out and defy him. I want it with every living, breathing cell in my body.

But I don't kid myself. What I want is of no consequence. I've known JD my entire life, and he's not going anywhere until he has said everything he came to say.

I edge my backside onto the corner of the desk—*surely this qualifies as sitting*—and pull back my shoulders with my head high and proud. Only the fingers twisting in my lap hint at how anxious this man makes me.

"I'm sitting. Get on with it."

He says nothing.

JD plays a wretched little game when he wants the upper hand—which is pretty much all the time. He doesn't talk. He just observes and listens with the utmost patience, absorbing every nuance, every stutter, every tic of his victim's unease. He's cool and calculating, like a chess master, or a predator preparing to swoop in for the kill. When he decides you've suffered enough, he speaks carefully. It's mesmerizing to watch, unless you're the one caught in the cross hairs. I witnessed it dozens of times when we were younger, but even so, it's my undoing now.

He runs a thumb across his full bottom lip, arching a single disapproving brow at me.

I don't care. The extra height gives me confidence and helps me feel in control. But it's an illusion. And I know it.

"Your father took a loan from me. A loan he'll never be able to pay back."

"*What?*"

He might as well have said Martians landed on the Flag Tower at the Citadel, and they're occupying downtown Charleston as we speak. The idea of my father accepting a loan from him is *that* preposterous. "I-I-I don't believe you."

He says nothing.

How could my parents go to *him* without first talking to me? They weren't privy to any of the ugly details, but they know he hurt me. Yet, they went behind my back, told *him* things they kept from me, and took *his* money without a single word about it?

I struggle for composure, trying to make sense of why my parents would possibly go to him for money. I can't come up with a single thing.

I glance at him. He's watching from the catbird seat, waiting patiently for me to make a wrong move, say the wrong thing, so he can pounce. I imagine him backing me into a corner, swatting with his oversized paws like a big tomcat, toying with me until his hunger consumes him. Then devouring me in a single bite.

Gabrielle, get a grip. Do not let him do this to you.

I take a few calming breaths.

"My mother's very sick." It's the only reason I can come up with, but it doesn't make much sense. "If they needed money, they would have come to me." *Yes, of course they would have come to me before going to JD.* "I can't imagine why they'd go to you without talking to me first."

"And what would you be able to offer them?"

You smug bastard. "I own the hotel. I—"

"Oh stop. You don't have a prayer of coming up with the kind of money they need. You took every cent of equity out of this place to renovate and get it open. You're in debt over your head."

"You don't know a damn thing about me or my hotel."

"I know everything I care to know."

His voice is low and gruff, the sound achingly familiar. A small tug at the base of my belly fuels the anger and confusion.

"What do you want?"

JD leans back with an elbow draped casually over an arm of the chair. He deliberately brushes a piece of lint from his trousers before answering, as though even the most inconsequential matters are more important than responding to me. "I'll get to that soon. First, let me fill you in on what's happening with your mother."

"What do you mean, *fill me in* on what's happening with my mother? What's going on with my mother?" *Lower your voice, Gabrielle. The hotel's filled with guests.* But right now, all I really care about is my mother.

"She's in good hands. Your parents left the city last night to get a second opinion about your mother's illness."

"They said they were going to the beach for a few days to spend some time alone before she begins treatment." Anger. Betrayal. Fear. Swirling and twisting until they're indistinguishable. "She already had a second opinion. Two additional opinions," I choke out.

A lump gathers in my throat as I remember those appointments. How the doctors explained everything in excruciating detail. Painting a vivid picture of the disease and how it would progress. It was sobering—for me, for my mother—but especially for my father, who would do anything to change the course for her. *Anything.* Including making a deal with the devil, it appears.

"She had an appointment with a world-renowned immunologist today. He's running some tests and is likely to confirm the diagnosis, but he might have a more promising treatment to offer that'll give her more good years."

"Where are they?" And why didn't they tell me any of this?

"It's up to them to tell you where they are. They don't want to give you false hope in case the long-term prognosis doesn't change. Your mother insists on keeping you in the dark until they have more information."

I swallow my pride, and like a big, tasteless wad of chewing gum, it catches at the back of my throat going down. My parents are still keeping vital information from me as though I'm a child. It never changes. "They don't want me to know about any of it. Yet here you are."

"I have it on good authority the appointment went better than expected."

"So much for privacy laws."

The smallest of smiles plays on his lips, but his eyes don't twinkle. "Your mother will talk to you when she's ready."

"She'll talk to me now." I reach over and grab my cell phone off the desk and call my parents, but it doesn't go through. I text them, but the messages aren't delivered.

"You won't be able to reach them, Gabrielle."

"I don't care how powerful you think you are, even the president himself doesn't control the damn cellular network." My voice is full of bravado, but in my heart, I know there's very little the Wilders don't control. Especially now, with DW a presidential candidate.

I lean over the desk, pick up the landline, and dial my parents' number from memory. I still can't get through. Panic begins to fill my chest, squeezing and tightening until it's difficult to breathe.

"Don't underestimate me, or my reach. There's no end to what I can make happen if it suits me."

A myriad of emotions roll through me, breaching the dam I

painstakingly built in the last fifteen years. Pushing and pushing against the walls until there is nothing standing between visceral emotion and him. "I hate you."

My voice is raw with the hurt and betrayal he's dredged up. I don't want him to see the vulnerability, but I can't stop myself. "It wasn't enough to break my heart, to humiliate me and rub my nose in it. *No.* You won't be satisfied until you've taken everything."

Pain flashes in his eyes like a bolt of lightning slicing through a dark, empty canvas. I see it. It's there for just a brief second and then it's gone. But I'm certain it was there.

He's a heartless bastard and you are a fool, Gabrielle.

He crosses one leg over the other, an ankle resting on a knee. "Your parents can't afford the treatment." The tip of a long finger traces the inner seam of his shoe, gliding through the ridge where the soft cordovan leather meets the sole. "It's considered experimental even though they've had some success with it. Insurance won't cover any of it."

"When did you get to be such an expert on a rare autoimmune disease? And exactly why did you lend them money?"

"Before I agreed to pay for the cost of your mother's treatment, along with all their living expenses while they're away, I did some research. I don't throw around money idly."

He's calm, and I'm feeling just short of hysterical. I want to shake him. "*Why?* Why did you agree to help? What could you possibly want from them?"

He doesn't speak for at least a full minute, maybe more. It feels like hours slip away while we stare at each other. With each passing second, the silence grows louder until it shrieks like a banshee heralding my demise. This will not end well for me. I can feel it in my marrow, and the wait is excruciating. "What do you want?"

He doesn't answer right away, but when he does, it sucks all the oxygen from the room.

"You. I want you."

I wait for the punch line. Maybe a cruel laugh, and him to tell me I'm not fit to carry his trash to the curb. And I wait. Surely, I misunderstood. But one look at his stony face and I know there's no misunderstanding.

"*Me?*"

His gaze is penetrating. "I say what I mean, and I mean what I say. Always have. Nothing's changed."

Maybe he's not talking about sex. Maybe I've let my mind run away. Maybe he wants to use the hotel for some half-cocked scheme. Maybe. Maybe. Maybe.

"What do you want from me?"

"Whatever itch I need scratched."

Whatever itch I need scratched. Sex. He wants me to be his plaything. His whore.

My knees tremble until they can no longer support my weight. I grip the edge of the desk, and slump into the chair beside him. I'm done. It's been a long, trying day, and he's beaten what little fight I had left right out of me. I can't bear to hear any more from him. From the man who once professed his love for me. From the man who promised to protect me from all the evil in the world.

The room whirls, and a sour taste tickles my throat. My face is damp and clammy, and I can't decide if I'm going to vomit or faint first. Gripping the sides of my knees, I lower my head between my legs to stop the spinning.

He curses, and I hear the echo of my name and the faint rustle of his trousers, but it all seems so far away. I don't know how long I'm hunched over before he crouches next to me and pulls back my hair with a long, gentle sweep. "Take small sips," he instructs, wrapping my fingers around a paper cup.

I sit up slowly and do as instructed. Small sips until the nausea subsides and the room stills again. JD sits beside me, his chair angled toward me, assessing quietly while I pull myself together.

"Do you need to lie down?"

I shake my head and swallow the last drops of cool water, staring into the empty cup as though I might find some wisdom there.

"You want me? For—sex? You can't. Can't possibly. After all these years, why me?" I'm rambling. Barely managing choppy fragments between the short pants. My mind can't process any of this. Or it won't.

"It means exactly what you think it means."

I look up at him. He's tapping his fingers on the arm of the chair, his gaze devoid of any compassion. I search frantically, but can't find a single shred of decency anywhere in his face.

"But why me, JD?" My voice is louder now. Stronger. My thoughts more coherent. "Of all the women in Charleston. Of all the women who stalk your every move like you're a goddamn rock star. Why does it have to be me?"

He slides his wrist along the chair arm, as though he's polishing a scuff from the exposed wood. "Opportunity. Never been one to pass up a good opportunity, especially when it falls into my lap." His icy eyes meet mine. "Maybe I want something familiar. Or maybe I like the challenge. Take your pick."

He's not joking.

I'm stuck in his trap. Snared without a single hope of freeing myself. My pulse pounds loudly in the silence while I search for an escape. "I'm engaged," I plead. It's a lie, but I'm desperate.

"*Pfft.* Engaged. Don't go there. Just don't."

I start to argue it's true, but I don't bother. It won't take much for JD to figure out that Dean and I broke up. Gossip travels through Charleston like a tiny hamlet. In a matter of days, everyone will know.

There's no way my father would have agreed to terms remotely like this. He would never do that to me. But JD is manipulative and cunning, and I wouldn't be shocked if he managed to trick my parents. I grip my seat and push out the words. Mentally preparing myself to be ripped apart. "My father agreed to this?"

Please say no. Please. I fill my lungs and hold the breath while waiting for an answer.

He looks aghast. "Don't be ridiculous."

I slowly release the breath, and relax my hold on the chair. "Then why are you here?"

"I'm not interested in his money."

"This has nothing to do with me. It's between you and him."

"Not anymore."

"What if I don't—agree to your terms?"

"I turn off the tap, and your mother doesn't get access to the beneficial treatment."

My hand instinctively flies to my mouth to cover a gasp. Of all the terrible things he's said today, this stuns me most. "Even you wouldn't be that spiteful. Not to my mother. You wouldn't."

"Don't underestimate me." He sits back in the chair, lifts his chin, and stares straight into my eyes. "I would hate to see her suffer. Your parents worked for my family for a long time. As far back as I can remember. They were always good to us, especially after the accident. But business is business."

2

Gabrielle

B*usiness is business?* His cruelty re-energizes me.

"Is that what you think? Is that how you think about life? About relationships? It's all transactional? God help you."

"I've never been a fool who turns to God for help."

No, JD doesn't believe in God. Not after his mother died. Praying to God is for the rest of us foolish mortals. I tuck a loose curl behind my ear, plotting a way forward. "How much does he owe you?"

"After all is said and done, I expect it will end up to be somewhere in the vicinity of three hundred and fifty thousand dollars. That's a conservative estimate. It could be more."

I gasp at the sheer magnitude of the number.

He's right. There's not even the slightest possibility my father will be able to repay him, and I'm not sure I'll ever be able to either. Certainly not in cash. "This will take some time, JD. I'll need a week. Maybe a month. Add additional interest to the debt. I don't care. I'll come up with the money."

"And how are you fixin' to do that?"

He's smug and comfortable, his long legs stretched out in front of him. I hear it in the informal cadence of his speech, the way his Ivy League education yields to his Southern roots. He asks the question like he already knows the answer. But I suppose only a fool wouldn't wonder how I expect to raise all that cash. JD is many things, but he's never been foolish. Calculating and clever, but never foolish. I doubt that's changed. "I'll go to the bank. And my fiancé will help."

When he says nothing, I glance up nervously.

His body is tight and a storm is brewing in his eyes. "Your fiancé is a worthless piece of shit who has about drained his bank account, and given the opportunity, would siphon every dime out of this place, too."

"You don't know a damn thing about my fiancé, or our relationship. So just stop."

"I know he hangs around sleazy bars on the dock, looking for a game to lay a bet on or a whore to stick his tiny dick into."

I swallow the humiliation and lift my chin. "I don't believe you."

"Suit yourself. You always liked fantasies."

JD edges forward in the chair, his arm resting on his thigh, his face closer to mine. "Think about what I'm offering," he murmurs. His fingertip trails a path from the crook of my elbow to my inner wrist, the callused pad rousing the sensitive skin. He hovers brazenly over my racing pulse. "Nervous? Or is it something else?"

I shiver and jerk my arm away, rubbing my hand up and down over the place where his has been, hoping to wipe away the sensation.

JD gets up and smooths his trousers with a ghost of a smile that mocks me.

He knows. He knows that no matter how much I hate him, my body hasn't forgotten. Even after all these years. It both shames and angers me, so I do what any well-raised Southern woman in my situation would do. I take a swing. Not with my fists, but with words, delivered in a syrupy voice dripping with sarcasm.

"You want me to be your whore? That's all you need from me? It really is no bother. Let's start right now." I make a big show of unzipping my boots and flinging them across the office, one at a time. Then I take off my jewelry, piece by piece.

While I'm behaving like a woman possessed, he's standing with his back toward me, scrolling through his phone, completely unmoved. It's not until I slam my ivory bangle onto the desktop that he glances over one shoulder.

"Don't push me unless you want to end up bent over that desk with your skirt around your waist. I don't have the patience for it tonight. And stop acting like a petulant child. From what I remember, you're getting the best of the deal."

"Bastard," I spew, from somewhere deep and ugly.

He swivels to face me. "Unfortunately for you, darlin', I'm my father's son. Inherited every one of his despicable genes."

The hair at the back of my neck prickles. His father is a monster, and we both know it. I understand *exactly* the message JD's sending.

"Enough about me." He reaches down and encircles my wrist with one hand, pushing up the bell sleeve of my dress with the other, exposing the fading purple bruises on my upper arm where Dean grabbed me. "This is what I want to know about."

Long, embarrassing minutes pass while he examines each black and blue mark. The disgust on his face causes me more pain than the bruises.

"What happened?"

"I bumped into an armoire. It's nothing."

"Don't you lie to me. Those are finger marks on your skin."

I yank my arm in an effort to escape his hold, but he clenches my wrist tighter. Still, he doesn't dig painfully into the flesh the way Dean had. "It's none of your business."

He lets go of my wrist and I sit behind the desk, putting some distance between us.

But JD isn't finished.

He reaches over and unloops the scarf from around my neck, and before I think to secure it, it's in his hand. There's a long, angry hiss while he glares at the bruises on my throat. They're fading too, more green and yellow than purple, but they're still large and ghastly. I instinctively reach to cover them, but he swats my hand away.

His fingers skim my throat, lingering over each bruise. I squeeze my eyes tight, but a small tear escapes and slides down my cheek for him to see.

"Do they hurt?"

I shake my head. "Not anymore."

"I don't have all night and I'm not leaving before you tell me what happened."

"You knew exactly where to look for the bruises, so you already know what happened."

"I want to hear it from your mouth. All of it. The truth."

"He had too much to drink. It was only one time."

"*Only one time?* He choked you, Gabrielle. That's one fucking time too many." His voice is a whisper. A menacing whisper he's fighting to control.

It takes all the strength I have not to cower as the tremor of his barely restrained rage reverberates through the room.

"Did he hit you?"

My hands are trembling, and I clasp them on my lap to steady them. I didn't do anything wrong, but still, I feel small and ashamed. "You've seen the damage. Does it really matter?"

"Did. He. Hit. You?"

"Yes," I mutter.

JD takes half a step back and brushes a loose curl off my cheek. His touch is careful, gentle and warm, and my eyelids droop with a heavy flutter. "Did he force himself on you?" His voice is softer and kinder now, too, and for a moment I feel like he's the man I once knew and loved.

I shake my head. "No."

It's a lie. Another lie tumbling off the tongue of the woman who always chooses truth over lies. But I don't dare tell JD the truth about that night.

"I cannot believe that sonofabitch had his drunken hands around your neck tight enough to leave those kinds of marks. He could have killed you." JD growls like a grizzly caught in a steel-jaw trap and stumbles back, running a hand over his head to the base of his neck. He squeezes the muscle a few times. Then swivels to face me.

"Tell me you love him," he demands. "Tell me you cling to him and scream his name when he fills your pussy. Go ahead, tell me." He's looming over me now, both hands planted on my desk, disgust oozing from every word. "You won't say it because you can't bear to hear the filthy lie come out of your own mouth." He drops the scarf in my lap. "And this is the man you expect to save you? This is the man you want to marry? What the hell is wrong with you, Gabrielle?"

My fingers find the scarf, rubbing the silky fabric between them for comfort.

"That relationship is over," he fumes.

I've had more than enough of the paternalistic attitude. "What do you mean, it's over? You can't—"

"I already did."

His words are final. Spoken as though what I think, what I care about, is of no importance. My anger mounts again. "What did you do, threaten to make him your bitch?"

He glares at me through squinted eyes and dismisses my question as though it's nothing. And in a way, it is nothing. Nothing more than an insolent remark requiring no serious response. I want to jab at him. That's all. I want to hurt him the way he hurt me.

He straightens and buttons his suit jacket. "I have a victory party to get to."

"Your father won?" The surprise in my voice is unmistakable. It was possible, but I never expected he would actually win. Not many people did. *God help us all.*

He nods, but his face gives nothing away.

Unless things have changed markedly, JD has little use for his father. But still, I would have expected him to be more pleased about the outcome of the election. Instead of poisoning just South Carolina, the Wilders can now spread their special brand of misery all over the country.

Before he leaves, I need to put an end to this. And I make my final stand with as much bravado as I can muster. "I will not be your whore."

"I don't expect you to be my whore. You'll get as much pleasure from our arrangement as I will. Maybe more, if you can manage to stop snarling and calling me names long enough to enjoy it."

I don't know what I ever saw in him. He's nothing more than a vile, self-righteous hypocrite dressed in expensive clothing. And I want at him. I want it in the worst way.

"Lay it out, JD. Go ahead. You can stand there all high and mighty, but you're no different than Dean. You might not leave the kind of bruises that are visible to the eye, but don't think for one minute you're *any* better than him."

As soon as the words tumble off my tongue, he's towering over me, one hand gripping the back of my seat. He's trembling. I feel his rage through the bones of the chair. My heart thumps wildly, and I know the instant he spits out the first word, I pushed too far.

"Your mother gets the care she desperately needs to stay alive. Your father's debts are forgiven." He leans over, so close his breath heats my scalp, but it's not a soothing sensation. It's biting and bitter, like his words. "In exchange. You. Are. Mine. To enjoy as I like. Take it or leave it."

I glance up when he quiets. His face is screwed up with a fury I don't recognize. I'm the one trembling now, not in anger, but with fear.

Before I can calm myself, his shadow recedes, and he strides toward the door. My hands are balled so tight, the white-tipped nails leave bloody crescents on my palms.

He turns in the doorway. "The offer stands until tomorrow evening at eight."

I don't respond, and JD doesn't leave. Instead, he stands there, appraising me, as though he has more to say. I've already heard plenty from him, so I open my desk drawer and begin organizing the gel pens and index cards, sorting each by size and color.

"Gabrielle?"

I glance at him, and immediately wish I hadn't.

"If you breathe a single word about this to anyone, you'll watch in horror as your mother's body is ravaged by disease. You have my word."

For the first time in my life, I'm truly afraid of him. Terrified of the rage I unleashed. I knew better than to push and push, to compare him to a man like Dean, but I did it anyway.

"Antoine will meet you in the hotel lobby tomorrow at eight. We'll have supper at Sweetgrass and discuss the terms in more detail. I'll answer any questions you have. If you're not interested in what I'm offering, just send word with him, and I won't bother you again. I'm not forcing you to do this. Come willingly, or don't come at all. It's entirely up to you."

He saunters out of the office as though he hasn't just dropped a bomb on my world. As if I actually have a choice. Without thinking, I pick up a bud vase off my desk and hurl it at him through the doorway. It misses, hitting the corner of Georgina's desk. The vase shatters dramatically and water splashes onto his elegant suit, but he doesn't stop. Doesn't flinch. He just keeps walking.

3

Gabrielle

Once I'm certain he's gone, I grab a small trash bag and get down to clean the wet shards from the rug, trying to concentrate on picking up glass without pricking my fingers. It's an impossible task. Each time I think I'm done, another sliver winks at me.

Somehow, I'm always left with a colossal mess to clean up when JD's around. So this should come as no surprise.

I would love to blame it all on him, every bad idea we indulged, every risk we took, all the adult-themed parties for two we threw for ourselves. But I did it all willingly. Sometimes it was me who led him astray. Me who seduced him into the darkness.

I was fifteen and he had just turned seventeen the first time we ventured into the shadows, playing games that neither of us were anywhere near ready to play. He was the teacher, and I the compliant student, eager to show off everything he taught me. Eager to use my hands and mouth in ways that elicited desperate gasps and shudders from the all-powerful JD Wilder. Eager to submit fully, while he stripped me bare and tethered me to a hitching post, stroking my body with colorful ostrich feathers until a damp sheen covered my skin and nothing but muted whimpers and pleas for more escaped my lips.

We were nothing more than a push and pull of hormone-driven bodies, capped by minds too young to understand the implications of the physical pleasures we explored. At least that's how I remember it—until he had his fill of the common girl with humble roots.

Don't feel sorry for me. I had no business taking up with him in the first place. I fell prey to an age-old cliché. Servant's daughter falls in love with the master's son, something girls like me are repeatedly warned against. But lustful desires and fairy-tale endings obscured all good sense. That, and a beautiful, sweet-talking boy with a mouth like velvet.

I've kept in touch with his brothers off and on, but until today, I hadn't spoken to JD since the night I discovered him balls deep in Jane Montgomery, the lieutenant governor's daughter. They were both naked. Jane on all fours, squealing like a stuck hog, her Junior League pedigree and dignity discarded in a heap with her clothes.

Julian—I called him Julian then—was behind her, gripping her slim hips with two hands, pounding her pussy while the sweat dripped off his body.

I stood there, feet glued to the floor, both hands covering my mouth, until he noticed me. "Get out," he hissed, never breaking his connection with her. Never interrupting the punishing rhythm.

I stumbled out of the stable, but got no more than fifty feet before I keeled over and emptied the contents of my stomach under a mulberry tree on the horse path.

Two weeks later, I was whisked up North to an all-girls boarding school. Ripped away from my family and friends and a life I so loved, all without a good explanation. At least not one that I believed.

My parents and the school principal behaved like co-conspirators, pretending that a hostile environment filled with snooty teenage girls was a fabulous opportunity for someone like me. Never questioning how a scholarship to an elite Connecticut boarding school fell like manna from heaven, midway through the school year, and found its way to *me* in Charleston, South Carolina. They could pretend all they wanted, but I knew exactly who was behind it.

And I never forgave him.

Not when I left Connecticut with a full scholarship to Cornell. Not when I traveled Europe, interning in the finest hotels. Not when I had the opportunity to return to Charleston and buy this hotel for a song from the city. Not even after the renovations were complete, and the doors opened to accolades. I never forgave him.

And I never will.

What could he possibly want with me after all this time? *Sex?* No. JD doesn't need me to satisfy some sick fantasy. Women are lined up from here to Greenville to indulge his fantasies.

He wants to ruin my life, crush me completely this time. Yes, I know it's dramatic. But like last time, I can't come up with a more plausible explanation.

I toss the white trash bag into the incinerator. Well, I have news for him. As long as I have a breath in me, that is not happening. I'll go to the bank tomorrow and beg the loan officer to let me establish another line of credit. The hotel is fully booked every night for the next year, and the restaurant is booked six months out. That has to account for something.

Maybe I should call Dean. *No.* I don't have the stomach to crawl back to him. Despite what I told JD, Dean did try to force me into sex that night but he was so stinking drunk, he couldn't get it up. Though, booze or no booze, it wasn't a unique phenomenon. But that night was different. That night he held me by the hair and slapped my face, again and again, when I refused to suck him off. That night he wrapped his hands around my neck and squeezed while I teetered in and out of consciousness, choking for breath. That night I prayed he wouldn't kill me in a drunken rage.

No, I'll never go back. I'll take my chances with whatever JD has planned. He won't beat me, not the way Dean did, but he'll hurt me in other ways. Crueler ways, leaving invisible scars that last a lifetime. But he won't kill me.

Sweet Jesus. How did my life get to this? *How?*

There has to be another way. I say it so convincingly, I almost believe it myself.

4

Julian

Most Charlestonians would deliver their acceptance speech from a historic hotel in the storied downtown. Most presidents-elect would be concerned about the optics of holding an election night celebration on a plantation where slaves were once forced to pick rice and beaten on a whim. Not my father. He revels in it, and his fuck-you attitude is exactly why he was elected president today.

After passing through a half-dozen checkpoints, I pull up in front of the main house and toss my keys to the valet. "Don't bury it. I'm not staying all night."

The party is out back under a tent. Large screens are set up so revelers can follow the election results. I hear the victory cries over the raucous music. *Idiots.* They'll get exactly what they deserve.

The Secret Service agents stationed at the front door let me pass with nothing more than a curt nod. I barely have a foot in the foyer when my brother Gray pounces. "The president-elect is in his upstairs study. You've been summoned."

"It's nice to see you, too."

"You should have been here hours ago if you wanted pleasantries. That time is long over," Gray says, dragging me into a hug. When he pulls back, he doesn't immediately let go of my shoulders. "You look like hell."

"Nothing a little dirty water can't cure."

Gray shakes his head and grins. He resembles my mother, with dark hair, prominent cheekbones, and a small cleft in his chin. That, and he's always reaching for straws where DW is concerned. Always giving *Dad* the benefit of the doubt.

"Chase and I were starting to worry you weren't going to show, and we'd be stuck holding the bag."

"I thought about it." *At least a dozen times, just today.* "But I didn't want to leave you to deal with the fallout. Besides, not showing up would put a kink in my plans." As soon as it's out of my mouth, I want it back. But it's too late.

"Your plans?" Gray studies me carefully, his slate-blue eyes piercing. "What are you up to?"

"Nothing for you to worry your pretty little head about, princess." I have it all under control.

"Be smart, JD."

"Always."

"For what it's worth, the old man never doubted you'd be here. When Shelby fretted about it, he told her he wasn't worried in the least."

Gray knows DW's despicable, but he's forever searching for evidence to the contrary. Worse, he's always trying to convince me to cut DW a break. But I never do. He doesn't deserve any breaks from me.

I blow out a breath and crack my knuckles. This is going to be one long fucking night. It already feels like it's gone on forever. "I'm going to get a drink, and then I'll be up."

"Don't dawdle. He's already pissed it's taken you so long to come kiss the ring."

"*Kiss the ring.* He can kiss my ass."

On my way to see the president-elect, I pass his wife Shelby, in the upstairs hall with two women fussing over her like she's a helpless child.

"JD! You're here. I was starting to worry. You know how your father gets."

As she inches closer, I can almost feel the scratch of her bubble lips on my cheek. Parched and ice cold, injected with toxins to plump them, and brushed in a vile burgundy. The color is garish against her lily-white skin. I duck out of her reach, my precious bourbon sloshing near the rim as I escape her clutches. "It's almost time to go down to the party. Don't want to ruin your makeup."

Her smile fades quickly, much like her good looks did. She was stunning when DW married her. Now she's just an aging beauty queen, more caricature than human. "Don't spoil tonight for him," she pleads. "He worked so hard."

Shelby is nothing more than a gold digger, and even costly French perfume can't hide the stench, but she's more than he deserves.

"I wouldn't dream of spoiling your evening. Why don't you finish getting ready, and let me go say hello to the president?"

"He's not the president just yet," she calls after me, giggling like a little girl.

Shelby. I can only tolerate her in small doses. Very small doses.

Right after they married, I thought about bending her over my father's desk and fucking her until she screamed *my* name. Spraying *my* seed over her pale skin. Don't doubt for a second that she would have been a willing partner. But what would it have accomplished? Short-sighted vengeance, that's all. Nothing more than the momentary satisfaction of defiling something pretty that belonged to him. But the thought of sticking my dick where his has been always made my stomach turn. Never more than now.

I pause at the door of my father's study to pull myself together.

My mother, bless her soul, rolled over in her grave today. Probably a dozen times. The worst of her unrest was undoubtedly caused by my visit to Gabrielle. But it couldn't be helped.

Gabrielle doesn't know it yet, but she needs to be under my protection. DW will use her to keep me in line, especially once I begin to dig deeper for answers. I fell prey to that tactic once, but it won't happen again.

I contemplate bolting down the stairs and out the door. But I won't do that to my younger brothers. They're both already here. The two who can be. Gray, with his tie loose and sleeves rolled to the elbows, and Chase, with a tablet tucked under an arm. Zack can't be here. My father made sure of that.

Gray and Chase worked on the campaign for the past two years while I stayed in Charleston to take care of Wilder business. Gray has people skills. He was born with the gift of bringing complete strangers together and putting them at ease.

Chase, the youngest Wilder, lacks Gray's social acumen, but he more than makes up for it with tech know-how. The kid can hack anything, anywhere, get in and out without leaving a fingerprint. He's that good.

And me? I'm a moody bastard who doesn't suffer fools easily. I don't kiss ass any more than I kiss rings. Apparently these are not useful campaign skills, so I was mostly left in peace while my brothers scoured the country doing the devil's bidding.

My father pauses mid-sentence when he catches me in the doorway. We have the same coloring, same eyes, same nose, and the same chestnut hair that curls at the ends, when it's wet or too long. The resemblance is uncanny.

Some days, when I look at myself in the mirror, I see him.

When I was a child, strangers would comment on how much we looked alike. Back then, I would puff out my chest and beam. Now when someone says I'm the spitting image of my father, it takes all I have not to puke.

"So glad you found the time to join us, JD. Come in."

While ring kissing isn't my style, I extend the sonofabitch my hand. "Congratulations. It appears everything went as planned." I glance at my brothers. "Congratulations to you two clowns, too. Nice work." I elbow Chase, and am rewarded with an impish grin.

"Thanks." He's still smiling, and I smile, too. There were months and months, when he was a kid, that Chase didn't smile. Especially after the accident, when my father shipped Zack off to that dreadful place where he withered instead of thrived.

"What's the plan for tonight?" Chase asks my father.

"Collins will concede after the polls close on the West Coast. As soon as he delivers his speech, I'll give mine, with my sons standing behind me, pleased as punch, showing the appropriate deference and support."

That part about deference and support was for my benefit. *Pleased as punch.* Fuck me.

"I think we should all take a minute to appreciate the history made today. When I started, there were nineteen other candidates. The voters picked me, primary after primary, to represent the party. And today, the country chose me to lead them into the future. By the time the votes are all counted, I'll have won both the Electoral College and the popular vote. It's big. *Huge.* Do you appreciate the significance?" He looks from me to my brothers. "Do you?" he roars when we don't answer.

"Yes," Gray and Chase say in unison.

I nod. *What an asshole.*

"The voters have handed me a mandate to govern as I see fit.

Think about what that means for us. For Wilder Holdings. Looser regulations, lower corporate taxes, stronger employer protections. We can sell our drugs all over the world. Hell, we can sell them on the streets of America if we want."

I can't take one more second of his self-aggrandizing bullshit. Even if it means my grandfather's pharmaceutical company will flourish. The money means nothing. My brothers and I inherited more money from my mother's parents than we can spend in ten lifetimes.

"Maybe we should let you meet with your speechwriter." I try to sound helpful. Anything to get me out of here. "You probably need to make some last-minute tweaks before you face the country."

"The world," he says.

Christ. I don't dare so much as glance at my brothers, who I'm sure are thinking that DW is an insufferable bastard. Even Gray can't deny it. It would be laughable if he wasn't just elected president. It would be laughable if he was someone else's father.

"The speech was final months ago," DW says proudly. "It's all up here." He taps an index finger against his temple.

I imagine a loaded gun against his head in the very place his finger lingers. Maybe after I'm finished. First I want him to suffer through long, excruciating days and longer sleepless nights. I want every creature comfort stripped away. I want him begging for mercy that never comes.

My hand tightens around the crystal tumbler and I throw back the deep tawny liquid, welcoming the burn at the back of my throat. But even before the warmth subsides, I need another.

"We have family business to discuss. So don't think about going anywhere yet. The bar's open all night." DW glances warily at me. "Sit down, JD."

"I've been sitting all day. I'll stand." I wait for him to tell me to sit again, but he doesn't. When it comes right down to it, he's got no balls and won't take the risk that I'll refuse. Not in front of my brothers. He can't afford a mutiny on his hands. It's a small victory, but it's tasty.

"We've talked around the edges, but now it's real. Once I'm sworn in, I can no longer keep the business in my name. My shares will have to go into a blind trust. There's no choice. I'll push it off as long as possible, but there's a limit to how long I can wait. The three of you will run the day-to-day operations, and make whatever decisions are necessary in the best interest of Wilder Holdings."

My brothers nod.

"Exactly how will the responsibilities be divided?" I ask.

"Gray will go back to running Wildflower. Full-time after the transition is over. With everything it entails. Being more careful than ever. *No* mistakes."

Wildflower is Gray's baby.

It's an upscale social club. The very proper front for a not very proper, but very private, sex club. A place where the most discriminating South Carolinians go to play. It's a high-risk, high-reward kind of place. Lots of interesting people and toys to play with. But if you get caught with your pants down, strapped to a spanking bench with a plug in your ass, your constituents won't like it. Neither will your clients, your boss, or your wife. Especially your wife.

My father is still droning. He likes to hear himself talk. Always has. "Chase, you'll oversee the technology arm of the company, just like before. But I want you to stay with the transition team, too. After I'm sworn in, I'll still need you from time to time, but your main focus will be in Charleston, helping your brothers.

"And JD, you'll continue to oversee all of Wilder Holdings, but your responsibilities will also include Sayle Pharmaceuticals now. That's significantly more responsibility than you had during the campaign. Are you up for it?"

Does he expect me to say no? "Of course."

I try not to look as smug as I feel—no reason to piss off DW more than necessary tonight.

It must kill him to hand over the reins to me. But my brothers don't have the experience or interest in managing the company, and according to the terms of my grandfather's will, Sayle can only be managed by an outsider, if my brothers and I, or our legitimate offspring, are unable or unwilling to serve.

"Secret Service detail? Anybody change their mind?"

"I have plenty of security. I don't need handouts from the government," I answer. *And I certainly don't need strangers peering over my shoulder while I search for evidence to destroy you.*

My brothers each grunt something in agreement. I'm not worried about their safety. They have excellent security and my father can't afford to kill off any more of his family members. If he could, I'd already be dead.

"I'd turn it down if I had a choice," DW mutters. "I have Olson. He's all I need. Can't stand having all these government hacks watching my every move. I don't trust them." He waves his hand dismissively. "There will be paperwork you'll have to sign, but you're all of age. They can't force you to accept it."

"So you're backing completely away from everything? Even Sayle?" I ask.

"You two," he points to my brothers, "go make sure everything's in place for the speech."

"Don't you have people for that?" Gray asks.

I gnaw on the inside of my cheek not to laugh. *Don't we have people for that* was my father's most uttered phrase during the campaign. Maybe Shelby's too. The old man has no idea Gray's mocking him.

"Go," he says, dismissing them like they're unruly children. "And shut the door behind you."

Just what I need, a little father-son time. Like this night hasn't already sucked enough life from my soul.

"You'll be the face of Wilder Holdings while I'm president.

And that includes the pharmaceutical arm. But I expect daily briefings."

"Daily briefings?" *Jesus Christ.* He expects to talk to me every day? That is not happening. "I thought the whole point of putting your shares into a blind trust is so you won't be privy to the day-to-day operations."

"No one's going to listen in on, or question, a friendly conversation between a father and son who miss one another. You will miss me, won't you, JD?" He snickers, and I want to slam my fist into his jaw.

"Don't you think you'll have enough on your plate running the country?"

"My interests and those of the country dovetail nicely. I can multitask. It's how Sayle Pharmaceuticals got to the top. Despite what your grandfather believed, you don't get to be one of the big boys unless you play the game."

"I don't think *my* grandfather or *my* mother saw *their* beloved family business as a game. And I certainly don't."

He pounds a fist on the desk.

I stand perfectly still, ignoring his antics, like an adult watching a toddler throw a tantrum. Apparently, he doesn't appreciate being reminded who lawfully owns the company.

"No one's indispensable, JD. Least of all you." He leans back in the chair and clasps his hands over his stomach, like he's the fucking king issuing a proclamation. "This is my business, including Sayle Pharmaceuticals, until the day they inter my body. Maybe even after."

He flashes me a blinding toothy smile as fake as his wife's tits. "Do your job, JD, but stay out of things that don't concern you or you'll force my hand. Your job is to babysit the company, not to make policy, or implement changes, or to harass the employees. The babysitter is supposed to keep things running smoothly and follow instructions until Daddy gets back. If he snoops in the bedside table, or in the medicine chest where he doesn't belong, he's promptly disposed of."

"You mean fired."

"You can take it to mean whatever you like."

Sayle Pharmaceuticals is my birthright. I would have to die for that to change. DW doesn't have the balls to do it himself, but he's not above having me killed. I'm sure he's thought about it over the years, and I'm even more certain he regrets I wasn't in the car with the others when it went over the embankment. But this is the closest he's ever come to saying it.

Power is intoxicating. It makes people careless. The more people feed his ego, the more careless he'll become. Eventually he'll make a mistake. And I plan to be standing right there when it happens.

"I think we've said everything we need to for tonight. I'll be downstairs." I turn to leave, but I don't escape quickly enough.

"JD, how's that girl you used to bang in the back of the stable like she was a bitch in heat? Vivien and William's daughter. Gabrielle, right? I bet she had a sweet little cunt, didn't she, son?"

I freeze with my hand on the doorknob, rage and terror flooding into every crevice of my body, until I can barely breathe. *Do not let him see it, JD.* My fingers squeeze the cold metal knob until they ache. "She's fine, I guess. Lally says she's engaged."

"That's too bad. I've always wanted to tap that tight ass. Engaged makes it more complicated. Sometimes more complicated than married. But I'm the president now...all things are possible."

Focus on the endgame. Don't let him distract you with shiny objects he knows you can't resist.

My only job this evening is not to scowl while my father accepts the presidency. If I can do that, everything else will fall into place. One small step at a time. *You've waited a long time for this opportunity. Breathe, JD. Breathe.*

I picture him with an orange jumpsuit yanked down around his ankles, beefy inmates waiting in line to spear his virgin ass with long, thick cocks while he cries like a baby. The image settles me.

I turn to him with a practiced smile and ice water barreling through my veins. "I think it's about time to go downstairs and face the world, Mr. President."

5

Gabrielle

"I'm sorry, Ms. Duval. The bank would love to help, and we certainly appreciate how you've turned the blight of the neighborhood into a shining jewel, but there's nothing we can do in this situation. You haven't built enough equity in the hotel for the bank to extend a line of credit."

He might be doing his job, but there's not a less sincere man than Jacob Lott, the vice president of State Street Bank. My friend Georgina calls him *smarmy*, and he is. But there are so many other things about him that are off-putting, too. His bulbous nose is always bright red, like a man who drinks too much, and he always smells like he's just eaten pickled onions. And while we can't help our genetics, the man surely earns enough to find himself a decent tailor and a bottle of shoe polish.

"The Gatehouse is fully booked a year out, and the restaurant doesn't have an available table for months," I explain, trying to appeal to reason. "We've been invited to join the Blackberry Inn and the Hotel Savannah for the Christmas celebration this year."

"I did hear about that. That was so good of them to invite you."

"We've worked very hard. I like to think we deserve the honor."

A woman knocks on the glass partition, between the offices.

"Will you excuse me for a moment?" he asks as he scurries out the door.

"Of course."

Nice of them to invite you. What a prick. The Gatehouse is celebrating Christmas with two other small hotels in Charleston. They're exquisite hotels with an upscale clientele. Not so different than us in that regard, but they've been around for decades.

The Blackberry Inn will serve Christmas Eve dinner for guests from all the hotels, the Gatehouse will host Christmas brunch, and Savannah will pull out all the stops for Christmas dinner. It's genius, and there's been so much excitement about the holiday event that all three hotels were fully booked on the day of the announcement, six months ago. For the Gatehouse, it's an opportunity to showcase our best to a group of people who normally stay elsewhere in Charleston. It has the potential to change everything for us.

"Where were we?" Lott asks, on his way back into the room.

Nowhere good. "What about the underwriter?" I ask. "You've turned me down without even talking to him."

"Ms. Duval. I haven't turned you down. You haven't even filed an application." He sighs, a long, exasperated breath that distributes the tang of pickled onions into the tiny office. "I'm just trying to save you the trouble. As you know, the loan process is lengthy and very involved. I'm just apprising you of the almost certain outcome before you embark down that road."

"What if the underwriter feels differently?"

"He doesn't."

"You've discussed it with him?"

"I spoke with him after you called. He's sorry to hear about your mother's declining health, but his initial commitment was to the restoration and preservation efforts in Charleston, not to the hotel specifically, or to you."

I nod. "I understand, and I'm very grateful for his generosity."

"There are so many people in need, we can't possibly expect him to solve everyone's financial woes."

That might be the case, but I'm not taking your word for it. "No, I don't expect that, but I would appreciate a loan application."

His tongue clicks softly in disapproval.

"My mother always says you never know unless you try," I add, with a smile sweet enough to make rhubarb palatable.

Five minutes later, my loan application and I are on the sidewalk, headed toward the parking lot. There's no way I'm getting the loan. I insisted on the application in part because Lott was so condescending. But I will submit the paperwork. All I have to lose is time—something I don't seem to have much of these days.

I pull into the driveway of Georgina's house. It's a cute bungalow with a newly painted picket fence. Georgina Bressler Scott has been my best friend since before I could walk. And she was with me from the beginning, when the Gatehouse was little more than an empty shell, badly in need of a facelift and some love.

Georgie's waiting at the door when I come up the porch steps. "I want to hear why you were at the bank. I take one day off, and you're already borrowing money?" She pulls me into a hug.

"You look great," I tell her. "Those pregnancy hormones are good for your skin. It's all glowy."

"Don't lie. I look like a whale." She rubs her hand over her expanding belly. "Can you come in for a few minutes? I have cookies."

"What kind?" I ask, following her into the kitchen.

"Lemon sugar."

"I would never say no to a sugar cookie. Especially a lemon one. Did you make these?"

"Yes. Can you believe it?" she says, pouring iced tea into the tall glasses embellished with bees that she usually saves for company. "I think it's a nesting thing. I read somewhere that around the third trimester all of these maternal instincts kick in as you prepare for the baby. Maybe I'll become the next Martha Stewart."

"There's about as much chance of that happening as there is of me becoming the next Julia Child. But about our baby." I hand her a bag from Mimi's, my new favorite store.

"Gabby, you buy this baby more clothes than you buy for yourself. *Oh my God.* Look at this!" She holds up a onesie with newly-hatched chicks on it that will be perfect for spring.

"It's adorable, isn't it? It was on sale, and I couldn't resist. She can wear it Easter morning before she puts on the cute ruffled dress we're going to buy her. The one with the matching shoes and tights."

"She could be a he, you know."

"I don't think so, but maybe. That's the only reason the ruffled dress is still in the store. Before I forget, here's the paperwork you wanted. It's not so adorable."

"Thanks. Wade's away tonight and it'll give me something to do before bed." She takes the color-coded folder and puts it aside. "So tell me about your appointment with the bank that I didn't know anything about."

"Like I told you earlier, I was trying to persuade them to loan me some more money, but I wasn't successful."

"Why do you need money? Is it for the quarterly insurance

bill that's coming up? Don't borrow money for that. I have a few dollars put away. I can help."

I shake my head. "My mother has been offered some experimental treatment that might prolong her life. Or at least make it better."

"Oh Gabby! I'm so happy to hear it. I've been so worried about her since you first told me she was sick. And worried about you, too."

I nod.

Georgina doesn't take her eyes off me. "Experimental treatment. It sounds expensive. That's why you need money?"

I draw a breath before I say the words out loud. Even as they come out of my mouth, I still can't believe them. "JD helped my parents find the doctor and loaned them the money to make it happen. I was hoping the bank would lend me the money to pay him back. Then I could get him out of our lives. Things were better for me that way."

The color drains from Georgie's face, and I haven't even told her any of the ugly details. It's startling to watch.

"*JD Wilder?*" she whispers, like she might summon the devil himself if she says his name too loud.

I nod. "I don't like it either. But it is what it is. My mother needs the treatment, and Jacob Lott said they aren't giving me any more money. I'm still going to apply for the loan, but it's not likely to come through. It might be her only real hope."

"Nothing good happens when he's anywhere near you. Remember that whole boarding school thing? Instead of breaking up with you like a normal boy, he had his father send you away."

I cover my face, making small circles over my tired eyes. "I know. Believe me, I haven't forgotten. It's all I've been thinking about since I found out my parents took money from him."

"Isn't there another way? Being indebted to those Wilders is—it's not good."

"No." I sigh. "It's not good. But the treatment is very expensive. Believe me, I'm searching for another way to come up with money."

She looks at me with those round hazel eyes, framed by soft, inky lashes. I see the worry in her face. The pity. She knows about my history with JD. Not all the things we did in the stable, but everything else. I cried on her shoulder the night I found him with Jane, and for months and months after.

"When we were kids, I was always jealous of you," she says softly.

"Oh, come on. You talk about this like you committed some big sin. Kids are kids. And I've told you a hundred times, I don't remember you being jealous of anyone."

"I was. I loved you, but in my heart, I always wanted what you had. It didn't matter how much you shared with me. I coveted every single thing about your life, like an unrepentant sinner. A mama of my very own, and a father who didn't stumble around drunk while kids taunted him. And JD—I wanted him most of all."

She gets up and pours us each some more sweet tea, wiping the lip of the pitcher with a pale-yellow dishtowel. "I was closer to his age, and it never seemed fair that he wanted you instead of me. But it didn't matter how much I flirted, or paraded around in shorts that were practically indecent, or showed off my belly button to him. None of it mattered. He chose you. Every day he chose you."

Every day he chose you.

Until he chose someone else.

A ball forms at the opening of my stomach, and even the tea can't go down smoothly. "Everyone wanted his attention—boys or girls, it didn't matter. I never noticed you flirting with him more than anyone else did." And I would have noticed.

"Because you always saw the good in everyone. Especially in me. Even when I didn't deserve it."

"You always deserved it, Georgie. And JD didn't turn out to be much of a prize. Consider yourself blessed."

"*Mmhm*. I do." Her voice trails off, as she smooths the wrinkles from her cotton skirt. Her left hand finds a soothing rhythm, but it does nothing to ease her crinkled brow. "Do you remember when I visited you at that school in Connecticut?"

"Yes." I nod. "I counted the minutes until you arrived. I was so lonely and homesick."

"All those terrible girls who called you Black Brie and Brie Noir, like you were some wretched French cheese gone bad. You put on a good face, but I knew how broken you were inside. How awful it was to be around those girls with too much money, who couldn't get their noses out of the air. My heart hurt when I said goodbye that Sunday. Leaving you there in that dreadful place, full of mean and spiteful girls who talked with funny accents. I cried all the way home. It was the very last time I was jealous of you."

I wrap my arms around my middle, cupping my elbows. "I cried after you left, too. Cried for hours until I fell asleep. I was so miserable." Those first few months at boarding school, when I was the strange new girl, were the worst.

"I never told you this, but that visit changed my life, Gabby. It made me grateful for what I have." She twists a small section of hair around her finger, and for several seconds her mind is somewhere else. "I never again wanted to be you. I asked God to forgive my envy, and thanked him for his mercy. Thanked him for sending JD to you instead of to me. I'm so sorry."

"A lot of the girls were awful. But looking back now, after the first semester, it wasn't all bad. My parents coddled me. I was too soft. At boarding school, I learned to tune out the noise, and to push through adversity. It proved to be an important life lesson. Painful, but important. And just so you know, they're quite sure that we're the ones with the funny accents. I can't believe you remembered they called me Brie Noir."

"It was terrible. It sounded exotic, until I found out they called you that after they saw the picture of your mother."

"*Mmhm.*" My mother is biracial. Her skin isn't particularly dark, but she has tight, tight curls, that she wears natural. The girls didn't know what to make of it. They only knew she wasn't white. White women don't have that kind of hair. And biracial wasn't part of their elite vocabulary.

Georgie is quiet and calm now. But I feel like there's more she wants to tell me. I don't know what dredged all of this up today. We haven't talked about any of it in more than a decade. Maybe longer.

"Did I ever tell you Brie Noir is a real cheese? I tasted it when I interned at that hotel in Paris. I thought about those nasty girls while I enjoyed a sliver with some pink champagne."

She doesn't smile. "You have so much, Gabby. You worked so hard. He'll ruin it. If you let him near you again, he'll take everything. He can't help it. It's how he is. How they all are."

She's right. But it won't do any good to tell her that. And it won't do me or my mother any good to wallow in self-pity. "I won't let him. I'm prepared, and my brain isn't filled with fairytale endings anymore. I know his game this time."

"Be careful. Be careful of all of them."

Georgie is afraid of something. Her face is still ashen, and she's pushing back her cuticles, like she does when she's anxious. "What aren't you telling me, Georgina Bressler Scott?"

Georgie opens her mouth, then presses her lips together.

I wonder if something happened with JD when we were younger. Maybe they made out behind my back. There was a year or two in there—it doesn't matter. Not anymore. I love her, and nothing she can say will change that.

I'm going to be late meeting JD. I stayed longer at Georgina's than I planned, and now I'm stuck in traffic. I'm sure he'll have plenty to say about it, too.

What am I going to do about his proposal?

I tried to reach my parents again last night, and all day today, but I still can't get through to them. I'm not getting an error message, but the calls are going directly to voicemail. Despite his warning, I can't believe JD can block my calls. Can he? *No.* Maybe my mother is tired from the trip and the tests, and she hasn't bothered recharging her phone. My father refuses to deal with the cell phone, so he wouldn't think to recharge it. He probably doesn't even know how.

It's all drivel, but it's distracting me from the bigger questions. The ones I'm about to be faced with. What am I going to do about JD's *business proposal*? That fucker.

Do I become his plaything? He wouldn't really stop my mother's treatment if it can help her, would he?

Gabrielle, he showed up yesterday after all these years and he wants you to have sex with him to pay off a loan. He's capable of anything.

I don't know.

When JD's mother and sister were killed, my mother held his brothers while they cried. She bathed and fed his brother Zack, changed his diapers until DW sent him away. My mother nurtured those boys. Doled out real hugs and an endless supply of love when there wasn't anyone else who cared about them. Surely that has to count for something.

I'll go to Sweetgrass, talk to my parents, and feel JD out. Maybe I can change his mind. When we were kids, JD was tough, and he could be really mean, especially to anyone who picked on the younger kids. He was always the leader. Always the boss of everyone and everything, but he had a sense of honor and decency about him. Fairness was important to him, and he was loyal to everyone he cared about. *Loyalty*. That was one of the hundreds of reasons I was so crushed to find him with another girl.

Snippets of my life flash in front of my eyes as I sit in traffic. Running on the lawn at Wildwood as a child, JD tugging playfully on my braids. How he always hid the last cookie for me in a small copper tin behind the flour sacks in the pantry. And those long nights we spent wrapped in a blanket under an enormous sky teeming with stars, or in our little corner of the stable, kissing and petting, until nothing, *nothing,* seemed as important as chasing the ultimate pleasure.

What happened to that boy who gazed at me under the stars, his bright-blue eyes shining with what I foolishly believed was love? "I'll take care of you," he whispered into my damp skin, after we had sex for the first time. "I won't ever let anything bad happen to you. I promise."

What happened to him? Some part of him must still exist under the custom-made suit and expensive haircut. Surely, it must. People don't change that much. He's still beautiful, but his eyes don't sparkle anymore, and his features are cold and hard.

Maybe they do.

Or maybe I can find some of that decency. Maybe it's still there, hidden beneath the trappings.

6

Julian

Lally doesn't keep a goddamn thing in this place to make a decent sandwich. I find a wedge of cheddar in the refrigerator door and a stale baguette in the bread box, and toss them on the counter.

The casserole Lally made for dinner tonight is still sitting on the stove. I lift the lid and peek inside before shoving it into the fridge. I don't feel like eating it alone. And I'm tired of looking at it.

Gabrielle. Damn woman.

She pissed me off tonight. Threw a wrench into my plan before we even started. I never thought she'd back out upfront, not with her mother's life on the line. She's going to be an even bigger challenge than I anticipated. But somehow, I need to make it work with her. *Somehow.*

There's no way I can go after my father unless she's wrapped up. She needs to be on board before I make any overt moves. Otherwise, it's too risky. I won't take that chance. Not with her.

Gabrielle, you never make things easy.

If the stakes weren't so damn high, I'd enjoy her insolence. But the way things stand, it's just another hurdle on the road to hell.

I'm pouring the third drink of the night when my phone buzzes. I turn it over. *Security.* This better not be any more bullshit. The election speeches went on much too long last night, and now with Gabrielle being a huge pain in the ass—I'm out of patience.

"Yeah?"

"Gabrielle Duval is at the front gate. Says you're expecting her. She's on the list for tonight, but I thought Antoine was bringing her by the house. Did something change?"

I almost laugh out loud at her audacity. "Nothing's changed." *Oh Gabrielle, you will learn to listen and obey. Even if it kills me.* "Send her away."

"Will do."

"Smith?"

"Yeah?"

"She's not to be roughed up or hurt in any way. Not an eyelash harmed. No one lays a finger on her for any reason. *Ever.* Anyone who doesn't understand that will answer to me personally, and it won't be pleasant. Tell your men."

Smith was a member of the Special Forces before he started overseeing security for me and my brothers. He doesn't normally man the gates, but the election has made his job a whole lot more complicated. And it's going to become more complicated still. Before this is all over, I suspect Gabrielle will have him longing to be back in uniform, patrolling the darkest corners of Jalalabad.

I turn on the kitchen monitor and watch Gabrielle stomping around outside the front gate. She's waving her hands around and yelling at Smith like she's oblivious to the fact he's got nearly a foot on her and at least a hundred pounds of solid muscle.

She's always had fire in her blood. And I've always enjoyed it. My dick's hard just watching her little scene.

Sending her away is a risk, but it's important to show her right from the start I mean business. Otherwise, she'll do whatever she wants, and that is not an option.

Not five minutes pass before Smith calls back. "JD, the woman refuses to leave until she has a word with you. She's wild, and not much we can do without putting a hand on her. If you give the okay, we can fold her into the car and send her on her way. We'll be gentle, though she's a live one, and I'm not sure she won't just ram the gate," he mutters.

I can still see those bruises the asshole *Dean* put on her. She can cover them all she wants, but they're etched on my brain. "Not a goddamn finger on her. I don't give a shit how gentle it is. This is the last time I say it. Put her on."

Smith offers Gabrielle the phone.

She yanks it out of his hand and presses it to her ear. "You demanded my presence at eight o'clock. It's eight twenty-five, and I've been out here for at least ten minutes arguing with your goons. I got caught up in a meeting, and then in traffic. I'm fifteen minutes late and you won't see me?"

Tonight can't be on her terms. I can't afford it. *And neither can she.*

"Good evening, Gabrielle. Did you have a pleasant day? I'm sorry things didn't go as you hoped with the bank. That's normally how polite conversations begin. After all these years, I figured you'd need a little training on how to suck my cock, but if I have to teach you the most basic of courtesies, you'll be paying me back for a long time."

Her breathing is ragged. I glance at the monitor. She has one hand on the hood of the car, as if to steady herself. I can practically see the fumes spilling out of her luscious body.

"The instructions were to meet Antoine at eight o'clock in the hotel lobby. You were to either get in the car or send him away. There was no option of driving that piece of junk you call a car to my house."

"But . . ."

"No buts. I'm not interested in excuses."

"Should I cross-stitch that on a sofa cushion?"

"Whatever it takes for you to remember."

She kicks the car tire and hobbles back. *Jesus.* Gabrielle, this could be so much easier on both of us if you would just do what I ask.

"How do you know about the bank?" she demands.

"I already told you. I know everything I care to know."

"There was a time when you were a decent human being."

That was aimed right at my chest. But I deflect it before it finds the target. "I'm in a benevolent mood tonight, so I'll give you another chance. But before you begin to question my parentage in front of the security detail, I would think twice. My mood isn't that good."

Her full, pink lips part, and I swallow hard. *Fuck, she's gorgeous.* Tall and lithe, her dark mane sprinkled with wispy highlights that sparkle under the security lights.

And all that sinful hair curling around her breasts. I don't need to touch it. I know exactly how it feels sliding through my fingers, wound tight around my hand, or tickling my stomach while her hot, silky mouth torments me.

I massage my cock through the coarse denim, trying to soothe some of the need. Trying to get it to calm the fuck down before it owns me completely.

But she wets her lips and looks directly through the monitor at me with those soulful brown eyes, rich and deep. And I almost call the whole thing off. I almost come clean. I almost beg to lick her pussy so I can taste for myself if it's as sweet as I remember.

But I don't have the luxury of indulging fantasies or placating my base drives. Fortunately, Gabrielle opens her mouth before I do anything foolish, and her words are a harsh reminder of reality.

"What exactly do you want from me? Spell it out so there's no confusion."

There is no surrender in her voice, and the part of me that doesn't require her surrender is proud. Proud of the way she refuses to cower and bend to my whims. This pride will be my undoing if I'm not careful. I will not let that happen.

"What do you want?" she demands again, in a huffy voice that might accompany a churlish foot stomp. She's sexy as hell when she's pissed off.

"I have a list, kitten. And don't worry, you'll learn quickly not to get confused. But that's for another time. First you need to show me you can follow simple instructions. Antoine will be at the hotel tomorrow at eight. Get in the car with him, or don't. But there won't be any more chances."

"So help me God, if you call me kitten again, I'll chop off your balls with a rusty axe while you sleep." She ends the call, tosses the phone to Smith, and stalks off.

Smith knows I'm watching, and that sonofabitch stares directly into the camera, not even bothering to bite back the smirk. If he wasn't my closest friend, I'd fire his ass.

7

Gabrielle

I don't bother to shower after work. I'll need to wash away the slime after I meet with JD anyway.

After pulling my hair into a severe ponytail, secured by the fattest, ugliest hair tie in my drawer, I scrub off all my makeup, and throw on a pair of unflattering sweatpants, ballet flats, and a stained T-shirt I wore when gilding hotel furniture in an effort to save money.

Maybe if I make myself unappealing, he'll look elsewhere for a little side piece. Deep down, I know this thinking is childish, because it's not about sex. I don't know what's going on, but it isn't about sex. It just isn't.

I catch my reflection in the mirror. It's not a pretty sight. I can't believe I'm setting foot outside my suite looking like this. *Southern women don't leave home looking like they haven't bothered. It's not about vanity. It's just impolite.* My mother's disapproving voice booms inside my head, as though she's standing beside me. For a half-second I think about changing, but decide against it. He wants me? This is what he gets. And it's too good for him.

I select the longest coat in the closet, one certain to cover my fashion sins, and belt it tightly, so I'm not walking through my beautiful hotel looking like something the cat dragged in from the woods.

When I arrive in the lobby, Antoine is already waiting.

"Ms. Duval," he says with a polite nod and a wide smile. I want to hug him, and for a minute he looks like he wants to hug me too. But he doesn't. "The car's just outside. Follow me," he says in a much too formal, stilted voice.

Antoine grew up on Wildwood Plantation, just like me. His parents worked for the Wilders, too. He's five years older, so we were never really friends growing up, but he was always kind to me. When I was six, he rescued me from the loft in the stable where I hid while playing hide-and-seek. I knocked the ladder over by accident when I reached the top and was too frightened to jump down. I was terrified I'd be stuck there all night, but afraid to yell for help because I had wet my pants. After he helped me down, he tied his sweatshirt around my waist so no one would see my soiled clothes. He never said a word about it.

"Here we are, Ms. Duval," Antoine says, holding the car door for me.

Ms. Duval. The formality stings. "Antoine, we've known each other forever. Please call me Gabby."

"Gabby was a skinny little girl in braids. You don't look much like her."

"I'm still me."

"If you say so."

"How are your parents?"

"Getting old. Happens to all of us if we're lucky."

"Please send them my best."

"I will."

I feel like there's so much to say, so many things and people we can talk about, so many questions that I want answers to, but we ride in silence. It's loud and uncomfortable, at least for me. "Do you like working for him?" I ask, hoping to draw him into conversation.

"Mr. Wilder?"

Mr. Wilder? This surprises me, and I speak without thinking. "JD has you call him Mr. Wilder?"

"Do I like working for him? Very much. I've always liked him."

Antoine ignores my last question, and I don't press. I know enough about how these types of relationships work to know that regardless of what he calls JD in private, he would always refer to him as Mr. Wilder in public. Even in front of me.

"*Hmmm*. He seems different."

"He's a man now. More responsibilities. Bigger problems. That's the only real difference I see." He catches my eye in the rearview mirror. "I'm going to put up the partition now. Keep us both out of trouble. Especially me."

Before Antoine left to join the Marines, we threw a big party for him. Lally, who ran the Wildwood kitchen back then, cooked for days, and my mother baked a dozen peach pies. They were his favorite.

It was the Fourth of July, and the air hung thick and salty, crackling with the promise of fireworks over Charleston. That night, Julian kissed me for the first time. It had been all day in coming.

When no one was looking, he dragged me behind the stable under a starless sky, and pinned me between his solid frame and the vast wooden structure. I was breathless while his mouth worked magic on mine. I had never been kissed before. Not like this.

The heat surged between us, smoky billows wafting and curling, until we were wrapped in a hazy fog. My fourteen-year-old heart pounded, and waves of pleasure rippled through me as he brushed loose tendrils off my face. His strong fingers slid all the way to the silky ends, skimming my newly developed breasts ever so slowly. My nipples furled and tightened for him, greedy for some attention. When his tongue slipped between my wet lips, I swayed into him.

He was hard, *there*. I had watched horses mate, so I wasn't completely naïve, but I'd never been anywhere near a boy's cock. I dug my fingers into his shoulders, rocking and grinding against the long, thick bulge, my young body tingling and quaking as it awakened. Time stood still while a flurry of fireworks exploded around us. They were nothing compared to what was happening inside me. It was sublime.

In the last fifteen years, I've seen JD on television, in newspapers, and gracing the pages of glossy magazines. And I've caught sight of him a handful of times from a distance. But that's it. When I came back to Charleston, I heard he'd grown harder and meaner with age. Some said his soul was as black as his daddy's. My parents, Lally, and Antoine don't seem to share that view, although my parents never say too much about him.

From the outside looking in, the Wilders seem like ordinary rich folks. The kind living all over Charleston. But when you get up close, they're nothing more than a crime family, and Wilder Holdings, a criminal enterprise. They control all of Charleston, and most of South Carolina. The darkest elements of their *business* lurk in the shadows, but the rest is out in the open. Why not? They have no shame and much of law enforcement is in their pocket. When that doesn't prove to be enough, they have fixers, corrupt lawyers, and thugs who do the dirty work, and clean up the messes they invariably leave behind.

DW is the devil in disguise. He has no conscience, no remorse, feels no empathy. Never has. People from around here figure he wants to be president as a way to fill the company coffers. Others feel he craves the legitimacy of the office.

Half the city believes he had his first wife killed, the other half is skeptical because the children were in the car when it happened. Apparently murdering your own blood is a bridge too far, even for the likes of him. I've always thought it possible.

It's a quick trip to Sweetgrass, the Sayle family home, where JD's mother grew up. I haven't been here in ages, but from what I remember, it's a magnificent antebellum property with rich history. The family had an army of servants at their beck and call, but slaves never worked there. JD took it as his own when he returned to Charleston after business school.

Antoine lowers the partition as we pull up. The car stops briefly at the gate, and we're waved through.

"How do they know you aren't hiding someone in the trunk?"

He catches my eye in the rearview mirror. "They know." His gaze is deadly serious, and I don't doubt for a second he's telling the truth.

We drive down the quaint lane lined with live oaks rustling in the breeze, the Spanish moss draped over the sprawling branches like a scene from a gothic romance. It's stunning, lulling me into a lush, sleepy fantasy, and I almost forget why I'm here. *Almost.*

But as we approach the main house, even fanciful daydreams can no longer distract me from the purpose of tonight's dinner. I wrap my coat tighter to ward off the sudden chill.

Antoine enters the circular driveway, and I can't help but admire the gracious piazza that extends the full length of the house. Its haint blue ceiling and white wicker swing with striped cushions strewn casually across the back exude effortless charm.

The car stops directly in front of the house. My heart is heavy as I gaze at the clusters of manicured evergreens flanking the entrance. They stand tall and proud in decorative urns, welcoming guests. They're lovely, but not meant for me.

I am not a guest. And I won't pretend to be. I can have transactional relationships, too. I'm here to do a job, like the housekeeper, or the plumber, or the man who cleans the fallen leaves from the gutters. Only my job is to *scratch any itch JD might have,* isn't that how he put it?

"Where's the kitchen entrance?" I ask when Antoine engages the emergency brake.

"Around to the side." He points toward the far end of the main entrance.

I don't remember exactly where it is, and that side of the house is dark. "Would you mind dropping me there?"

"I don't think Mr. Wilder would appreciate guests arriving through the kitchen."

I'm not a guest. But I don't want to make trouble for him. "I'll get out here." Before Antoine can come around to open the door for me, I'm out of the car. I'm behaving like a selfish brat. I know it, but I'm jittery and can't seem to control my emotions now that I'm here.

None of this is Antoine's doing, and the greatest respect I can afford him is to allow him to do his job with dignity. I know this. I feel a small pang of regret, but I want JD to have to let me in through the servant's entrance. I want—I *need* to make the point with him.

I start down the walk toward the side of the house.

"Ms. Duval, where are you going? The front door's behind you."

"Don't worry. I'm sorry for all of this. I promise there won't be any trouble for you."

"I'm not worried about trouble for me. You've been away from here for too long." He jumps back into the driver's seat, inching the car forward, lighting my path while keeping me in his line of vision.

I ring the bell at what seems to be the kitchen entrance. After a couple of minutes, the light comes on, and JD opens the heavy wooden door and unlatches the outside screen that I'm sure Lally insists on keeping up, even in November.

He pushes the screen door open and searches over my head, past me. "Did Antoine leave you here?"

"Good evening, JD. It's so nice to see you again. Did you have a pleasant day? That's how polite conversations normally begin. I figured after all this time you'd need some training on how to lick my pussy, but I didn't think I'd have to teach you the most basic of manners. And no, Antoine insisted on leaving me at the front door. But I know my place. The help always enters through the kitchen."

One side of his mouth curls, and the smile, with all its playful light, reaches his eyes. At least I thought it did.

"Cute. I opened the back door for you tonight because it's dark out, but next time you pull a little stunt like that, I'll make you walk around the front to come inside. Don't play games with me, Gabrielle. You'll never win."

I slip off my coat, shrugging away his assistance. He takes it from me, and hangs it on a hook in the back hall. I keep the scarf. It adds to my unkempt look and hides the bruises he can't seem to keep his eyes off of.

"How about a drink?" he asks.

I desperately want a bourbon. Something to numb me before the onslaught of emotional pain that's sure to come. But I should have my wits about me for this discussion. "I'll have a glass of wine. Red if you have it."

He looks so young and relaxed mixing drinks in the kitchen, like this isn't some sick horror show. Something about him in a pair of faded jeans and a Gamecock T-shirt softens me, too. I've always thought the University of South Carolina could have chosen a more dignified mascot, but JD always loved the damn thing.

I'm fascinated as he painstakingly measures the gin and fresh lemon juice, and adds simple syrup to a cocktail shaker. By the time he finishes with a splash of a brand of French cassis—that's not easy to find—my fascination has given way to a quiet unease.

He hands me the chilled couplet with a brandy-soaked Luxardo cherry suspended from the glass stirrer laid across the rim. It's the signature cocktail at the Gatehouse, my hotel. And this is exactly how we serve it. I catch myself with my mouth open and press my lips together to hide my surprise.

"We'll have wine with dinner. You look like you could use something stronger. Rough day?"

Oh, how I want to slap that smug look off his face, but I savor the icy pink liquid instead.

"How is it?" He sips his bourbon, watching me over the rim.

Delicious. Exactly the way I like it. "Not bad," I tell him.

"Not bad, huh? You're still a terrible liar."

"How do you know about the Gatehouse's signature drink? It's something we created in-house. And we don't share the recipe."

"I make it my business to know everything that happens in these parts." He nudges a small bowl of spiced nuts toward me and clinks his glass against mine. "To a long, satisfying relationship."

My stomach roils in protest. First, he gets access to the executive suite of the hotel, and now he knows about the drink. It's as though he has a spy on the inside. Maybe Gray—no, Gray didn't have anything to do with the bar and he certainly doesn't have a set of keys to my office. Although I don't know who else would have shared that information with him. "Did Gray tell you about the drink?" I blurt it gracelessly, not bothering to smooth the sharp edges.

"How does my brother know about your drink?"

"Gray helped me with the restaurant and made some connections for me."

JD licks his bottom lip, and then scrapes his teeth over it.

He doesn't know Gray helped me.

"I thought you knew everything about the hotel?"

He shrugs. "Everything I care to know. Dinner will be ready in about twenty minutes."

I set down my drink, harder than I mean to, and the stirrer with the bloated cherry plops into the glass, splashing a few drops onto my wrist. Before I can reach for a napkin, JD grabs my arm and sucks the sticky liquid from my skin. It's audacious. But no more so than demanding I trade my body for my mother's health. He catches me by surprise, again, and it takes several seconds before I even think to pull away.

"*Mmmm.* Delicious," he murmurs. "Could whet any man's appetite."

I yank my glistening wrist from his clutches and rub it on my leg. The friction dries the skin but doesn't erase the memory of his mouth.

His lips.

His tongue.

Or the rasp of his teeth over the sensitive flesh. The sensations are all still there, each one bold and haunting.

I need to get out of here. *Now.*

"I'm not hungry. Let's stop dancing around, pretending like this is a pleasant evening between old friends. Let's just get it over with."

JD leans across the center island and fingers my ponytail. "Always so impatient for the climax. Didn't matter if it was a storybook or an evening in the stable. But when you get there, no matter how sweet it is, darlin', the thrill is over. Anticipation is the first leg of every satisfying journey. Learn to enjoy it."

I adjust my scarf to hide my nipples peeking through the threadbare T-shirt. The last thing I need him to know is how his words affect me. "Pearls of wisdom aside, I'm really not hungry."

"Well, I'm starved. And you don't want to negotiate with me when I'm hungry. You'd do better to ply me full of Lally's cooking and some decent booze first."

The doorbell chimes, and there's barking outside the kitchen. JD opens the door and a yellow Lab wearing a blue and white bandanna leaps over the threshold, his silky tail wagging furiously.

JD gets down and rubs his hands over the golden fur. The dog licks his face in return. It's genuine and sweet, and it reminds me of a young JD. For several seconds, I forget I'm here to negotiate for my mother's life, and I smile, an honest smile, for the first time since I arrived. Maybe for the first time since he walked into my office.

"Thanks," he calls to someone outside. "He smells so good I might even let him into my bed." The door shuts, and I hear the lock click. "Sumter," he says, approaching me, "we have company."

The dog circles me once, then sits at my feet. I let him sniff my fingers before I run my palm along his glossy coat. He's a beauty, strong and lean, and far more civilized than his owner. When I scratch behind his ears, he lifts his snout, his lids fall shut, and he practically purrs. Sumter is a lovable ham, and I can't stop smiling. "You have a dog?"

"Don't act so surprised."

"It's just—"

"That monsters don't have pets? Even Hades kept a dog."

It's not too far off from what I was thinking, but of course I don't say that. "You must work long days. I didn't think you'd have time for a dog."

"I make time for the things that are important."

"*Sumter.*" My heart clenches tightly. "That was the name of Zack's stuffed bunny. The one he dragged everywhere by the ears."

JD chews on the corner of his bottom lip. "Lots of things around here named Sumter."

I stare right at him. Hold those brilliant blue eyes in a tight lock until I can practically see into his soul. The intensity would unnerve most people, but he doesn't look away. And he won't. Not before I do. It'll make him appear too weak. But he shifts his weight from one foot to the other. It's a subtle move, but for JD, it's the equivalent of squirming.

"I'm surprised you remembered."

A whole host of feelings grabs hold of me, and without any

warning, the past, with everything we shared, seems far more important than why I'm here tonight. I reach for him, in spite of myself. In spite of the terrible circumstances he's created for us. My hand and his arm. A magnetic pull, orchestrated from somewhere beyond my control. "Of course I remember. I loved Zack."

For several seconds, he looks young and lost. Not so different than he looked the morning they buried his mother and Sera. It's a side of JD he rarely lets anyone see, and for a few seconds I struggle with the overwhelming emotion.

"Your brothers are always uncomfortable when I ask about Zack. Even Chase doesn't really like to talk about him. Do you still visit him? How is he?"

JD nods. "The same. He'll always be the same, until the day he takes his last breath." He looks down at where my hand rests on his skin. "I'll be right back. Sumter, let's go, buddy."

The whiff of humanity lingers in the kitchen after he leaves, competing with the delicious smells from the oven. And right now, I'm the one who's lost.

Something is going on here. There's more to this than he's telling me. He hasn't really changed. I see too many glimpses of the past in him. I look out the kitchen window onto the sprawling yard. The moon shines through the trees, creating lacy shadows on the cold ground. *Or maybe I just want to see the flashes of good. Maybe I need to believe I wasn't a foolish teenager who fell in love with a boy who only wanted her for dirty sex. Maybe I need to believe that the tiny, tiny place in my heart, wedged into a far distant corner, the one that will always belong to him, isn't simply wasted space.*

Gabrielle, you're a grown woman. No more excuses. No more fairy tales. You can't rewrite those chapters of your life.

The timer goes off just as JD returns. The vulnerability is gone, replaced with that cocky swagger he hides behind. He grabs a pair of quilted mitts from a hook above the stove and pulls a casserole from the oven.

"*Whoa*. This sucker is hot."

Clouds of steam rise from the baking dish, and I hear the cracklings sizzle and pop. I crane my neck to get a better look. It's Lally's special red rice, with sausage, chicken, bits of ham, and shrimp.

"Why don't you have a seat. I usually eat there." He points to a table tucked between a large bay window and a cavernous stone fireplace with a potbelly stove tucked inside. The warmth from the fireplace soothes my frazzled nerves.

"I think it's more comfortable in here," he says, "but we can eat in the dining room, if you prefer."

Comfortable.

Everything this isn't. Everything it will never be.

"This is fine." I place my glass on the table and cling to the back of a padded chair. I recognize the handwork on the fabric. Neat, precise stitches in a multitude of colors. My fingers graze the raised pattern. I feel his eyes on me while I examine the cross-stitch.

"They were a housewarming gift from your mother."

"*Mmhm,*" is all I can muster. *A gift from your mother—the same mother I'm using to blackmail you.*

The scent of humanity has evaporated. All traces gone, as though it never existed. There really are no words to describe how surreal this whole scene feels. How depraved he is. It's as though I'm wading through a swamp in the black of night, unsure when the monstrous creature will emerge to drag me into the murky water. I only know it will happen.

He sets a plate in front of me. Rice, okra, and a generous wedge of cornbread. Growing up, it was my favorite meal. I requested it for my birthday every year. *Oh, God!* My face burns with shame. "You—you told Lally I'd be here."

He shakes his head. "No. She's always nagging me about what to prepare for dinner. I asked her to make it for last night." He shrugs. "It's better the second day, anyway."

Lally cooked at Wildwood for all of us. She's ten years older than me, and has always been like a big sister or a young aunt who I went to for advice and trusted to keep my secrets. She can't know anything about my arrangement with JD. *If* there is an arrangement. I would die if she knew.

It's all delicious, but I can't swallow more than a couple forkfuls. Even after the drink, my insides are shaking. My grandmother always told me if you don't lie, you'll never have to worry about keeping your story straight, and if you don't do shameful things, you'll never be ashamed. *Easier said than done.*

I can feel his eyes on me as I push the rice around the plate.

"You should eat. Lally would be so disappointed to know you just picked at her food."

"What would disappoint Lally is you treating me like a toy. Like I'm less than a person. Like I'm as disposable as a paper napkin. She'd beat your ass with a broom if she knew."

"That she would." He breaks off a piece of my untouched cornbread and pops it into his mouth. "Tell me about the Gatehouse."

If you don't like the subject, just change it to something you do want to talk about. *Right, JD?* "I thought you knew everything you cared to know."

"I want to hear it from you. The kinds of things you worry about, and things about the hotel you love. When you own a business, there's always something to worry about, but the worries should always be outweighed by the things that bring you satisfaction. The stuff that makes you happy." He shrugs. "Otherwise you should find something else to do."

"Why do you want to know? So you can have something else to hold over me?"

He pushes his empty plate away. "It doesn't have to be like this, Gabrielle."

JD watches while I stare into my dish, seeing nothing. I feel the sear on my skin for long, excruciating minutes, while I try to figure out a way around this lunacy. My mind races in circles, until I'm ready to scream.

"Do you want some coffee?" he asks quietly.

"*No.* No more. I want to know where my mother is. And Dean. His sister called me late last night. His phone is off, and they haven't heard from him in over a week. They're worried something terrible has happened to him. Did it? Is he still alive?"

JD taps a finger on the edge of his plate, hard enough to make the fork rattle. "Your former fiancé has relocated to a warmer climate. Last I heard, he was alive and well. I'll pass the message along and make sure he gets word to his family."

My head is pounding. "You bought him off?"

"It sounds so unsavory when you put it like that. But yes, in a manner of speaking, I suppose I did."

I couldn't care less where Dean is, as long as he's alive, but the idea that JD would barge into my life and buy off my fiancé because it suits his plan—and that Dean would take the money and disappear—it's infuriating. All of it.

I glance at JD. He was livid about my bruises. *Livid.* There's no way he rewarded Dean with a wad of cash. I don't believe it. "Where is he?"

"Are you sorry he's out of your life?"

"Did you kill him?"

JD digs his fingers into the tabletop, and the long, sinewy muscles in his forearms contract. "I am not a killer. At least not yet. But if you keep talking about him, that might change. Because every time I hear his name from the woman with bruises on her throat, bruises he put there, I want to find the sonofabitch and murder him with my bare hands. Not one more word about him," he snarls.

This might be over for now, because you're not going to tell me anything more tonight, but we will revisit this conversation, JD. "My parents? I want to speak to them."

"You can call them when we're finished."

Fine. I'm anxious to speak to them, but this will give me a chance to iron out the details before I talk to them. It will be good to have some sense of exactly what I'm dealing with here. Is this a one-time thing? Weekly? Nightly? I need to know before I make any decisions. "What exactly does this—arrangement—you're proposing entail?"

"I won't delve into every salacious detail, because I know you're fully aware of what it entails."

Not an answer. "What do you expect from me?"

"You don't really want me to spell it out."

"But I do. Spell it out, JD. Tell me exactly how you plan on degrading me, as though I'm not human. Go ahead," I challenge. "I'm sure it'll bring you lots of *pleasure*."

"Gabrielle, you test my patience too often. One day you'll get more than you bargained for."

He's fiddling with his knife. He can't meet my eyes. He doesn't want to say it. Something about it makes him uncomfortable. Somewhere inside he knows it's wrong. I'm a bit relieved, but I won't let him off the hook. I want him to squirm with discomfort. I want his stomach to churn until he tastes the bitter bile in his throat. I want whatever spark of conscience is left to keep him awake at night. If he wants to do this to me, he's going to pay. "Spell. It. Out. Unless you're too ashamed to say the words out loud."

His eyes are black when he drags my chair to him, pinning my legs between his until I can't move. His right thumb finds my chin, forcing me to meet his eyes. "It takes a lot to shame me. But we're about to find out where you draw the line."

I jerk my chin from his hold. In return, he squeezes his thighs around mine, holding them in a vise-like grip, the exquisite pressure forcing a bloom between my legs.

"You'll get on your knees and put my cock in your sassy mouth any time I tell you to. After I come, you'll lick every drop off your lips, and you'll enjoy it. Just like you enjoyed it before.

Like you enjoyed every filthy thing I did to you. Are you ashamed yet, Gabrielle?" He lowers his head and the heat from his mouth grazes my temple. "I don't think you are."

My heart is racing. I can't control it.

"Remember all those times I buried my face in your sweet pussy while you writhed under me? How you begged me to sink my cock into you? How you screamed and clawed before you trembled? It'll be just like that. Only *nothing* is off-limits this time. You were a dirty, greedy girl who begged shamelessly for release. I bet that hasn't changed." He runs a finger over my bare arm, and I shiver. "You loved it then, all of it, and you'll love it even more now."

I maneuver back and swing my arm to slap his face. But he catches it before I make contact. "I hate you."

"You don't hate me. You hate that you want to be under me again. If I stick my fingers in your pussy, it'll tell the real story." He lowers his head again and murmurs near my ear. "Want me to do that? Slide a finger or two inside you? It'll feel so good. Remember how much you liked it? This is just too much for you to process right now. You don't know how you feel. I can help you figure it out. Let me."

I'm aroused. Disgracefully aroused by his husky voice, his filthy words, and the memories of him pleasuring me. My core is throbbing. And I don't need him to check if I'm wet. I'm drenched.

He's right. I don't hate him. I'm filled with unresolved anger, resentment, and hurt. And I'm confused. So confused. But if he stroked my breast, or brushed his fingers over the slick flesh between my thighs, I would press my pussy into his hand. No, I don't hate him. I hate myself for being so weak.

I draw a breath through my nose and let it fill my chest. It does little to calm me. "I want to speak to my mother."

He takes out his phone and scribbles down a number. "Call her."

And I do.

"Mama? How are you?" Her voice is strong and familiar, and I want to crawl into her arms like a little girl. I want her to rub my back and tell me this is all a misunderstanding. That she's not really sick. That my father didn't borrow a cent from JD. After indulging my inner child for the briefest of moments, I pull up my big girl panties and ask hard questions, befitting the adult I am, not the little girl I long to be.

"It's so good to hear your voice. I've been trying to reach you."

"They say the reception isn't good in the hospital. Before we hang up, I'll give you the direct line to my room. JD explained to your father that he told you about Houston. I'm sorry we lied to you, but I couldn't bear to see your face if the news was bad. I just couldn't put you through it again."

"JD didn't tell me much. I don't care about the lie." *Not right now.* "Just tell me what's going on with you."

"The doctors here are hopeful. Very hopeful. Not like in Charleston. This is promising." Her voice is thick with emotion. "They have a treatment—gene therapy—it's experimental, but they've used it for several years, and have had great luck with it."

"Is it safe?"

"Yes. But there can be some side effects. And because not many other places have had experience with it, I'll need to stay in Houston, near the hospital, so they can keep an eye on me. But I won't need to be in the hospital the whole time." Her speech is wobbly. She's on the verge of tears. "Once they're satisfied I'm tolerating the treatment, I can go back to Charleston. I could be here six months, but it's something I think we need to do."

"Of course you need to do it!" It's a gut reaction, but even if I thought long and hard about it, even if I considered how I'd be paying for the treatment, I wouldn't have said anything different. The truth is, I would prostitute myself in the darkest corners of hell if it would save my mother's life. "Six months will go by so fast, and I'll visit as often as I can. Do you need anything? Anything I can bring with me when I come to visit?"

"We have everything we need. More than everything. I've been here, but your father is staying in a hotel. We're more than fine, honey. What about you? How's my baby?"

"Now that I've been able to talk to you, I'm fine."

"Gabrielle, I'm a great candidate for this treatment. But I'm counting on you to be strong. It might not all be smooth sailing, but I feel like—like I have a real chance. Like I might be around long enough to spoil grandbabies." She's crying now, and so am I. I can barely understand what she's saying through the tears. "Your father wants to say hello," she snivels, handing off the phone.

"Sweet pea, we miss you."

"Hello, Daddy."

"Don't cry," he says, choked with emotion. "Your mother—we—we have a real opportunity here. I feel so blessed—I'm nothing without your mother," he sobs.

Apart from when my grandmother died, I've never seen my father shed a single tear, and I can't stop my own deluge of tears.

I'm so consumed with my parents, I forget JD is in the room, witnessing the intimate moments with them, until he places a tissue box within my reach, smoothing my hair before he walks away.

"The doctor's just come in to see your mother," my father says. "Let's talk later."

After giving me a few minutes to compose myself, JD sits beside me. He says nothing. But it's a different kind of silence. A quiet silence. Like he's not looking for the upper hand. Probably because he knows he already has it.

I need to do this. My mother's life depends on it. It's really that simple. Only it's not.

Yes, I've already had sex with him. Filthy sex, even. And it's not as though I didn't like it. I loved it.

But I had a choice then. He never forced me into anything I didn't want to do. It wasn't a business arrangement. I loved him. And I was sure he loved me.

But this—this lacks human decency in a way that our dirtiest sex never did. And what scares me the most isn't that I'll hate every second of his touch, but that I'll enjoy it. Begin to crave it, like I craved it before. The signs are all pointing to the fact that no matter how much I lash out at him, no matter how much I want to hate him, my body—and my heart—remember. They miss him.

I might let him back in my bed. But I can never let him back into my heart. He can live in that tiny corner, but he's never taking over the whole thing, again. *Never*. And I might be his whore, but I'm not giving up everything I worked for, everything I've become. I won't.

I sniff a couple of times. It's loud and unladylike. "You win. I'll agree to your sick little arrangement." I reach for a tissue and blow my nose, balling the used paper in my hands. "But you will not mark me. You will not collar me. I will not do anything that involves other people or animals. I need to work—I have an important Christmas event that I'm planning. It will require a lot of my time. The future of the hotel hinges on it."

He nods. "What else are you worried about?"

"You need to make it easy for me to travel to see my mother. And I don't want the staff here to know anything about what we're doing." I couldn't bear if Lally or Antoine, or any of the others, knew I was whoring myself, even for my mother. "Those are my rules."

"You're allowed concerns, but you don't make the rules, Gabrielle. You follow them. When you do, you'll be rewarded." He squeezes my hand, his thumb pressing firmly into the sweaty palm. "When you disobey, you'll be punished. It's that simple."

I chew on my bottom lip until it stings. There's nothing simple about this. Not a single thing.

"Of course you'll work," he says, as though I'm crazy to think otherwise. "I work too. The hotel is important to you. Owning a beautiful hotel downtown has been your dream forever. I remember when you outgrew the dollhouse your father built, you used scraps of velvet and brocade to turn it into a glamorous hotel. You and Georgina—and Sera—made a huge mess on the driveway with gold spray paint."

JD tucks some strands of loose hair behind my ear. It's almost as though he's forgotten why we're here. As though he's let himself get lost in the past, and for a few seconds he pulls me back with him. His words are like a balm. I feel myself softening, growing malleable.

But just as the confusion begins to abate, he speaks and I'm left brittle, searching for answers again. "I'm not interested in destroying your dreams or hurting you." He pauses, as if to let the words sink in.

Not interested in hurting me? Then what the hell does he think he's doing?

"I'm not looking for another pet, or to share you with anyone or anything else, and despite what you believe, I'm not like your ex-fiancé. I won't leave those kinds of marks on your skin. But if you disobey me, if you push me too far, I'll redden your ass until sitting down is next to impossible, and then I'll fuck you until you scream." The words are threatening, but his voice is smooth, like freshly whipped cream that melts into a sweet, milky puddle on a warm tongue. "But that's more about pleasure than pain," he murmurs. "There are far better ways to punish you than to beat you."

I swallow hard. My skin is overheated, my cunt pulsing with need. My breasts are heavy and swollen, slip-ripe peaches wrapped in intricate lace, the silken threads deliciously coarse against the smooth, taut flesh.

"Do we have a deal?" I don't answer right away, so he prods. "Do we?"

Yes. No. I don't know. "For how long?"

"Until I'm done."

"I need an end date. Something I can focus on when it gets to be too awful."

"If you don't fight it, it won't be awful. Not even close."

No, it won't be awful. I want it to be awful, so I can hate him, but I know it won't be. "I need an end date."

"Can't give you one. Unless you want me to lie."

"When does—*it* begin?" I need something. Even a small crumb will suffice. Anything, to help me have some control over my circumstances.

"It begins when I'm ready." He pulls my chair closer, until his legs are brushing mine. "Listen carefully. Above all else, I want you to remember what I'm about to tell you. Tattoo it on your skin, or cross-stitch it on a sofa cushion, do whatever you need to do so you won't forget. You answer to me. *Only* to me. You obey me over everyone else. Regardless of who it is. Regardless of what kind of power they claim to have over you. Do you understand?"

"No! No, I don't understand, Julian."

He freezes at his name. *Julian and Elle.* No one but me called him Julian, and no one but Julian called me Elle. That's who we were. Who we had been so long ago. Before betrayal, manipulation, and lies. Before he threw me out like yesterday's trash. Before he insisted on absolute control over me. That's who we were.

"Do you understand what I just told you? No one but me. *Only* me."

"I don't see that there's another choice."

He nods. An arrogant nod that's the privilege of men with power.

Call it an arrangement. Call it whatever you want, but this is rape, Gabrielle. It doesn't matter how much you miss him, or how your body responds—he's forcing you into sex. And it doesn't matter whether you end up loving it. That's completely irrelevant.

I lift my chin and go straight for the jugular.

"I wonder if the man who raped my grandmother told her it wouldn't be awful. If every time he shoved his cock into her, he told himself she loved it. That she should be honored to have it. How do you think she felt when she carried my mama, knowing it was a rapist's baby? Do you think she thought to herself, *It wasn't that awful*? What do you think, JD?" I shove his arm, but he doesn't flinch.

My skin isn't dark like hers, and my hair doesn't curl like hers did, because my granddaddy, the *rapist*, and my daddy are white.

"I don't work for you, but will you think about me like that while you fuck me? Will you tell yourself that I love it? Tell yourself that no matter how light my skin is, I'm nothing more than the ancestor of slaves, and I should be honored to have your pure white cock inside me? Is that how you'll ease your conscience?"

He's motionless. Cold and stony like the statue of John Calhoun in Marion Square. His face reveals nothing. No sign that I pricked his conscience. But I am not done. "Do you remember how you reacted when I told you my grandmother's story? When I told you she said it wasn't really rape, because she never said no. Do you remember what you said? '*If he was still alive, I'd make him pay for it, Gabrielle. For every time he hurt her, he'd pay twice.*' That was what you said back then. You knew it was wrong when you were sixteen. But for some reason, now it's your God-given right to behave like an animal." I take a minute to catch my breath.

"Antoine will take you home." His voice is controlled, but I hear the rage knocking at the surface. He starts to leave the kitchen, but turns before he reaches the doorway, and comes back. Inches from my face, he pulls out the dreadful tie securing my ponytail, and my hair falls down my back.

"You can pull back your hair and scrub your face clean all you want. Did you think you made yourself unattractive to me? Is that what you think? Because all you did was remind me of the fifteen-year-old who cried out under me as I stole her innocence."

I bite down on my bottom lip, remembering the boy who treated me like a porcelain doll that night. Gentle, loving, and careful. It was his seventeenth birthday, and my virginity, wrapped in white lace panties adorned with a petite satin bow, was my gift to him. "You did not steal it. I gave it to you willingly."

He lifts my face, forcing me to look into his frosty eyes. "Just like you'll give me everything now. Willingly."

I'm not ready to surrender. I still have some fight left. "You might take my body, but you get nothing else. My soul will hover above it and watch while you violate me like the demon you are."

"Not a chance, darlin'. You'll be fully present for all of it. Mark my words. And Gabrielle, by the time I'm done, I'll own your body and your soul."

And just like that, he turns and walks out, leaving me standing in the middle of the kitchen, angry, and—dammit—aroused. My head is spinning with a whirlwind of emotion that only JD can stir up in me. I clutch the counter, gasping for breath until Antoine appears to take me home.

8

Gabrielle

I'm at my desk trying to wade through paperwork while it's quiet, but I might as well have stayed in bed. The memory of last night keeps intruding, making it impossible to get anything done.

I was all over the place last night. One minute, I wanted him, wanted everything about him, and the next, I hated him. Hated the position he's put me in. Truth be told, I've been all over the place since he sauntered into the hotel on election night. Hell, I've been all over the place since I saw him with the other girl in the stable. My mind and body warring. My mind and heart warring. Yes, dammit, my heart. It's the biggest traitor of all.

JD was all over the place, too. One minute, he was sweet and considerate, serving me my favorite meal, and the next, threatening to steal my soul. It's almost as if he's as confused as I am. As if he's conflicted in a way I don't really understand.

That's ridiculous. He engineered it—all of it. He is neither confused nor conflicted. He's playing a game. Do not forget that.

My private line rings, pulling me from the agony of the unknown. An outside call before seven thirty in the morning. *It can't be good.* "Hello?"

"Ms. Duval?"

"Yes."

"This is Patrick, JD Wilder's personal assistant. I hope it's not too early to call." When I don't respond, he keeps right on talking. "Mr. Wilder asked me to assist you with visiting your mother."

"My mother? Has something happened?"

"As far as I know, everything's fine. I didn't mean to alarm you. Mr. Wilder thought you'd like to spend some time with your parents this weekend."

I push out the breath that's stuck in my chest, but my hands are still shaking. "Yes, of course. I guess I didn't expect anyone to be calling so early."

"We get started awfully early around here. Especially Mr. Wilder." He chuckles, as though it's some sort of a private joke. "Normally his plane would be at your disposal, but things are a bit more complicated since the election. We'll get it straightened out, but in the meantime, he didn't want your visit to wait. I apologize for the inconvenience."

I wonder if Patrick knows about our *arrangement*? Could JD be so careless he'd tell people? Could he have so little regard for my reputation? I don't know. I don't seem to know anything anymore.

"How did you get this number? Only a few people have it, and I'm quite sure I didn't give it to JD."

"I'm sorry. Is there a different number I should use to reach you?"

Nice dodge, Patrick. I hope JD pays you well. "No. This is fine. But I would like to know how you got the number."

"Mr. Wilder gave it to me, but I don't know how he came to have it."

His tentacles are wedged into everything Gabrielle Duval. That's how he came to have it, Patrick. It's unnerving, and I'm furious that JD's defiled the one place I always felt safe. The little sanctuary I built for myself, that until four days ago didn't have a single memory attached to him. He's shattered all of it. And I'm still struggling to figure out why.

"I took the liberty of reserving a ticket for you. I'll email the itinerary, and if it works with your schedule, I'll purchase the ticket. Antoine will take you to the airport, and a car will be waiting when you arrive in Houston. The driver will take you directly to the hospital. Your parents are staying in a two-bedroom suite at Celene. There's plenty of room, but I'm happy to book you separate accommodations, if you prefer."

"My parents are at Celene?" *Jesus.* "No. I'll stay with them, thank you."

"The hotel is not as elegant as the Gatehouse, but it's quite comfortable."

I did demand that JD make visiting my parents easy. But even so, I want to tell Patrick that JD can shove the over-the-top luxury hotel and the private plane where the sun doesn't shine. But I don't. I'm relieved and grateful my mother is getting state-of-the-art care, and that my father has everything he needs.

I guess I'm surprised. I assumed he'd want me to spread my legs before letting me see her. *Assumed or hoped, Gabrielle?* I try to bury the thought, but it's alive and screeching, pecking at my conscience mercilessly with a strong, pointed beak.

"Thank you for making the arrangements."

"My pleasure, Ms. Duval. My contact information will be in the email. Let me know if there's anything I can do to assist you with the trip."

I say goodbye, still shaken that JD has somehow wrangled my private number. It's a small thing, but it's emblematic of what's to come. If this were a play, we'd call it foreshadowing. But this isn't make-believe. This is my life. There will be nothing, no part of my existence that won't be open to him. He as much as said so.

But I will fight to keep some modicum of control, some small part of myself that is untouched by him. Sure, I'll probably lose, but I will not go down quietly.

Georgie pokes her head into my office. "Good morning."

"Morning. You're here early."

"I'm having a sonogram this afternoon and I don't know how long it'll take. They're never on time at that office. I thought I'd get here early to get some things done before my appointment."

"Take as much time as you need this afternoon, Georgie. You work hard, and Lord knows I can't pay you what you're worth. But a few hours, here and there, is the one thing I can afford. Is Wade going with you?"

Georgie nods. "I don't know how I'd ever keep him away. Wade's like a little boy let loose in a candy store with a pocketful of change. He can't wait for this baby to be born."

"What about you? You seem a little anxious today. Are you okay?"

"I'm excited. I really am, but some days the nerves get the best of me. The doctors aren't really worried about post-partum preeclampsia. So far, there's not even a hint it might be a problem, but it killed my mother and my aunt. Some days, I just can't get it out of my head."

"Things are different now than they were when you were born. Maternal healthcare is so much better. It's all going to be fine, Georgie. I'll be there with Wade, and we'll be watching out for you every step of the way. We won't let anything happen to you or the baby."

"I know I'm being silly. It's just this feeling I can't seem to shake."

I get up and go to her, cocooning her in my arms. My mother is so much better at this, but I try to make my friend feel safe.

Sometimes I worry about Georgie giving birth, too. But I try not to go there. The thought of anything happening to her is too much to bear. "It's going to be okay, darlin'. You're going to cry at her wedding. And I'll be right beside you, bawling too. I know it's a girl, and we're gonna have so much fun spoiling her rotten."

"Damn hormones." She sniffles. "They're the cause of all that's evil in the world."

I hate to see her like this. Georgie puts on a brave face better than anyone I've ever met. Her mother died two days after giving birth, and she was an only child, raised by a drunk.

She slowly pulls out of my embrace. "I should get to work."

"Sit with me for a minute. I have a favor to ask."

She lowers herself onto the edge of the chair. "You never ask for favors. Is everything okay?"

"Everything's fine. I'm sorry to put this on you at the last minute, but any chance you'll be around this weekend?"

Her features relax, and she wiggles back in the seat. "Wade and I don't have any special plans. We're just cleaning out the spare room to get it ready for the baby. Do you need me to work?"

"If you wouldn't mind popping in for an hour or so on Saturday, and then again on Sunday, I'd be grateful. You can take Monday off."

"Happy to. Please tell me you're getting out of town, and maybe having a little fun for a change."

"I'll be in Houston, visiting my parents. I want to talk to the doctors and see for myself what's going on there."

Georgie nods, but the sour look on her face is unmistakable. I wait for her to bring up JD, but she doesn't mention him. "Hardly fun. And here I thought maybe you were sneaking away with a hot guy and putting that miserable bastard Dean behind you."

"I'm done with hot guys. They've been nothing but trouble for me. The next guy I date will be middle-aged and balding, with a slight paunch and a double chin."

Georgie chuckles. “If you don’t mind pickled onions, I hear Jacob Lott is looking for a bride.”

I stick my tongue out at her. “Thanks.”

“Do you want me to purchase the plane ticket or make hotel reservations for you?”

I shake my head. “JD’s assistant made all the travel arrangements for me.”

She nods and gets up, shoulders slumped. “I hope you know what you’re doing, Gabby.”

9

Gabrielle

On Saturday morning, I pause in the doorway of my mother's hospital room, and smile wistfully. Mama's asleep, her hair wrapped in a cream satin scarf, and my father's dozing in a recliner near the bed. They both look so peaceful, I almost hate to disturb them.

It's a spacious, private room with a bouquet of fresh flowers on the windowsill. It looks more like a room in an upscale hotel than in a hospital. Bright and fresh, immaculate, without the sterile decor and antiseptic smells I associate with hospitals.

My father opens his eyes and blinks a few times when I walk in. He seems a bit disoriented, and frailer than I remember. My mother's illness has taken a toll. I remember when my grandmother was dying—spending days upon days in a hospital, even when you're not the patient, exacts its own toll.

I go over to him and press a kiss to his cheek. He pulls me

against his chest. His heartbeat is steady and strong. And familiar.

"Let's step outside," he whispers, patting my arm. "She needs to sleep so she'll be ready for Monday."

In the hall, my father slings an arm around my shoulder and pulls me into his side. "I'm so glad you're here, sweet pea. Dean with you?"

It was inevitable they would want to know about Dean, but with everything going on in the last few days, I hadn't given much thought to what I would say when they asked. I shake my head. "I gave him back his ring."

He pulls away from me. "Did he hurt you?"

I hate lying to my father, but the truth would serve no purpose but to upset him. "The relationship wasn't right. Not for a marriage. I'm just glad I realized it in time."

My father studies me for a few seconds before pulling me back under his arm. "You're young. You'll find your soul mate."

"I wish you or Mama had told me you were coming to Houston. I would have made the trip with you."

He shakes his head. "Your mother and I talked about it at length. As much as we miss you when you're not around, I can hold down the fort here while your mother's having treatment. You need to stay in Charleston and take care of the hotel, sweet pea. That's your future. We'll be back before you know it."

"It's just—"

"Just what?"

"Mama cooks a special diet for you, and makes sure you take your blood pressure medicine, and that your shirts are pressed just the way you like them."

"I'm perfectly capable of taking care of myself. I'm not helpless. I can take care of your mama too."

He sounds a bit wounded, and I try to smooth things over. "I know you can. I can't help but worry. It's in my genes."

He chuckles. "Don't worry about me. Have you eaten?"

I nod.

"Daddy, I know we talked about it on the phone, but can you explain to me again how this all happened? How JD got involved? I'm still a little confused."

"Me too. It all happened so fast. JD called us after he heard your mama was sick. Said he wanted to help, asked some questions, and told us he'd get back in touch in a day or two. He came by to see us the very next day, and we were on a plane to Houston the day after that. He made everything easy for us."

I can't even begin to reconcile the man my father's talking about with the one who showed up in my office, wanting to use me for sex. This JD, the one helping my mother, this is the one I knew. Except back then, he would have never demanded sex in payment for his kindness.

"Your mother—she's going to beat this." He's crying softly. "I know you don't have much use for JD, but our faith was faltering, and he brought us hope. A miracle maybe."

I can't stand to see him cry. I squeeze his hand. It's smaller than I remember, and my heart clenches. "It doesn't matter what I think. I'm so grateful JD got involved."

And while I'm standing there with my father, I mean every single word. I am grateful he got involved. *Even if the terms are exorbitant.*

I ask a few questions, before it hits me—something he said earlier. My parents didn't go to him. He went to them. "How did JD find out Mama was sick?"

"Lally told him."

Lally. Of course. She knew about the bruises, too. Georgina and Lally were the only ones who knew about what happened. I bet she told JD all about Dean. The little traitor. She and I are going to have a little heart-to-heart when I get back to Charleston.

My father hates when I ask about finances. In part, it's a source of pride with him, but more than that, he isn't very literate and only knows what my mother tells him. But we need to talk about it. "Is there enough money to pay for the treatment? And for living expenses? I heard you're staying at a pretty swanky place."

"I don't understand too much of it. Your mother—she's always taken care of the finances."

I detect a bit of a bruised ego.

"And you've always taken good care of Mama and me."

He kisses the top of my head. "JD didn't want to add to your mother's burden, so he made the arrangements for us. And his assistant Patrick took care of a lot of it too. Nice boy, Patrick. The money comes out of some kind of healthcare trust that even your mother doesn't fully understand, and the hotel bill goes straight to him. We were embarrassed he put us in such a fancy place. Have you seen it?"

I shake my head. "Not yet. But I'm staying there with you tonight."

"I got to hand it to him. JD calls every day to make sure we don't need anything. He's a busy man. But even when he was a kid, he could do a dozen things all at the same time. Always been sharp, that one."

A busy man, indeed. "Is there a plan for paying him back?" I hold my breath, hoping for—I don't really know what I'm hoping for. Answers. Just some answers.

My father shrugs and shakes his head. "When he called to tell us he found a specialist, your mother asked how much it was all going to cost. He told her she wasn't to worry about the money. Said he has more money than he'll ever need, and no one to leave it to. And he's never forgotten how good she was to him and his brothers after their mother died. Said they wouldn't have made it without her. He told your mama he was humbled by the opportunity to pay back a small portion of her kindness and generosity."

My head is spinning. I don't understand any of this, and I'm at a loss for words. He goes out of his way to take care of my parents, then he comes to me for payment. Either he is the most conniving person to walk the earth, or it makes no sense.

"Daddy, would it be okay if I speak with the case manager to find out more information about the finances? I don't want to run out of money at any point during the treatment."

"I would appreciate that, sweet pea. It would be one less thing to worry about. Your mother signed a bunch of papers. You can talk to anyone you want. The doctors, nurses. Anybody. Then maybe you can explain it to me. I'd like to understand it."

Mrs. Dupres is the case manager, but she's off for a few days. I finally hunt down the person covering for her, Ms. Sanders, and she agrees to meet with me in her office. It takes me more than an hour, and a good deal of persistence, to pin down the moving pieces. No wonder my father can't figure any of it out.

"Thank you for seeing me on such short notice. Before I go back to Charleston, I want to know how the hospital bills are being paid. And if there's an outstanding balance on my mother's account."

She nods. "I understand. It's hard to be so far away when a parent is hospitalized." Ms. Sanders scrolls through her computer screen. "Okay, let's see what we have here. It appears your mother's care is being paid through a healthcare trust."

My father got that part right. "Is there enough money to cover the entire cost of the treatment?

"There's nearly three million dollars in the trust."

Oh my God. "Three million dollars?" I squeak. That can't possibly be right. JD said the treatment could cost up to five hundred thousand dollars. "There must be some mistake."

"I don't think so. The lawyers set it up. It's pretty routine. But I'm not the case manager assigned to your mother, so let me take another peek to make sure I didn't make a mistake." She continues to scroll. "No. There's no mistake. The money is to be used for healthcare and living expenses. The definition is loose. If something happens to Vivien Duval, William Duval is the beneficiary. If there is money left in the trust once they're both deceased, Gabrielle Duval is the beneficiary of the trust. It's an irrevocable trust. A couple of pages, and the language is pretty basic."

Three million dollars? Maybe she has my mother confused with another patient. "Did Julian Wilder fund the trust?"

"I'm not at liberty to share information about the trustee. I've probably already said more than I should. You can call the legal department on Monday for more information. They'll be able to answer your questions about the trust."

An irrevocable trust. The hotel had been deeded to the city as part of a revocable trust, which is why they were able to dissolve the trust easily and sell the building without any issues. My lawyer had said if the trust had been irrevocable, it would have been next to impossible. "Just one more question, please. You said it's an irrevocable trust. Does that mean the trustee can't change his mind?"

"I'm not a lawyer, but I'm quite sure that's what it means. The hospital lawyers look closely at these trusts. This is a very costly course of treatment, and it behooves no one to run out of money midway through. That's just not how we do things here."

"Why so much money?" It's a rhetorical question and I don't expect an answer. Not from her, anyway.

She shrugs. "For this type of treatment, we would normally require that a patient could demonstrate that they had a minimum of fifty thousand dollars at their disposal. He certainly was very generous."

My mother's awake when I get to her room, and she persuades my father to take a walk so we can have some time alone. I sit by the bed and hold her hand. It's warm and has plenty of fight in it. When I think about the future the doctors in Charleston described—my father is right, if this treatment works, it will be nothing short of a miracle. We've been blessed.

"Now that he's gone, I want to know how you really feel."

My mother chuckles. "He's worse than a mother hen sometimes. I'm fine. Just tired. Being in bed makes me feel old and tired. I need to keep moving. What about you? You okay?"

"I'm just fine, now that I'm here with you."

"Your father told me about Dean. Tell me what you didn't tell him."

I want to share everything with her but then I remember I'm an adult, and she's very ill. I'll tell her one day, but not now. It would upset her too much to know Dean had been abusive. "He wasn't the man I wanted to spend my life with. Deep down, I always knew it, but I'd given up on finding the perfect man. I'm not getting any younger, and I really want a family." I smooth the bedsheet. "And I don't want to end up alone. But in the end, all that wasn't enough."

"Oh, Gabrielle." She squeezes my hand. "You're too young to settle. There's plenty of time for babies in your future. I'll be honest. I never thought he was good enough for *my* baby."

"You'd say that about anybody. What's this?" I ask, holding up an opaque glass spray bottle from the bedside stand. "Pretty bottle. Looks almost like sea glass."

"It's a mixture of rosewater and rose oil to mist my hair with before I put on my scarf, so the air conditioning doesn't dry it out."

I take the cap off and spray a little on my wrist. "Smells amazing." I bet it would be great for dry skin too. I rub the oil into my arm and sniff. "Where did you find it?"

"It was in a basket of toiletries they brought especially for me when I was admitted. This is some kind of VIP area of the hospital."

"And they know about black girl hair?"

My mother laughs. “Yes, they know about black girl hair.” She shakes her head. “They know about everything here. Nothing is too small to escape their attention. I might never leave this fancy ward.”

“You deserve it. All of it.” I take a deep breath. “Mama, can we talk about JD?”

She nods. “I was wondering when you’d bring him up. JD. He’s a complicated man.”

“That’s for sure.” I catch myself rolling my eyes, something my mother always chides me about.

“Careful,” she teases. “One day they’re going to roll out of your head.”

I smirk. “Hopefully it’ll happen on Halloween. Otherwise, that would be just plain gruesome.” It’s a private little joke we’ve shared forever.

“Honey, it might be time you got over your hurt feelings about JD. Holding a grudge weighs you down.”

“I am grateful to him for all of this.” I wave my hand across the room. “More grateful than I could ever put into words. But it was more than a few hurt feelings, Mama. When he didn’t want me anymore, he had his father send me away. It nearly killed me to be away from you and Daddy.”

“I understand how a sixteen-year-old girl thought about the circumstances like that, but you’re a grown woman now, Gabrielle. A smart woman. Is that what you still think? That he was tired of being your boyfriend so he had you sent to a fancy boarding school?”

It sounds so ridiculous when she says it, but it’s exactly the kind of thing the Wilders did. I was simply another mess to be cleaned up. “Well, since you and Daddy refuse to be honest about it, my imagination is left to run wild. I never bought the story that I won a scholarship. I’m not that special.”

“You are that special.”

I know she's not going to tell me. Not today. Maybe not ever. For some reason, it's a subject too hard for my father to talk about. I think she would tell me if it was just up to her. I do. She won't go against him on this, but I push anyway because I want to know. I want to know that they didn't scheme with JD to send me away. In my heart, I believe they didn't, but sometimes—sometimes I'm not as confident about it, and it's all because the whole damn thing is some big secret.

"Daddy won't talk about it, but maybe one day you'll tell me. Over a cup of milk tea and a lemon sugar cookie."

She closes her eyes for a few seconds, and when they open again, she doesn't look at me. "It's painful for your father, in the way few things are. I know JD being back in our lives like this has dug up the past. But please let it go. Please." She squeezes my hand. "For me." Her lids droop again, and she looks too tired to hold them open any longer.

"Why don't you take a little nap, Mama? I'll be right here when you wake up."

She nods off, and I sit alone, watching her shallow, even breaths. Except for the color of her skin, she looks so much like her mother.

My maternal grandmother, Meme, was Creole, from Louisiana. She had high cheekbones and chocolate-brown eyes, like my mother's. And like mine. But neither my mother nor I inherited her beautiful dark skin.

Meme wore ruby-red lipstick whenever she left the house, and kept a special glossy tube in her stocking drawer just for Sundays when we went to church. The color was stunning on her, and the lustrous sheen made her seem glamorous, like a movie star. I always wanted to look like her. To be like her.

When I was a little girl and my parents were out for the evening, she would paint my lips ruby red, and hold up a tissue for me to kiss, to set the color. I would always put the tissue with my lip print under my pillow before I went to sleep. "So you'll dream of your Prince Charming," she'd tell me while tucking me in.

When she was just seventeen, Meme got pregnant by the man she worked for, a sandy-haired man with blue eyes and a wife. She always said he didn't force himself on her, although she felt she had no choice but to go along with what he wanted. She insisted that every bit of shame was worth it, because he gave her a beautiful, healthy daughter. Now that I'm older, I wonder if in her heart she really believed that, or if it was something she said to make herself feel better. To make all of us feel better.

My grandmother made sure her beautiful daughter had choices. And even though she never found her own happily ever after, Meme always believed in a fairy-tale ending for her daughter and granddaughter.

Unlike her mother, my mother did get her happily ever after. She also met a fair-haired man, but my father is loving and loyal, nothing like the man who made Meme pregnant.

I am the watered-down version of those two wonderful, strong women. My skin is more golden, slightly lighter, than my mother's. But every time the sun winks at me, I turn dark brown. My mother has tight curly hair that breaks easily, like my grandmother's. I have a head of dark waves that morphs into a mass of unruly curls in the humidity.

I look white on the outside. And aside from boarding school, I've never shared their struggles of being black and biracial. *Or the joys*. My struggle is different. My struggle is not being like the women I so admire.

I smooth the blanket over my mother.

Unlike my grandmother, I have a choice. The healthcare trust JD set up is irrevocable. Regardless of what he says about turning off the tap, he can't do it. This gives me control over my life. Over my body. It gives me power.

I can play JD's game, if I choose, on my terms. It might be an opportunity to work through the past. A past that even after all these years I can't seem to let go of. I can also exact some punishment for his betrayal, if I decide I want it. This time JD can be the one left searching for answers.

A part of me wants what JD is offering, never stopped wanting it. I know I'm overmatched and can easily have my heart stomped on again if I let him get too close. If I'm not exceedingly careful. But I'm willing to take the risk.

Okay, JD. None of this makes any sense, but I'll play. If for nothing else than to see what you're up to.

10

Gabrielle

My mind is still reeling as I make my way to the arrival gate in Charleston to locate my ride. When Patrick emailed, he wasn't sure who would be meeting me, but promised someone would be waiting to drive me home.

I'm confident my mother is in good hands, and God willing, she'll have many more years on this earth. And I have JD to thank for it. Although I'm not any closer to unraveling the mystery. Why is he doing all of this? There's something I'm missing. Something behind all the money he's throwing around. Something behind the control he wants over me. *Something.*

"Good evening, Ms. Duval."

Antoine. I'm happy to see him, but a small, pathetic part of me hoped maybe JD would be waiting at the gate. "It's wonderful to see you, but don't you ever get a day off? Even God rested on Sunday."

He takes my bag out of my hand. "I get plenty of time off.

Don't you fret about me. But if you don't mind me asking, how's your mama?"

"Of course I don't mind. She begins treatment tomorrow. She's exhausted from all the tests they put her through, but in good spirits."

"I'll keep her in my prayers."

He opens the car door for me and hands me a sealed envelope after I'm settled in the backseat near a navy and white gift bag with gold tissue paper peeking out the top. "Mr. Wilder asked me to give this to you. He said to tell you he highly recommends you read it before you leave the car."

"Does he?" I'm too full of pride to have Antoine see me snapping to obey JD's commands, so I stare out the window until the partition is up, before discreetly opening the envelope. The scrawl on the embossed notecard is familiar. I'd know it even without the initials engraved at the top.

"Take the bag on the backseat with you when you leave the car. There's a gift for you inside."

I glance at the small striped bag on the seat beside me.

"We made a deal. I sent you to your parents in good faith, before demanding a single thing of you. I expect you to uphold your end of the bargain."

I reread the note several times. It speaks volumes, yet says nothing. It has me agitated. A little aroused. Maybe even a little frightened. The combination acts as a potent cocktail, and it has me squirming and fidgeting, like I've just gulped a supersized coffee laced with something sinister.

I glance at the handsome paper sack. *Every pleasurable journey begins with anticipation. Learn to enjoy it.*

The bag is a tease. There might be something wonderful inside. Like hand-dipped chocolates from Renaud's, or a sugar cookie from the little bakery on King Street. Or maybe something that brings me a different kind of pleasure. Something that fills me, or pleasantly stings my skin. Or there could be nothing at all in the bag. Maybe it's all a ruse. My fingers skim over the matte stripes, itching to crawl inside.

After a few minutes, my curiosity becomes too much to quiet, and I place the bag on my lap. It's too heavy to be empty.

Antoine can't see back here. At least I don't think he can. *I'll be careful.* I remove each fluffed sheet of tissue paper with the utmost care. Giving it a small shake to be certain nothing's lost for Antoine to find later. There's a mesh pouch with a small tube of lube, and a satin hinged box resting at the bottom of the bag. The kind of box that might hold a piece of jewelry. But I know it doesn't.

I lift the lid, and inside is a pair of shiny silver balls. Guilt, or maybe shame, pricks my conscience and I look up to make sure the partition is still raised. It is. I run a fingertip over the perfect spheres. They're smooth and cold. I take one between my fingers. It's heavy. Heavier than I expected. Heavier than the pair I experimented with in Paris.

There are instructions tucked inside the lid. I smile. Did you think I didn't know how to use these, JD? Did you think all my fun stopped the day you sent me away?

There's something else in the lid. Another note. This one written on a neon Post-it. *Slip these in before you leave for work tomorrow. I'll be by to check. Don't disappoint me.*

As I finger the smooth balls, the ache between my legs begins to throb. *I'm not sure I can wait until tomorrow, JD.*

11

Julian

I'm in Gabrielle's chair with my feet propped on her desk when she returns to the office. A laptop full of work in need of attention rests on my thighs. But it's nothing more than a prop. I haven't accomplished a damn thing in the hour I've been here.

Those steel balls vibrating in her pussy, and the remote burning a hole in my pocket, have consumed me. I'll either watch the flush spread over her skin while her slick walls clench around the stainless steel, or slap her ass if she defied me. Either way, it's a win.

"Make yourself at home, JD. Please," she calls from the doorway, in that sassy voice that makes my cock weep. The sweater dress wrapped around her lush curves doesn't help either. It accentuates every peak and valley. Whispers all her secrets.

I bite down hard on my knuckle before I dare speak. "Never

been the kind of man who needs an invitation to make himself comfortable."

"What are you doing here, JD?"

Her dress is pink. A soft knit that begs to be petted. Thin and lustrous like fine cashmere, but I know she can't afford that kind of luxury. It doesn't matter what it's made from—I ache to touch it. Ache to buy her closets full of beautiful clothes, and anything else that makes her happy. I catch myself venturing into dangerous territory, fraught with perils, and I get the hell out while I still can. "Might want to shut the door behind you."

She bristles at my tone, freezing for a minute as though she's contemplating a response.

"I don't care for myself, but I would shut it if I were in your shoes," I say.

She lifts her chin and her head tilts back, just a bit, but enough for me to see the small ripple in her throat when she swallows. Gabrielle inches the door shut, handling the knob as if it was a piece of delicate china.

"How's your morning been?" I ask, activating the remote in my pocket.

"You can't just waltz in here anytime you get the urge to toy with me. Georgina is out today, but normally she would be sitting right outside this door. You promised me I could work."

"You didn't follow my instructions, did you?"

"X-ray vision?"

I slide my feet off the desk and push out of the chair. My eyes don't waver from her face as I stalk over to where she's standing. Her lips are parted, and I can hear the shallow pants, but she doesn't move a muscle.

"I don't need x-ray vision. I know. I know just how you'd look with your pussy clenching around those balls. I know the stain that begins right below your left clavicle and spreads across your chest and neck. I know the labored breathing and the high color in your cheeks right before you come." My voice is low and rough. And she is mouth-watering. I dig deep for whatever sliver of control is left. Fighting the urge to take her hard against the wall, or drag her to the floor and mount her until she screams. But I don't do any of that.

Instead, I cup her head in both hands, tracing the outer shell of her ears with my thumbs. She lets my fingers glide through her dark tresses. Allows my knuckles to scrape her cheeks as I wade through the soft waves. She doesn't protest when my hands rest against her gorgeous tits, until the last silken wisps of hair slip through my fingers.

Her breasts are still pert, but they're the breasts of a woman now. Heavy and firm. The nipples, hard and greedy, push against the soft knit. I squeeze the tight buds with a quick, firm pinch.

"*Ahhh.*" The moan comes from deep in her belly, and she arches instinctively. It's barely a perceptible movement, but I've always been attuned to the nuances of her body. There was a time when I knew it better than my own.

I taught her the language of sex: cock, cunt, fuck, cum, and so many other words. Taught her to ask for what she needed—all without shame. And I'm the bastard who taught her to savor a small bite of pain with her pleasure. It was me. All me.

I should have known better than to drag her down that path. Because once she tasted dirty sex, once it was hardwired into her developing brain, she craved it like an addict craves the next fix. And nothing, *nothing* less, will ever give her the same kind of high.

Did I enjoy it? Every second. But the guilt has dogged me for years.

They should burn me alive for leading her there. Tie me to a stake while the flames of damnation engulf me, until all that remains is a pile of ashes and the teeth I used to mark her flesh. That's what I deserve.

And now, JD—now you're going to lure her back into the dark. Use her addiction to control her. Jesus.

I draw in a breath, and release it. "Where are the silver balls?"

"Upstairs."

"Upstairs. Is that what I told you to do with them? To leave them upstairs?"

She shakes her head. "I have a business to run. They're too distracting. I need to work."

"Too distracting. How do you know they're distracting?"

"I've—I've experimented with them before."

"Have you?" I can feel the corner of my mouth curl until the impact of her words hits me. *She played with someone else the way she played with me.* Of course, I knew it was possible, likely even. She was engaged, for chrissake, but hearing it still guts me. "When?"

"Paris."

"With whom?"

"That's none of your business."

I tip her chin and force her to look at me. "With whom?"

She jerks her chin away from my hold. "I used them alone." Her cheeks are flushed, and my cock is throbbing.

"Just in Paris? Was that the only time?"

"And last night," she whispers, lowering her eyes.

Last night. Fuuuck. "You had them in last night?"

"Yes." Her voice is soft. Her tone pliant.

"Did they make you feel good?"

"*Mmhm.*"

I twist her hair into a ponytail, winding it loosely around my hand. Enjoying the silky fibers against my skin more than I should.

"Did you touch yourself while they were in your pussy, dirty girl?" I tug gently when she doesn't answer.

"Yes," she whimpers.

"Did you come without me?"

She says nothing.

"Did you, Gabrielle?"

She starts to nod, but the movement is halting because I have her hair in a firm grip now.

"No orgasms without me, Gabrielle." I lower my head, and my voice. My mouth grazes her ear intimately, so close, the heat off her skin warms my lips. "I want you needy and wet when you come to me at the end of the day. You don't get to take the edge off. You don't get to make your greedy little cunt happy. Only I get to do that."

She lifts her chin defiantly. The movement must hurt because I'm still holding a fistful of her hair. But she doesn't blink. And her voice is strong and clear, like a fucking queen. "You don't get to tell me what I can do with my body. That was *not* part of the deal."

I want to smile. Because I love her feistiness, her courage, because she's telling me to fuck off while I tower over her with a fistful of hair in my hand. But I don't. I can't.

"The next time you come without my permission, I will tie you to my bed and spend hours bringing you to the edge without letting you have even the tiniest bit of relief." I lower my head again to whisper near her ear. "You will be a whimpering, sweaty mess, floating helplessly in subspace. You won't even know your own name."

A small moan escapes, and she sways closer to me. Closer to my cock. My control is fraying at the edges. I can feel it unraveling, one strand at a time.

"Do you remember what I said I'd do if you didn't obey?"

Her fleshy pink tongue darts out and wets her bottom lip. "Spank my ass red, until I can't sit down, and then fuck me until I scream." Gabrielle gazes up at me through thick, dark lashes, as the words glide off her tongue. She's gauging my reaction. The cheeky look on her face is stunning.

She's not afraid. Her lips are pulled into the smallest of brazen smiles. Her eyes gleaming. She wants me to punish her.

I let go of her hair and force my hands down, curling my

fingers into tight fists. I watch as she flicks that sweet tongue over the bow of her lips. I feel the rumble of desire in my chest. And right now, there is nothing, nothing in the entire sordid history of dirty, filthy things, that I don't want to do to her.

If I was a God-fearing man, now's the time I'd get on my knees and pray for forgiveness for every indecent thing I have planned —and for the ones that I haven't planned—the ones that will be driven in the moment by primitive lust. Basic and pure. Hers and mine. But I'm not a good man, and there's only one thing I fear, one thing that haunts my dreams, and it sure as hell isn't God.

I suck in a breath and smooth her hair. "Such a good girl. You remembered what I told you. I need you to remember everything I tell you. I need you to obey me—always. Will you do that?"

She lowers her eyes and nods.

And more than anything, I want it to be the truth. It's the only real hope I have for keeping her safe.

"Maybe I'll go easy on you today. Would you like that?" She bows her head, and pushes it gently into my hand, like a sleek feline currying favor. If I didn't know better, I might believe she's surrendered. I press my lips to her crown, knowing full well that her claws might be in for now, but they're sharp and can strike without warning. "Let's go upstairs and find the pretty silver balls. I want to slide them inside you and watch your pussy quiver. Tell your assistant you'll be out of the office for a couple hours."

She squints, and her head falls back. The mood shifts dramatically. "A couple hours? I have a staff meeting."

"You should have thought about that before you disobeyed me."

She stands inches from me, with those pouty lips I desperately want wrapped around my cock. The claws have emerged. The wheels are spinning, and I'm not sure if she's going to tell me to go to hell, or follow my instructions. Just as my patience grows thin, she picks up the phone.

12

Gabrielle

We take the back staircase up to my living area. When we get to the top, JD flicks the overhead lights off, leaving just the low emergency lighting to illuminate the stairs. He pins me to the wall behind the exit door, my hands firmly above my head.

His long fingers slide through mine, and I close my eyes to privately savor the rough hands on my skin. All those years of riding, gripping the reins, grooming the horses, have left their mark on his hands. I can feel the wear. Every callus. Every coarse patch. It's electrifying. I push the hollow of my back into the cool wall to steady myself.

Even with my eyes closed, I know his face is near mine. I can feel the heat of his breath on my cheek. The smell of his boozy cologne mixed with the musky scent of him, the smell of sex. It's intoxicating. And if I could reach, I would run my tongue over his jaw, feel the rasp of the whiskers over the delicate flesh. I'm wet and needy, and aching for the zing of pleasure. Aching for him.

And dammit, it's not just about physical gratification. My heart wants in, too. *No, Gabrielle. No, no, no!*

JD touches my palate with the tip of his tongue, and I moan softly.

Every touch is painfully familiar, as if we did this just yesterday. The heat of his hands, his demanding mouth, and the strangled, carnal sounds that escape the back of his throat while he kisses me. My heart remembers it, all of it, even better than my body remembers.

"Gabrielle," he whispers, "look at me."

I'm afraid to open my eyes. Afraid for him to see how much I want him. Afraid he'll see the feelings that go well beyond those of wanton lust. Feelings of love that I thought sure I had banished forever. I don't want him to see any of it. I don't want to see it myself.

He lets go of my hands, but my arms stay along the wall, as though they've been anchored there. He cups my head, his thumbs grazing my cheeks. "Open your eyes."

I feel his hard cock on my belly, so close to where I need it, but just out of reach. It's excruciating. And while my eyelashes flutter open, I can think of nothing else.

My eyes begin to focus in the dim light. I see the torment in his face. The unmistakable need, twisted with something else. Something I don't know.

"Do you want this?" he demands. His voice is thick and rough, and my pussy is throbbing for him.

I open my mouth as his words begin to register. *It's an out.* He's giving me an out. *Is he?* Or is he asking because he knows I'm shamelessly aroused and won't say no? Would he really let me walk away? I don't want to know the answer. Not now.

I swallow, and nod, brushing against the thick bulge.

The knob in his throat dips and rises. "Say it," he commands. "I want to hear you say it."

"Yes." The word emerges breathy and needy. And as soon as it's out, his mouth is on mine, searing and rough, demanding, like him. He presses forward until there's not a scintilla of daylight between us. Not a smidgeon of space between my back and the wall. There's only his mouth on mine, his body welded to mine.

He's big and powerful, hard and unyielding. I gasp and shiver against him.

"You're mine," he growls, his knee wedging between my legs, pushing them apart inch by inch until a muscular leg is wedged between mine. I'm all sensation, every nerve screeching. The second, the very second his leg grazes my mound, I whimper. He does it again, deliberately brushing against my center, but this time, instead of pulling away, he lets his thigh rest against my pussy, tempting me to grind against the long, hard muscle. When I give in to the temptation, when I rock against that thick thigh, I feel his lips curl against mine.

I've lost all sight of where I am. Lost sight that one of my employees or a hotel guest could enter the stairway at a moment, or maybe I'm beyond giving a damn.

His eyes are molten when he pulls away. "Not here." He swipes at his swollen lips with the back of his hand. He's panting softly. Fighting for control. I feel it. I might not have a drop of control left in me, but he's struggling, too. It's intoxicating, and woefully arousing, and just when I'm about to sink to my knees, JD squeezes my arms. "Let's go."

He flips on the light switch as we leave the stairwell and drags me to my door.

My hand shakes while he watches me fumble with the key. As soon as we're inside, even before the door latches, his mouth is on mine. He's palming my ass roughly, canting my hips forward, and I squirm against him until I can make out the ridge of his cock through our clothes.

"Get the balls," he murmurs, but I'm not sure I can move, not sure my legs are steady enough to hold me.

When I slowly start to pull away, he yanks me back to him and digs his fingers into my flank, tracing the seam of my mouth with a pointed tongue. I open for him.

"I miss you. Miss you so damn much it hurts. I live with the pain every second of every day. It's crushing."

His voice is raw, the emotion on full display. When I hear it, my heart clenches so tightly, it forces a tear to fall. A lone, fat drop that plops on my cheek and rolls down my face. He leans in and catches it on his tongue. It belongs to him. Like so many of my tears, it's his.

This is the very moment I push away all good sense. Because I know. Because every part of my being knows he's telling me the truth.

This is how he lures you into trouble, Gabrielle. This is how it always happens. I swat the nagging voice away. It's barely audible —so easy to dismiss.

He sweeps the hair off my face, and I reach for his hand, placing a small kiss in the palm before pressing it to my cheek. The gesture feels fresh and honest, like they used to be, like they all used to be. His soft, warm eyes tell me he feels it, too.

A quiet intimacy rises between us. Sacred and enveloping, it wafts around us like frankincense in a holy ritual, purifying and cleansing our souls, preparing us for the next chapter.

"Trust me," he pleads, not just with his voice, but with his entire being. "Trust me, even though I've done shit to earn it." His finger smooths the furrow between my brows. "I'm trying to keep you safe. It's all I want. It's all I've ever wanted."

I search his face. It's guileless. *Now. Ask him, now, Gabrielle. He's vulnerable. He'll tell you everything you want to know. All the things that have tormented you for the last fifteen years. Just ask him.*

But I don't. I want him too damn much. All of him.

Make him tell you what's going on.

But right now I don't care about anything else but having him. Not revenge. Not about the upper hand. And I sure as hell don't want closure.

His mouth is on my neck. His hands on my ass, pulling me into him. I'm overcome by the sensations dancing inside, twirling seductively with long, sheer scarves trailing behind, flitting in and out of the shadows, playing an elusive game with each nerve ending, until I can barely stand. Barely breathe.

I miss you. Miss you so damn much it hurts. I live with the pain every second of every day. It's crushing. JD rains kisses on my throat, and my body rejoices, reveling in the warm rainfall after years of drought.

His words echo in my head, again and again, adding to the unsteadiness. I twine my arms around him more tightly to remain upright. When I moan, he sinks his teeth into a tendon right above my collarbone. *That* one. "*Ahhh.*" I feel the bite between my legs. It's exquisite.

"Go," he says, releasing me.

13

Gabrielle

Somehow, I make my way to the bathroom and locate the velvet box with the silver balls. I clutch it in my hand and gaze at the woman in the mirror.

Her hair is a colossal mess in that way curly hair can be when it's misbehaving. And a telling feverish glow covers her face and neck all the way down to her décolletage. Aroused. Sexed-up. Wanton. Whore. The adjectives are plentiful.

I touch a fingertip to my swollen lips. The stain I carefully applied this morning has faded to nothing. Much like my resolve and self-control.

What are you doing, Gabrielle?

I ignore the question, swatting it away while I spread a creamy balm over my bruised lips, rubbing until the skin is soothed.

But my conscience is relentless, and the questions keep coming.

Are you really going through with this? the woman in the mirror asks. I detect a judgmental tone in her voice. I lift my chin. *Yes*, I tell her. *Yes, I am*. When I can no longer bear the sanctimonious looks, I turn away. Away from her sharp eyes, boring through me, before she tells me how foolish I am. Before she warns me that my heart will surely end up in tatters again. I don't want to hear any of it. Not now.

When I enter the bedroom, JD's jacket and tie are hanging over the back of an oversized chair in the corner, where I curl up at night with a book and a cup of tea. His sleeves are rolled to the elbows, and the top three buttons of his shirt are undone, exposing a swath of sun-kissed skin. I catch a glimpse of the chain around his neck, the one his grandfather's dog tag hangs from. The one that rests near his heart. The one he never takes off. The one that caressed my skin, hundreds of times, while he reared above me. While he loved me, it rested near my heart, too.

Maybe he hasn't changed. Maybe nothing's changed. Maybe. Maybe. Maybe.

See, I can tell myself any lie I'd like. I can kid myself as much as I want. But he's the *only* man I've ever really wanted. The *only* man I've ever really loved. This truth has never loomed larger than right now. It scares me to death as I find my way to him.

He holds out his hand as I approach, and I carefully lay the box in his palm. He lifts the lid and takes out one of the balls. "So cold," he croons, placing the small sphere near my mouth. "Open up for me, darlin'."

I shiver as the cool steel breaches my lips and slides into my warm mouth. Or maybe I'm shivering at the memory of last night. Last night, when the balls breached other pink lips, and made contact with the hot slick flesh there. I feel the heat rise in my cheeks.

JD takes the other ball between his thumb and finger, and holds it in his mouth. "I can taste you."

I gasp softly. It's not true, of course. I scrubbed the balls clean and rinsed them well before putting them away. But it doesn't stop me from averting my eyes in shame.

He holds the ball in his left cheek and fingers the neckline of my dress, tracing the contours of the deep vee. There's something hypnotic about his actions. About his voice. And when his wrist brushes against my breast, I almost forget to breathe.

"I love this shade of pink on you. It makes your eyes milk chocolate and gives your skin a rosy glow. Your flushed skin makes my cock hard. Always has."

He presses my hand over his erection. I swallow and stare into his blazing blue eyes.

"Take off your dress for me."

I do as he asks. Without hesitation. The belt comes off with ease, but my fingers are clumsy with the hidden hooks and snaps. When the last hook is free, I let the dress slide off my shoulders to the floor. I'm in nothing but a lace and satin thong and a matching camisole. And my shoes. *My heels.*

JD once fucked me over a bale of hay, in nothing but a pair of black patent leather high heels. I remember how aroused it made him. How insanely wild. How hard he bucked when he came inside me. An uncontrollable shiver skitters through me for him to see. The left corner of his mouth curls.

His gaze travels over me unhurriedly, taking in every inch of skin, leaving a sear as it passes. He lingers longer at my bare pussy, winking brazenly at him, through the pink lace. The tingle of shame begins to crawl up my spine, and I fight the urge to fidget.

The ball is out of his mouth now. His fists are clenched at his side, his thumbs grazing each knuckle, one at a time, over and over, as he admires me. "Gorgeous. Even more gorgeous than I remember. How is that even possible?" JD says the words out loud, but he's not talking to me. He's merely voicing his thoughts. It's as though I'm nothing more than chattel—a sleek sports car, a luxury watch, a prized racehorse purchased for breeding. It's unsettling, vulgar and arousing at the same time.

He's a few feet away, but I can feel the tension in his body. I can feel him struggling for control. The power is heady, and my embarrassment begins to melt.

JD steps closer and rubs my camisole between his fingers. My core zings and pulses as the silky fabric yields under his fingers. The ball is heavy in my mouth now. It's not so big, but breathing is becoming a challenge.

"You look like an angel," he murmurs, twisting a small section of my hair, "but I'm still going to punish you. Come."

I follow meekly as he pulls me to a bench at the foot of the bed, where he sits and tugs my arm gently. "Over my lap, darlin'."

He uses the sweet endearment, as though it's an invitation he's extending, but it's misleading. There's no room for negotiation in his voice. No opportunity to say, "I'm sorry, but now's not a good time. I can't attend your party."

He will punish me. It will hurt. *Won't it?* Yes, but mostly it will put me in my place. Humiliate me. That's what this kind of spanking is meant to do. Isn't it?

A small part of me contemplates bolting from the room. Getting out while I still can.

No. I want this. I crave it. A little bite of pain can turn a small tremor into an avalanche of pleasure. I learned this at his hands long ago.

I take a breath, almost forgetting to control the ball in my mouth. I shudder at the thought of nearly swallowing it.

"Gabrielle."

He's impatient. But I'm not exactly sure how to drape my body over his lap. While he slapped my ass before, it wasn't like this. Not ever like this. I've never done anything like it. Not with him. Not with anyone.

Before the awkwardness consumes me, he guides me over his thighs. I'm not entirely graceful, but not as clumsy as I feared.

The left side of my face settles into the tufted upholstery. It's cool and welcoming against my skin.

His fingers glide over my back in long, fluid motions to calm me. "Relax. Just close your eyes and feel. Let yourself experience the sensations. That's all you have to do. I'll take care of the rest. I'll take care of you."

I'll take care of you. But you didn't.

I push the thought away and let my lids fall shut, enjoying his strong fingers on my back, coaxing the knots loose. His hand moves lower, and lower still, nimble fingers pressing into the hollow space, massaging gently. I wriggle with pleasure.

"Stop squirming, Gabrielle."

"I—I—"

"*Shhh*. No talking. I want you to close your eyes, listen to my voice, and feel. That's all."

He wants total control over me. This is where he'll take it. Everything that came before was foreplay. *Go ahead, JD. Take it. Take whatever you want*—that's all that's running through my mind as his fingertips make a slow slide to my pussy, stroking the wet folds.

I moan and squeeze the bench when he slides two thick fingers inside me and slowly strums my clit with his thumb, nudging me toward the edge. "You're so wet," he murmurs, adding a third finger. "I'm sliding in and out, darlin'. It's so easy. Nothing to stop me."

His fingers feel so good. I inch my legs farther apart to give him better access. To give him more access.

"This is exactly what I want from you."

There's a pleased smile in his voice, as my pussy rocks into his hand.

"Wet and eager for me, all the time. Just like this."

Yes. Yes, I want this all the time, too.

My body is humming when I feel the cool, foreign object near my opening.

"Relax. It's just a little ball. Like last night, only this time for me." He pushes it inside, and my walls clench, welcoming the intruder with a big, lusty hug. "Good girl." He strokes me tenderly for long minutes, like a cherished pet.

"I need this one, too," he murmurs, tapping my cheek. I open my mouth and let the ball fall into his outstretched hand. "This one is much warmer." He teases my clit with the smooth steel before pushing it inside. "Don't you think?"

I jump when the balls begin to vibrate.

"*Shhh.* Just a tiny movement so you know they're there."

The sensation is heavenly. And *so* unexpected. This didn't happen last night.

"Feels good, doesn't it?"

I nod. Because it does feel good. *So good.* The balls are barely moving, but my hungry cunt laps up every twizzle, and I purr like a well-fed cat as they whirl inside me.

But the languorous feelings are short-lived. They start to shift when JD circles my ass, one cheek at a time. Pulling and separating. It's embarrassing. And arousing. And I fight to stay still.

"Relax, Gabrielle. Just enjoy my hands on you."

I try. But it's something we've never done. Something he couldn't tempt my teenaged self into agreeing to do, and somewhere I haven't gone with anyone else since.

His fingers are in the small of my back, pausing there briefly, before sliding down the long crevice between the cheeks. It's humiliating and titillating, and I want *more*. At least I think I do.

He dips his fingers into my pussy and draws the moisture up the slit, to the pleated entrance.

I whimper. *Please, no. Please.* I'm mortified. So exposed. So vulnerable. My face burns.

"Has anyone been here?" he asks, like he might ask if I want milk with my tea. "Have you ever played like this?"

"No," I squeak.

"Good. All your virgin holes. All mine."

I bury my face deeper into my folded arms, as he presses a single fingertip over the most private of places. It doesn't hurt. But it does make me feel squirmy. *And dirty.* His finger is ruthless, pressing firmly, the pressure constant and threatening, but he doesn't push inside.

"Relax, Gabrielle. Tempting as it is, I'm not going there tonight. I just want you to get comfortable with my fingers here." He taps a rough fingertip over the sensitive skin, and my bottom wriggles. "I want you to learn to enjoy me touching you *everywhere.* Every inch of your body is mine to explore. To tease. For my pleasure, and yours."

His voice is melodic. Seductive. The room is hot, *so hot*, and my head is getting woozy. It's getting to be too much.

"We'll go slow," he assures me in *that* voice. That Pied Piper voice, with its irresistible lure. "A little at a time, until you beg for my cock right here." He wiggles his finger. "Until you love me filling all your holes."

I sense myself pulling away from my body. The embarrassment and uncertainty, *and the heat*, nosing out the pleasure. I'm not sure what I want to do, what I want to say, if I want to stop him. But it doesn't matter what I want, because I can't form the words anyway.

I feel the rasp of lace, a tickle on the back of my knees as the thong comes off. I shift my head as JD buries his nose in the pink lace, inhaling deeply before carelessly tossing the thong aside. It's dirty, and the twinges of shame are becoming stronger.

Just when I think I can't bear any more, he changes tactics, sliding off my shoes and releasing my cramped toes. I sigh and wiggle them as they're freed, enjoying the air flowing between my toes.

He massages each foot, lavishing special attention on the overstretched arch, circling the abused ball with a strong thumb until I writhe from the exquisite pleasure. "That's better, isn't it? I don't know how you spend all day in those shoes."

I sense him leaning in and feel the unmistakable scrape of his teeth on my ass. It startles me as it stings the tender skin. I cry out as the sensations race toward my center, burying my face in my arms to muffle the cries.

He presses a soft kiss where his teeth sank into muscle and lets his fingertip graze my pussy. Lightly. Slowly. It's not meant to bring relief, only to torment. A delicious torment that goes on and on. He adjusts the pressure and movement ever so slightly, so the orgasm stays just out of reach.

It's almost too much. I'm slipping again. And then it happens.

Crack, crack, crack. The sound blares, heralding the sharp stings that inevitably follow. It doesn't hurt. Not really. Not at first, but the fire sneaks up slowly. And then the small throb of pain comes.

He murmurs endearments while he rubs the burning skin.

Soothing gently.

Cooing softly.

Praising lavishly.

And then *crack, crack, crack* on the other cheek. This time, he catches the skin right above where the thigh begins.

His fingers are in my pussy again, moving maddeningly slowly, inching me to the edge. I grind against them, hoping to spur them on. JD laughs softly, and shame washes over my hot, sweaty face. But it's not enough to stop me from chasing those long, thick fingers and the promise they hold.

"Keep still, Gabrielle." He flattens his palm on my lower back, to stop my gyrations. "You're so aroused. I can smell it, and my nose is nowhere near your pussy. Not yet."

Oh God. I bury my face deeper, shifting slightly, and his cock becomes wedged against my hip. It's hard, *so* hard, and *so* tempting. I fidget, rubbing myself all over the thick length.

This time the hand comes down hard. Brutally hard, and he pulls his fingers from my cunt. "Stay still."

I whimper. Not in pain, but in need. I'm close. *So* close. I rock into his thigh. Rubbing my mound into the muscle. My legs are shaking.

"Don't you dare come, Gabrielle. Not until I tell you."

I hear myself whimpering, and even as I cling to the bench for support, I can't stop the pitiful mewls.

Crack, crack, crack. I'm already sore, and these slaps come down like a branding iron. He rubs the abused skin with one hand, and flicks my needy clit, once, *once*, with the other.

"*Please*," I beg. But I'm not sure what I'm pleading for. Release? His hand hard on my ass? For him to stop? *No.* Not that. Please, not that. "JD, please."

"Soon, darlin'. Soon."

When he lifts me off his lap, I'm a bit unsteady and curl my toes into the plush rug for support. JD stands, too, cradling my face while he kisses me. It starts with a gentle brush of his mouth, but in seconds it's an urgent assault on all my senses. When he pulls away, I'm breathless.

"Take this off," he demands, fingering the cami's satin strap.

And I do, shedding the final garment without delay.

Even before the lingerie hits the floor, my hands are on his belt. But he squeezes them when I attempt to unloop the burnished strap from the gunmetal buckle. "Not yet."

I'm naked, and he's fully dressed. The power differential has never been starker between us. *Is this what I've agreed to?* There's no time to protest before his thumbs are on my nipples, skating in small mind-numbing circles around the furled peaks until I don't care about power discrepancies and agreements. Until I don't give a damn about anything.

"I want you to get on that bed and show me how you made yourself come last night with the balls inside you."

A small gasp pushes its way from my chest. I might be beyond aroused. I might not be able to string a coherent sentence together, but there's still some part of me that's hesitant to do what he asks. It's been a long time since I masturbated for him.

And then I'd used only my fingers. But I do remember how much he liked it. How hard it made him. How savagely he fucked me after I finished.

And how much I loved it.

"Now, Gabrielle. Don't make me wait or you'll spend the rest of the day without coming. Think how uncomfortable that'll be."

It occurs to me, as I go to my bedside drawer to fetch the vibrator I pleasured myself with last night, that I'm naked. Instinctively, I reach for a blanket to cover up, but I stop. He's seen me naked before. More times than I can count. Besides, it seems silly, given what I've just let him do. Given what I'm about to do.

I glance over my shoulder. His eyes are on me. They're a startling blue. Virile and threatening. I was kidding myself to believe I had any control over this arrangement. Over him. It was a lie. *All a lie.*

A small panic hovers, but I look away before it squelches my desire.

JD pulls a Queen Anne chair near the bed. I watch him in my peripheral vision, the way a small animal tracks a predator. He settles in with an elbow resting on the wooden arm. The feminine chair with its sweeping lines and graceful curves makes him seem even larger than he is, stronger, and more sharply chiseled.

His jaw is tight. And his fingers dig into his thigh impatiently. I see the feral need in his eyes, the naked passion. It triggers a surge of power that rattles my spine and emboldens me with some unabashed courage that had started to slip away.

I lift my chin and stack two pillows near the foot of the bed, just like last night. The balls stir inside me, a gentle tremble against my swollen walls, ensuring my arousal never wanes. I lay the rabbit vibrator carefully on its side, atop the pillows. It's not my favorite toy, but it's perfect for this kind of play. When I'm satisfied it's positioned just right, I climb astride, using the wooden footboard to steady myself. After a small adjustment so the bunny, with its fluttering ears, hits my clit at the exact right angle, I flip the remote on low.

The whir fills the quiet room, competing only with the ragged breathing and the small gasps. Are they coming from me? From him? Does it matter?

JD's a few feet away, testosterone seeping through his pores, wafting into my nostrils. Musky. Sinful. Scathing. It's all I can smell.

I pull my head back and stare straight into his eyes. They're dark and hooded. *Oh, JD, you want this.* You want it more than your next breath. *You need it.* You can't resist the lure of filthy sex any more than I can. But this time it will be your downfall, not mine. This time it's your heart that will be left in a million pieces when I walk away.

He's clenching the arms of the chair, his knuckles ghost white. And I wonder if the delicate frame can survive his punishing grip.

With every forced breath he takes, I feel a tug of power in my chest.

"Do you like this?" I murmur, pulling on my nipples before letting my hands slide to my belly. He grunts, fingering his belt. I rock my hips side to side, while he frees his cock.

It's fat and hungry, the skin shiny and taut. So taut, the dark-purple veins are visible. I shiver, remembering how his cock stretches and fills me. How he works me with it until my legs quiver like jelly.

I want that again. *I want it now.*

I slow my movements to better inspect him. To see if his cock is everything I remember. It seems bigger now, thicker and angrier. But it's still magnificent, with its proud, dusky crown.

My pussy flutters with delight when he takes it in hand, rubbing the leaking cum onto the shaft. It's lewd—*so* lewd—in the very best way.

He tosses his head back. His scruffy jaw is slack. I sink lower onto the vibrator, grinding with abandon. The tightening is starting. The tug in my belly is urgent. I arch my back, shoving my heavy breasts forward. *Yes.* It's beginning.

This will all be over soon. For both of us.

JD's hand moves over the swollen shaft, with short, hard pulls, while his glassy eyes flicker over my burning flesh. It's mesmerizing.

My release beckons now, every muscle fully engaged. I begin to buck, and grip the wooden footboard to stay upright.

"Wait for me," he warns, jerking harder. The muscle in his forearm pops with every vicious stroke. He doesn't miss a single beat when he reaches over and scoops my discarded camisole from the floor. Gathering it in his fist, he fucks himself mercilessly with the soft fabric that covered my breasts only minutes before.

My mouth is wide open as I fight for air. But I can't take my eyes off him. Not even to breathe.

"Now, Gabrielle. Come for me. Take it. Take it, now."

Yes. Yes. I flip the remote up a few notches and roll my hips, sliding my slick pussy along the phallus, while the powerful pulses zing the swollen flesh. I bear down, squirming over the bunny, babbling nonsense. My womb clenches into a tight, almost painful ball, as I dive off the edge with jerky movements and strangled moans, collapsing onto the antique footboard in a shaky heap.

Somehow, I manage to push through the tremors, and force my head to the side and my eyes open to watch him. My efforts are richly rewarded with the last glorious pull. The one that comes as his hips jerk forward, and his mouth falls open in a long, anguished roar, as the milky seed gushes over his fist and onto the delicate pink fabric.

My eyelids are heavy. I try, but I can't stay awake any longer.

I don't know how much time passes, but when I open my eyes, JD's standing over me. "Let's take out those balls, darlin'.

Push down. Just like that." His finger curls inside me, helping the balls out.

He disappears into the bathroom, and I hear the faucet running. When he comes back, he brings water and ibuprofen, which I swallow without protest. He picks up some hand cream from the bedside table, and inspects the tube before spreading it over my backside. I'm too tired to be embarrassed as he soothes the bare skin.

"This isn't the best stuff," he says. "But it has aloe and it will make you feel better."

When he's finished, he settles me under the covers. The sheets feel like silk on my cheek, and I curl deeper into the mattress. JD sits on the bed beside me and brushes an errant strand of hair from my face. He pets and smooths, and I nuzzle into his hand and moan, without ever opening my eyes. God, I missed this.

"Sleep. I'm setting your alarm so you can get back to work in time for your afternoon meetings. I'll have lunch delivered to your desk. Sleep as long as you can."

I'm warm and content, safe in my bed. His voice lulling me toward sleep, quiet and gentle—until it isn't.

"You need to obey me, Gabrielle. If you don't, it won't end in a satisfying orgasm next time." He presses his lips to my temple, and the bed shifts as he rises.

The last thing I hear is the door click behind him.

14

Julian

After a mind-blowing morning with Gabrielle, I'm spending the rest of the day getting better acquainted with Sayle Pharmaceuticals. The company was started by my mother's father. When she died, her children were all underage, so Sayle became a subsidiary of Wilder Holdings. But my father can't change the name, or oust my brothers and me from the company. It galls him to have the Sayle name attached to the shining star of Wilder Holdings, reminding everyone he came from nothing, all his wealth inherited from his wife.

Over the years, DW has managed to keep many of the inner workings of the company a secret from everyone, including the board. But now he doesn't have any choice but to open the doors to me.

DW's not the only one unhappy that the curtain's being pulled back at Sayle. There's Leonard Simms, who I'm about to grab by the neck and throw against the wall. Simms is upper-level management. The senior VP of assholes, and my father's eyes and ears at the company. He's spent the last twenty minutes trying to get me to cancel a company-wide meeting I scheduled without his prior knowledge.

"JD, you're a busy man," Simms explains, like I don't already fucking know it. "You really shouldn't have a big meeting like this. It makes people nervous. Like they're about to be laid off. The transition meetings we'll be having with employees are enough."

"Sounds like you're the one who's nervous, Simms."

He ignores me. Mistake number one.

"We can still cancel," he says, as we approach the cafeteria where the meeting will take place.

He's still talking. Mistake number two.

"You can go back to your office," he tells me, "and I'll go in, and send everyone back to their workstations."

Okay, I'm done. I swivel around and trap Simms between my body and the wall. I'm a good foot and a half away from him, but trust me, he's caught like a weasel in a spring-loaded trap. "*We* are not doing any transitions. *I'm* doing the transition meetings, and I don't need an assistant beside me, nodding for emphasis. You're free to do some real work during that time."

"But your father—"

"I am not finished." I lean forward and give him a few long seconds to think about how close I'm standing before I continue. "I prefer all employees hear what I have to say at the same time, so there's no confusion. You do what you want, but if I were you, I'd pay close attention in there."

After a few more seconds pass, I turn and walk away. "And Simms—" He jumps back, like I'm going to hurt him. I've gutted live bass that aren't as squeamish as this prick. "I'm the person signing your paycheck now, not my father. If you prefer to work for him, the door's behind you. But if you stay, I don't want to hear his fucking name from your lips again."

I think he just pissed himself.

"Of-of-of course. I didn't mean to upset you."

"You haven't seen upset," I mutter, as I enter the large dining hall, with hundreds of employees already squeezed inside. Some sit, while others stand elbow to elbow with their coworkers.

As I look around the room, I can't help but think of my mother and my grandfather, and everything Sayle meant to them. Their images flash in front of me, clear as day, looking as though they're counting on me to do something big.

I won't let you down, I silently promise, as though they can hear me.

I stride to the front of the room and grab a portable microphone from a young woman—Deidre. Then corral a chair to stand on, so I can see all the faces. And so they can all see me. "Good afternoon," I call to the masses, my voice booming over the hushed whispers.

"Good afternoon," a few dozen call back.

"My mother was Julia Davis Sayle," I tell the crowd, "and her father, my grandfather, was Julian Davis Sayle. And in case you haven't guessed, I'm Julian Davis Wilder, but most everyone calls me JD."

As I face the room, the responsibilities I've assumed take on a sharper focus. This isn't just my family's business. It's the livelihood of many.

"My grandfather built this company from a dream. He worked hard and believed his employees, like all of you, were the very soul of Sayle Pharmaceuticals."

I pause for a moment. Talking about my grandfather this way, here, inside this building, in the midst of everything he cultivated, makes me more emotional than I expected.

"Julian Sayle ran his company on three guiding principles: keep your hand out of other people's pockets, don't manufacture any product you wouldn't want your own family to use, and treat everyone fairly. While I'm in charge, those will be my guiding principles, too."

There are lots of nods and murmurs, many coming from the front, where the old-timers who knew my grandfather are gathered. I'm sure they loathed working for DW, who has no character or integrity.

"My door is always open," I continue. "But don't look for me up in the penthouse offices with the rest of the suits." That earns me more than a few chuckles. "Beginning next week, I'll be occupying my grandfather's old office just down the hall. You pass it every morning on your way into the building, and every evening on your way out. If there's a problem you can't work out with your supervisor, come see me."

Now for the part where I remind them that the kid's in charge, and he's not a pushover. Those with allegiance to my father should take note.

"I have only one rule, only one thing I will not tolerate, and that's insubordination of any kind. You share Sayle secrets, you steal funds or ideas—you go behind my back, for *any* reason—there will be no second chances. I'll show you the door myself, and after I personally escort you out, I will ruin your life."

I scan the room. It's deathly quiet. Some are nodding, some are staring at their colleagues, and others are examining their hands or the linoleum floor.

"Any questions?"

No one says a word.

"Okay then. Let's all get back to work." I hop off the chair, hand the microphone back to Deidre, and walk out of the room while a sea of eyeballs bore into my back.

After grabbing a coffee, I head into my last meeting of the afternoon. It's with an elite group of scientists, PhDs and MD-PhDs. Their lab is called SOLO—Sayle Only Logistical Operations. From what little I've been able to garner, their work involves treatments that don't currently exist in the market. But everything about the lab is highly classified. No one seems to know a damn thing about what goes on there. No one except my father. SOLO is his brainchild.

Don't get me wrong. Secrecy is imperative in this industry. Pharmaceutical companies and the scientists who work for them are notorious for stealing ideas and techniques from each other. Like other companies, Sayle takes espionage seriously.

But still, I'm beginning to think SOLO's work is more covert than anything happening at the fucking CIA.

Scientists and doctors get their little feelings hurt easily, so I try not to let my suspicions spill all over the room.

"Tell me more about what's happening at SOLO." It's an open-ended question. A softball to start, but even that doesn't spur any discussion among the eight-person group. Three women and five men. I glance from one to another. If their sphincters were any tighter, they wouldn't be able to shit. "Anyone have anything to say for themselves?" I prod.

"Our work is classified. We don't discuss it," Rofler, who's in charge of the lab, finally says. "We're forbidden, by contract, to talk about anything we work on. Past or present."

I smile—it's not a happy smile—and make small circles over my temples. "I'm not a spy, Rofler. I own the damn company. And I want to hear what you do. Otherwise, I'm going to think you collect a paycheck for doing nothing."

Patience is not always my strength, and my voice might have been edged with a bit of hostility. Because Rofler's sweating. And everyone else is looking down at their tablets so I don't call on them for answers. It's like middle school again. Only this time I'm the teacher, and not easily dissuaded by cowardly behavior.

"All right," I say, startling the sheep. "Why don't we begin with this: What's the most important thing you're working on right now? Gentry, you have the ball."

Fiona Gentry looks at me like a deer in the headlights. Her eyes dart to Rofler before she speaks. "Antiviral initiatives."

I glare at her until she looks away.

Rofler pulls out a handkerchief from a pocket and mops his forehead while I wait for Dr. Gentry, or anyone else, to give me some meaningful information. But no one says a fucking word.

"What kind of antivirals?" I ask, looking pointedly at Gentry.

Rofler answers for her, before she can respond. "We work on a lot of antivirals. It's a guess as to which one is the most important. It's like asking someone to choose their favorite child."

Two people in the small group laugh. A few smile. Not me. I'm not amused.

Neither is Rofler. He's wiping his neck now.

This is going nowhere fast. I stand and push the chair in. "Compile a list of every project SOLO is involved in. Add a coherent sentence or two, describing each one. I want it within the hour. No extensions."

My hand is on the doorknob when I turn back around. "You were all at the meeting today in the cafeteria?" They nod. "Good." I make eye contact with each scientist, spending an extra couple seconds on Rofler. "Don't leave anything off that list."

15

Julian

The parking attendant nods and opens the gate for me. Gray and I are having supper tonight at Wildflower. Chase can't join us because he's still holed up in Washington with the transition team.

Before the campaign, the three of us had supper together once a week, usually on Monday nights when the club is quiet. After supper, we usually catch the end of a game, or shoot some pool—and the shit—for a couple of hours. It gives me a chance to lay eyes on them and preserves some semblance of family, small and pathetic as we've become.

My mother raised us to be there for each other. Good times and bad, show up and cheer. She always did—we were the center of her world. She also expected me to keep tabs on my younger siblings, to make sure they stayed out of trouble. I still look out for my brothers, and I show up for supper every week for her. It's the best way I know to honor her memory.

That's a lie.

I show up for myself, too, because I love my brothers. Because they're all I have left in this world that really matter. Sure, there are people in my life who are like family. People I'd do almost anything for. But my brothers—for them, I would do absolutely anything. *Anything*. They're everything to me. Always have been.

That's a lie, too.

Years ago, Gabrielle was everything. Everything I ever wanted. Everything I needed. She was mine. Plain and simple. But now, despite this bullshit arrangement, despite how many times I tell her she's mine, and how many times I make her say the words to me, she's not mine. And no matter how much I bribe, threaten, and blackmail, she never will be. Not really. Not in the way that counts. Not in the way I want her to be.

But that little fact doesn't stop me from wanting her, from closing my eyes and imagining her hands on me as I stroke my dick at night. It was her face I saw in every woman I've been with for the last fifteen years. And it'll be her face I see in every woman I'll ever be with. Her whimpers of pleasure I'll hear, her soft skin I'll feel under my fingers. Her sweet taste on my tongue. It's always been her, and it always will be.

I tried to forget Gabrielle, for my sake and hers. Tried to drink my way past the memory of her, tried to bang my way through the pain, but it didn't work. Nothing worked—not the booze, not the women. Nothing. I've just resigned myself to it. Made peace with the emptiness.

But it doesn't change a damn thing. Doesn't change how much I want her. Doesn't change the crater-size hole in my chest. And it sure as hell doesn't change the fact that I will protect her with my life if necessary.

One of the bouncers standing guard at the entrance to Wildflower holds the door open. I make a beeline for the bar, hoping to avoid the glad-handers. Since it's just the two of us tonight, I grab a seat at the bar.

The bartender sets a glass in front of me and serves me a generous pour of Pappy's. Like a skilled lover, he always knows exactly what I need. Although it's not like I'm that complicated when it comes to booze. Always want the same thing.

I'm not that complicated when it comes to sex, either. Get in, get off, get out. And by get out, I mean get the fuck out of her place before she can think straight and start pestering me about breakfast, or next time. Breakfast is never included, not even if you pay extra, and next time—there is no next time. I've never had a problem breaking the bad news to a woman, but I find it's less trouble to get out quickly and avoid the conversation altogether.

I savor the bourbon, letting it slide down my throat, enjoying the hint of sweet vanilla before it becomes a spicy heat. The first taste is always the best.

Gray slides onto the stool next to me. "Starting without me?"

"Figured you'd catch up. Busy in here for a Monday night."

Gray points to my drink and nods at the bartender. "It's been busier than usual since the election. People stopping out front to take photos." He shakes his head. "Security's been swamped. It's too damn much. I'm hoping things settle down soon."

The bartender brings Gray's drink and a couple of menus.

"The club puts us all at more risk now than ever before. I think it's always going to be like that now." My eyes are glued to the menu while I have this discussion with Gray, yet again. "We might need to reconsider the value of holding onto it."

"This is my life." Gray's voice is brittle, and I feel him tense up next to me.

He loves the club, almost as much as I despise it. If it were up to me, I'd have dumped it fifteen years ago. Burnt the whole place till it was nothing but a pile of ashes. I actually threatened to do it once. DW dared me to try, but I didn't bite. "You could start over. Buy another place, in another part of town."

"What is your problem with this place? *What?*" Gray tosses

his menu on the bar. "I'm sick of your piss-poor attitude about it. It's not like you have such high moral standards. You'll stick your dick into anything breathing who spreads her legs. Hell, I'm not even sure she has to be breathing. Or a she."

"Not that it's any of your damn business, but that's a yes to both, asshole."

"JD, we don't sell sex, and I don't allow any bad shit to go down inside these walls. It's all aboveboard and consensual. And you damn well know it."

I shrug. "Aboveboard might be a bit of an overstatement, don't you think? It's not about morality. It's just not my thing."

"Which is good, because you were banned until you get some basic training. It's been what thirteen, fourteen years? And you still haven't done it."

"Once again, I was twenty, and those women liked it. They were masochists. That's how they got off." And I was in a world of hurt, looking for some way to forget Gabrielle, looking for some way to punish my father, punish everyone who had anything to do with the club. I acted out all over the place.

"You were totally out of control. That can't happen here. Not on my watch."

"Of course not. Theme rooms filled with industrial-sized equipment that looks like it came straight from the Inquisition isn't out of control. Don't give me that shit. People wear masks because it's so fucking out of control."

"Maybe you should give it another try before you insist on selling it."

"I don't need carefully planned-out scenes and someone calling me Sir to get off." I drain my glass and motion to the bartender for a refill.

"But you need control. You need to be the one in charge, always."

I rest both elbows on the wooden bar and turn my neck toward Gray. "How do you know what I need?"

"*Pfft.* Like you're so hard to figure out. You've never done a single thing in your life where you weren't in charge. Where you didn't expect everyone to do it your way."

"I like people to listen, and to do what I tell them. So what? I've got no problem with kink, but contracts and agreements that dictate where you can touch someone and where you can't—takes the mystery out of everything."

"It's a safety feature."

"Sex isn't supposed to be safe. Not all the way. Anyway, I don't need that shit. And I sure as hell am not a sadist."

"There might be a couple of women who disagree with you on that point."

"Bullshit."

"Well, if you always need control, and you're not a dominant, or a sadist, that pretty much leaves just one other possibility."

"What's that?"

"You're an asshole."

I burst out laughing, and then Gray starts to laugh, too, until we're both practically sputtering booze out our noses. "I guess that's about right."

I need to go easier on Gray about this place. I know I should just leave it alone, but I can't stop myself. I might be a fucked-up asshole, but it bothers me that all his relationships with women are scripted. That he hasn't ever let himself just be with a woman. The club encourages that behavior. I want something more for him. Even if I'll never have it for myself again, I remember what it's like to be in the moment. To explore and discover a woman, inhibitions and prohibitions cast aside. To love. I want my brothers to have that.

But my hatred of the club, of the memories that get dredged up every time I set foot downstairs, stem from another reason. A reason so dark, so ugly, that I've pushed it as far back into my subconscious as humanly possible. Only sharing it with one person. *Ever.* And even then, not all of it.

I turn to Gray. "What's good tonight, besides the hostess you can't take your eyes off of? Has she been downstairs yet? Or up to your place?"

"No. And she won't be going down there, either, or upstairs. Not in the way you're implying. Even if he wasn't the president, she works for me."

I'm just giving Gray shit, and he knows it. But he's a little too defensive.

The hostess looks like she was tailor-made for Gray. Surprised my brother hired her. I would have thought her wide-eyed innocence would be too much of a temptation for him. There's nothing he likes better than introducing a newbie to kink, but he cares too much about the club to ever fuck anyone who works here. "I don't have any quarrel with the way you run this place. You've always had more self-discipline than me."

"Always been better lookin', too."

"Pfft."

The bartender takes our order and pours us each a beer. "Zack's about the same," I tell Gray. He never asks about Zack, it's too hard on him, but I bring him up every time we're together because Zack's our brother, and the goddamn accident didn't change that. And if anything happens to me, I need Gray and Chase to fight for Zack so my father doesn't get his clutches on him again. He won't survive next time. "We're heading into winter, and he's pretty susceptible to catching something he can't fight off. You should stop by and see him."

Gray takes a long swig of beer. "For what? It's not like it would do him a damn bit of good. He doesn't even know I'm there."

The bartender puts a small dish of warm nuts between us, and I scoop up a handful. "I don't believe that's true, but even if it is, you should stop by for yourself. Because after your stomach stops roiling, it'll make you feel better to spend some time with him."

"Is that why you do it? Does it make you feel better?"

"We're family." A fucked-up family who meets once a week for supper in a sex club. Misfit toys, every one of us, lucky we weren't sent off to some island. But yes, it does make me feel better. It doesn't assuage any guilt, but it settles me in some way. It just feels right. Always has.

"I can't do it, JD. Every time I visit, it takes me weeks to recover. You're a better man than me." He downs his beer and sets his glass down harder than he needs to.

"No. I'm not. I'm just a different man. Sure as hell not better. So, what's the hostess's name?"

"Mae. Didn't you meet her while I was traveling with the campaign?"

"I might have. She's cute. I can see why you like her," I say.

"Cute? *Pfft*. Get in the game, old man. She's hot as hell."

"And an employee."

"Fuck you."

The bartender brings over our burgers, and we order another round. A piece about the transition flashes on the television above the bar. Apparently it's moving forward smoothly. *Sure it is.* The sound's off on the TV, but images of the new administration are plastered on the screen.

"What is it with the cabinet officials who never met a war they didn't want to wage?" I keep an eye on the transition, but Gray works closely on it and knows the ugly details. "Defense, State, and National Security. It's like the holy trinity of old white guys. What's he thinking? He campaigned as a non-interventionist. Those guys are all hawks."

Gray takes a bite of his burger and wipes his mouth. "They're well-respected and battle tested. They can provide valuable insight. But it's mainly a show of power and strength."

A show of power and strength. Give me a fucking break. "Like buying a big-ass truck you can barely drive, and outfitting it with giant wheels and an enormous gun rack. God, he must have a tiny dick."

"You're too hard on him, JD. As far as you're concerned, everything he does has some sinister motive. He can be an arrogant jerk, I'll give you that, but a lot of people like him. A majority of the country voted for him."

"So he keeps telling anyone who's still listening. They don't know him the way I do. What's that PT Barnum said? 'No one ever went broke underestimating the intelligence of the American people.'"

"Most of his bullshit comes from insecurity. Cut him some slack."

"Cut him some slack? I've already cut him way too much fucking slack."

Gray shakes his head and pushes away the plate.

My mother's death was devastating. Losing a loving parent, our only loving parent, along with Sera and Zack, hit Gray harder than it hit the rest of us. He's never really recovered, and I always feel bad DW is such a sore point between us, but there is no way I'm cutting the asshole an ounce of slack.

"I'm leaving a week from Friday," Gray says. "I'll be gone for maybe ten days. Liam can manage most things that come up better than either of us can, but he's getting old and forgetful. Will you stop by once or twice while I'm away, just to make sure the place is still standing when I get back?"

"Where you going, princess?"

Gray shoves my arm, nearly toppling my plate off the bar. He's always hated me calling him princess, and I've always loved getting a rise out of him.

"The president-elect is holding a summit," he says, like it's the most natural thing in the world.

"*What?*" Presidents-elect don't hold summits. Anyone who's paid any attention to the news in the last decade knows this.

"He wants to squeeze in a little R and R, and get some world leaders together. It'll be a working vacation. This way he can hit the ground running when he takes office."

"Is that what he told you, or is that what you think?"

Gray ignores the question. "He's sending me ahead with a few of his closest advisors and some staff to assess the situation before he joins us." Gray shrugs. "It's a show of good faith with these people to send your son. Ideally, it would be you going."

"Fuck that." Gray is letting DW manipulate him. He knows damn well this is a bunch of shit. "Where is this *summit* happening?"

Gray walks around the bar and dumps some ice into an empty glass. "On the Mediterranean."

It's not easy, but I hold my tongue and toss my napkin onto the plate, waiting for him to sit his ass back on the stool next to me. "Tell me you are not going to a fucking summit in the Mediterranean with world leaders before the bastard takes office. Please tell me that."

"Get a grip, JD. I don't need you to protect me from my father."

I need to take a different approach here, but of course I don't see it until I've already opened my big mouth. "Gray, don't let him use you. No matter what he thinks, he's not a fucking king. There are laws and rules that govern the transition of power."

This is just like my father. He probably can't find anyone else dumb enough to go to his little summit, so he's sending Gray. He'll think nothing of selling my brother out if there's any blow-back. "If he wants to skirt the law, that's his business. But don't let him pin his bullshit on you. For all I care, he can rot in jail. But don't let him dirty you."

"He just wants to see who he can trust. Who his real friends are. I don't get why you're so bent out of shape about it."

I can't figure out if Gray is downplaying this for my benefit, or if he doesn't fully understand the implications. Either way, it's an issue. A huge fucking issue. "Who else is going to be there?"

"Not sure. It hasn't been finalized."

I look up at the television and my father is staring down at me. Big grin on his face, like he's mocking me. I want to take my beer and chuck it at the screen. But I don't let him reduce me to a complete heathen. Not tonight. "They still hang people for treason?"

"Pretty sure the Supreme Court ruled that hanging people violates the Constitution."

"I'd find out if I were you. You don't like ropes."

Gray slowly turns his head to look at me. "How the fuck do you know what I like?"

"I read it on your little form when you were away."

The temperature in the room plummets twenty degrees. My little brother is pissed, and there's ice in his voice sharp enough to cut through glass. "You went snooping through private client information in the locked file cabinets?"

"You're not a client. And I needed something to do while I was babysitting this place. If you don't like it, get your ass back here permanently and don't leave me in charge of this shitshow."

"You're an asshole."

"We established that already. You need to be on alert around those jackals. And for God's sake, familiarize yourself with the rules regarding transitions."

"And how should I do that?"

"They didn't teach you how to read big words at Brown? Look it up. Or ask someone. All those ball-lickers hanging around, waiting for someone to notice them? I bet one or two of them have memorized every regulation. This is serious shit. The kind you can't buy yourself out of. Think alphabet soup: FBI, CIA, NSA, to name a few."

"He's the president."

When it comes to DW, talking to Gray is like banging my head against the wall. I crack my knuckles to avoid shaking him. "I repeat. The man is not a fucking king. Come on, Gray. You're a smart guy. You're talking like someone who's hitting the weed too hard. Promise me you'll get a good handle on what you're permitted to do before you let him send you anywhere."

"Fine." He takes a mouthful of ice and begins to chew. "Anything to shut you up," he mutters.

I watch him out of the corner of my eye while I take a pull of beer, hoping some of what I said got through to him.

"I was having coffee at Misty Moon earlier today, and thought I saw you go into the Gatehouse."

He's steered the conversation away from my father, which is uncomfortable for him, to the Gatehouse, which he knows is uncomfortable for me. *Insolent bastard.*

If he's waiting for a response from me, he better not hold his breath. But I do have a question for him. "How come you never told me you helped Gabrielle Duval get her hotel open?"

"I don't tell you everything."

"That's bullshit."

"Gabby and I have always been friends. That didn't change when you dumped her."

That's what my brothers think. It's what everyone thinks. I was the bastard who cheated on her. At the time, it was easier for people to believe that I was done with her, though nothing could have been further from the truth.

"She never asked me to keep it from you, but I thought . . . Anyway, I just made a few connections for her. Answered some questions. That's pretty much it. She didn't really need much help. Why do you ask?"

I shrug. "I like to know what's going on." *But she won't tell me shit, although it sounds like you know plenty.* "Tough business. You think she can make it work?"

He nods. "It costs a pretty penny to lay your head on a pillow, but she pulls out all the stops. It's modeled after the small European luxury hotels. If the concept takes off, and it seems to be, she'll be able to expand when the surrounding buildings come up for sale. That's her plan, anyway. Seems solid to me."

"Hope it works out for her."

"You never answered my question. Was that you I saw going into Gabby's hotel?"

I motion for another round of beer without saying a word about the Gatehouse. Hell will freeze over before he gets a confession from me.

"Leave her alone, JD. She's in a good place."

Yeah, a real good place. If only you knew the half of it. "I never read your little fact sheet. Figure every man is entitled to a little privacy. Even pussies like you. Maybe you could repay the favor by staying out of my business." I lean over the bar, grab the nozzle that dispenses water, and fill my glass.

"Gabby's not your business anymore."

Before I can respond, a sly grin spreads over one side of Gray's face.

"And I know you didn't read my fact sheet, because if you had, you'd know I love ropes. My hard limit section is blank."

"You are one sick fucker."

"I hear it runs in the family."

16

Julian

It's after ten thirty, and I've poured down more than my share of booze and filled my belly with hot food. Now there's just one more thing I'd like to fill. Just one more thing that's missing from making this a perfect night. But that's not going to happen—not tonight, anyway. Instead of looking for trouble, I call Chase, again.

"Hey," he says, sounding a hell of a lot more relaxed than he did when I called him earlier, on my way out of Sayle's. "What's good?"

"We missed you at dinner tonight. You need to get your ass back down here."

"I'm workin' on it."

"Work harder. Are you still in meetings, or can you talk now?"

"Talk away. This is a secure line."

I smile. Sometimes I forget how clever and grown-up he is.

And sneaky. "Good. I've got a couple things I need your help with."

"As long as it doesn't involve hacking Gabby's security system or jamming her phone lines. I'm done with that. You need to leave her alone."

"Why? You're not trying to weasel in on my girl, are you?"

"I'm not a seven-year-old, and she's not your girl."

When they were little kids, Chase and Zack were always following Gabrielle around, trying to get her to play. I would always tease them about trying to steal my girlfriend, and Gabrielle would always pretend she liked them more than me. Life was simpler then. Everybody was happy. "You need to get a sense of humor."

"What do you want?"

"Do you know anything about some bullshit meeting on the Mediterranean with DW and some foreign leaders? I'm guessing they're from countries not aligned with ours, otherwise it wouldn't be such a huge fucking secret."

"They don't exactly invite me to high-level foreign policy meetings. But I'll poke around."

Poke around. *Jesus*. Before this is over, we'll all be in prison—my brothers for being careless, and me for strangling my father for compromising them. "Keep your eyes and ears open, but you are *not* to hack into anything that even smells like government business. They put you in jail and throw away the key for shit like that."

"Whatever."

"Whatever my ass. Stay the fuck away from that shit, Chase."

"When did you become so concerned with foreign policy?"

I draw in a breath and blow it out noisily. Sometimes I feel like I share too much with Chase. *Ah, fuck*. He needs to hear about this. "DW invited Gray. He's the front man. I don't want him involved in anything illegal. Gray's too trusting. DW won't think twice about dumping the whole mess in his lap if it turns sour."

"I'll look around. Discreetly, of course."

"The answer is still *no.* Do not hack into anything that involves the feds. But if your fingers are itchy, there is something you can hack into for me."

"I'm listening."

"Know anything about SOLO?"

"The red cups we use for beer pong?"

"Funny. Glad you found your sense of humor."

"What's SOLO?"

"That's what I want to know. It's an acronym for Sayle Only Logistical Operations."

"What a stupid name."

"Tell me about it. I spent all afternoon at Sayle. There's a small group of scientists working on some type of antiviral agents. They gave me some bullshit story that didn't make any sense. I can send you the write-up they gave me, if it'll help."

"Hate to break it to you, but you've always sucked at chemistry. It's not that hard to confuse you. A lot of the stuff they work on at Sayle is complicated, even for people who know the difference between RNA and DNA."

"I might not be fucking Einstein, but I understand English pretty well, and can follow a cogent point from A to Z. Something didn't feel right. And there was this one guy, Rofler, who was sweating like a pig the entire time I was there. The more questions I asked, the more he mopped his forehead."

"You make a lot of people nervous when you start asking questions. You have that charming way of turning conversations into interrogations."

Maybe. But that's not what happened today. Rofler's bad news. I know it. "This wasn't like that. See what you can find. But DW is looking over my shoulder when it comes to Sayle. You need to get in and out quickly without anyone knowing you've been snooping."

"Is there any other way?"

"Don't be a smart-ass."

"How's Zack?" Unlike Gray, Chase asks about his twin every time we talk.

"He's hanging in there. Kid's tough as nails."

"Yeah. I'll go by as soon as I get back in town."

"Look forward to it. I told him you were away saving the fucking world or some such shit."

"Hardly."

"You see much of DW?"

"As little as possible. He has me running programs for him, and spying on other tech people they've hired. He doesn't trust anyone."

"Make sure you watch yourself."

"Don't worry about me. I know the bastard for exactly who he is."

No, you don't. You just think you know him. "Still. Be careful."

I hang up with Chase and put down the top on the car. The air is thick and humid for mid-November. I can almost taste the salt. It reminds me of Gabrielle. Of the lone tear that rolled down her cheek and onto my tongue. I wonder how many tears I've caused her to shed these last fifteen years? Maybe none. Maybe she knew right away she was better off without me.

Well, like it or not, darlin', I'm back.

All afternoon, I kept picturing her straddling that damn vibrator, beads of sweat trickling down her throat, into the valley between her breasts. I wanted to catch the salty beads on my tongue, too. Wanted it so bad. And those little whimpers and moans when I slapped her ass. *Fuck me.* I can't believe I kept my own ass in the chair while she got herself off. Not going to lie, I wanted more. I always want more when it comes to her.

But right now, my needs and wants are not important. What's important is that Gabrielle remembers how much she loves dirty sex. How much she needs it. She might believe she beat the addiction. But no one ever beats it. The craving's merely dormant, waiting for a filthy kiss to awaken from the long slumber. It's still there. I made sure of that a long time ago.

I glance at the time on the dashboard—screw it. I need to check in with her to make sure she's okay. *Right.* There's no shortage of bullshit that I'm willing to swallow when it comes to her.

"Call Gabrielle."

Calling Gabrielle, the automated voice repeats. If only everyone in my life was that quick to obey, things would be so much easier. The phone rings a few times before she answers.

"Hello." She's out of breath.

"I was afraid I'd wake you up, but you sound like you've been exercising. Or going another round with that vibrator."

She's blushing. I don't even need to see her face to know her cheeks are crimson. "No exercise of *any* kind. I've been looking for my keys for the last two hours. When the phone rang—it's late—I worried something happened with my mother."

"Sorry about that. I didn't mean to alarm you. I'm on my way home and I want to make sure you're okay after today. Things got a bit intense."

She doesn't say anything for several seconds. I can almost hear her wheels turning. "If you don't want to wake me, or startle me, they have this thing called texting. Have you heard about it?"

My mouth curls into a broad smile, and a small laugh escapes. And just like that, my shoulders begin to loosen, the tension rolling off my back. "Now why would I want to text and miss the annoyance in your voice when you realize it's me on the other end of the call? Not to mention that sassy little smile you have going on. Can't hear that in a text."

"I promise to add LOL at the appropriate times. And I'm not smiling, JD."

"No, not now. But you were."

"I don't have time for this right now. I need to find my keys."

"Don't you keep a spare set?"

"Yes, of course. But that's not the point. It's the master keys for the entire building that are missing."

If I wasn't so busy thinking about my dick, I might have thought better about her missing keys. "Maybe they fell out of your purse. When did you last have them?"

"I didn't put them in my purse. I don't take them out of the building. They're always on a hook behind my office door."

"Do you think someone borrowed them?"

"No one borrowed them. I checked with everyone who works here. I've looked everywhere. I don't know where else to look."

She sounds frazzled. I can almost see her furrowed brow, and her playing with her hair. Tugging and twirling the dark curls behind her ear. It's a sure sign she's stressed. She's been doing it since she was a little girl. "Anything else missing?"

"Not that I've noticed. You think someone broke into my office?"

"It's not that difficult to access the back offices."

"How did you get access? Did you pay off one of my employees?"

"*No.* If one of your employees agreed to betray you for money, I would have fired them on the spot."

"Silly me. Of course you'd fire one of *my* employees if you didn't approve of their conduct."

"Your security system isn't hard to crack."

"You hacked into my security system? That's how you got in?"

"I'm coming over to help you search for the keys."

"*No.*"

"Gabrielle, you don't get to tell me no. That's not how our arrangement works. I'm going to help you find those keys so you can get some sleep."

"If you come here, we won't look for the keys. At least we won't spend long looking for them. And I need to find them." Her voice trails off to a whisper. "Not tonight, JD. Please."

She sounds bone-tired, and after today, I'm probably at least partly responsible for the exhaustion. Besides, she's right. If I go over there, the keys will never get found. "Why I really called was to see how you're feeling. Why don't you tell me, and I'll let you get back to your search."

"I'm fine."

"That's not how this works. You'll need to do better than that."

"I know all about aftercare, and checking in. But I don't have time for it right now."

"Like hell you don't. I'm taking the time for it, and so will you."

"What do you want me to say?"

"Let's start with the physical part. How's your gorgeous ass?"

"I'll live."

"How about your puss—"

"*Jesus*. It's all fine. Enough with the questions."

"Now tell me what's going on inside your head."

She sighs loudly, and I imagine her eyes are rolling, too. "I'm wondering why I'm standing here having a ridiculous conversation with you when the master keys are missing. I'll talk to you tomorrow."

"Don't you dare hang up unless you want to see my face tonight."

It's quiet for a long minute, but she doesn't end the call. "I don't exactly know how I feel," she says in a small voice. "I don't feel the way I'd like to feel. The way I should feel."

"There are no shoulds, Gabrielle. You feel what you feel. It's all good."

I hear her draw a long breath, and release it slowly. "You're a lot to take in, JD. Even more than I remember. Thank you for sending lunch. The restaurant here isn't open at noon, but you probably knew that." She's quiet for a few seconds. "I can't believe you remembered I like tuna sandwiches with potato chips and sweet pickle slices."

There's not a single thing I don't remember about her. Not one damn thing. I've lived off those memories for almost fifteen years. They've kept me warm during the bleakest nights, helped me find release when I needed it. But I don't tell her any of that. "Part of our arrangement is that I take care of you. You give me your trust and your obedience, and I make your life better. Easier."

"You don't need to do that."

"I do need to. And I want to," I add softly.

"So this is a dominant-submissive arrangement without the normal safeguards?"

"There are plenty of safeguards. But no, I don't think of it like that. Not exactly. Although we can shape it or call it whatever we want. Our arrangement, our rules."

"You mean our arrangement, your rules."

I smile. While she isn't entirely wrong, I'm not Attila the Hun, either. "With the right incentive, I could be persuaded to be flexible about certain things."

"How magnanimous of you. It still feels like a power play to me."

"All my relationships are power plays. But they're not all about sex. Let's have supper tomorrow night. We'll iron out whatever wrinkles are left, and I can see for myself if that gorgeous ass really is fine."

"I have a dinner meeting with a supplier."

"Is he local?"

"Yes, *she* is."

"Reschedule with *her*. Make it a breakfast or lunch meeting."

"You can't expect me to change my plans on a whim."

Yeah, Gabrielle, I do, and you will. "It's exactly what I expect. You'll leave on Friday to visit your parents for the weekend. I assume you'll want to go most weekends, at least until we know how your mother reacts to the course of treatment. On Sundays, you'll need to catch up on the things you left behind, and set yourself up for the week. On Monday nights, I have dinner with my brothers. That leaves Tuesday, Wednesday, and Thursday for us. Crumbs. And I expect sometimes even that won't work out, but a dinner meeting with a local supplier is something that can be easily changed."

"What time?"

"Antoine can pick you up at eight o'clock."

"I can drive myself. But eight is so late to begin the evening. During the week, I'm downstairs every morning by five thirty at the latest. If you can't make it earlier, maybe we should plan on Wednesday."

For a minute I'm torn, but I can't do it. Not even for her. "I have a standing appointment every evening between seven and eight that can't be changed."

"A standing appointment? I thought that's what I was for?"

"You sound jealous."

"Don't kid yourself. But I'm curious, what do you do at seven to eight every night that precludes you from meeting earlier?"

"It's none of your business."

"Normally I wouldn't care about what you do, or who you do it with. But—"

"But what, Gabrielle? I'm not fucking anyone else, and I don't plan on it while we're together. And I highly recommend you keep your legs closed when I'm not around, too. And don't tell me for one second you don't care where I put my dick, because we both know that's a bunch of bullshit."

"I have to go."

"Wait."

But she doesn't. *Sonofabitch.*

I pound both hands on the steering wheel. What I do is no one's business. Not even hers. Aside from Gray and Chase, and a few others who need to know, no one is privy to how I spend that time. And that's how I want it.

But you asked her to trust you.

You need her to trust you.

I can't. I can't tell her.

Fuck! I don't know how to do this with her. I thought it would be easier. I knew she would balk and complain, and there might be things I'd say and do to her that would disgust me—but I knew I'd find my balls and do them anyway, because it was necessary. But there are so many other things, like this, that I'm not sure about.

Why can't I tell her? *No reason.* She won't go to the press. I know she won't. No matter how she feels about me, she would never do it.

Trust begets trust, JD. You want her to trust you? You need to give her more than kink if you want her all in.

Screw it! I don't even bother calling, because she's not going to answer. Instead, I text: **I'm parked outside the hotel. Answer your phone or I'm coming in.**

A second later, I send another text: **And I will find you.**

It's a bluff. I'm nowhere near the hotel, but I'm counting on her not wanting to see my face tonight, badly enough to pick up the phone. I've been enough of an asshole with her that she won't doubt I'd show up and harass her.

I give her a few minutes before I call. There's a better chance she'll have read the text.

While I wait, I grapple with the prospect of going over to the hotel and hunting her down. I didn't leave myself any wiggle room, but I really don't want to have this conversation with her in person. Gabrielle might be my kryptonite, but Zack makes me human in a way no one else can. I don't know how she'll react when I talk about him, and I don't trust my own reactions. It's bad enough she might hear the weakness in my voice, but I don't want her to see it.

After ten minutes of driving in circles, I call her.

She doesn't answer until the fifth ring. "You weren't enough of a bastard before? What do you want now?"

I take a deep breath and squeeze my fingers around the steering wheel. "I spend that time with Zack."

Her choppy breathing fills the silence until she speaks. "*With Zack?*"

With Zack. It doesn't change a damn thing for him, but I do it anyway. "*Mmhm.* I do my best to protect Zack from all the people who are curious about him and want to exploit his condition for a good story. It's been especially bad since my father started his campaign, and now that he's president, there's no sign of it letting up. I would appreciate it if you would keep this to yourself." I sound like a robot. My voice devoid of any real emotion. I feel a bit like one, too.

"Of course. I would never say anything that would compromise him."

I don't doubt for a second that she'll keep her mouth shut. When they were kids, she doted on Chase and Zack like they were little dolls. Even if she wanted to hurt me, she would never hurt him.

"JD. I—I didn't realize—I didn't think he was responsive anymore."

"He's not. Not really. Although it's possible he's minimally responsive some of the time. Difficult to tell at this stage. We're not entirely sure."

Zack suffered a traumatic brain injury during the accident. At the time, he was diagnosed with unresponsive wakefulness syndrome—a permanent vegetative state. It was probably a misdiagnosis, or more likely, a convenient diagnosis. So my father could lock him up and throw away the key. But it's too damn late now to change things.

"*Hm.* What do you do with him every night?" Her voice is shaky and quiet.

"I read to him. Tell him stories. We listen to music." I sigh. I'm not accustomed to answering this question, and it makes me feel vulnerable—like I'm soft—human. What I do with Zack is between us. I've never thought about sharing the specifics with anyone—even my brothers—but somehow, I find the words to tell her. "Brush Sumter. Bedtime stuff." She's sniffling, and it slices into my gut. "Gabrielle—don't. Please don't."

"I'm sorry. It's only been a week since you barged back into my life, but it's been a long, trying week. It feels like an eternity. I'm so confused. I don't know what to think. Between you and what's happening with my mother—it's all too much. I've been going through the motions, but I've been neglecting the hotel. I can't go on like this. I'm working hard to process it all, but it's overwhelming."

"There's nothing to process. Not with regard to me. When I walked into your office on election night, your first instincts were correct. I'm not here to ruin your life, or to hurt you—but everything else you thought about me is true. Don't lose sight of it because I read my little brother bedtime stories. It doesn't change anything." *Even though I wish it could.* This was the risk. That she would see this for more than it is and start to think I'm some kind of nice guy who she plays sex games with, but that when it comes down to it, I'm a pushover.

"I would love to see Zack. I haven't seen him since he went away. Will you take me with you one day?"

"One day."

"Soon."

"*Gabrielle.* Maybe."

"He must be in a facility nearby. Where is he?"

"Go find your keys and get some sleep. I'll see you tomorrow night."

"Don't bother Antoine. I'm perfectly capable of driving myself."

"I'm aware of how capable you are. But I don't want you driving home. It'll be late and I plan on making you very tired."

17

Gabrielle

After work, I shower quickly and change into a skirt with a zipper down the back that runs from waist to hem. JD won't be able to keep his eyes off it all night. And no, I'm not the slightest bit embarrassed about choosing it for that reason.

The room still smells of him. Still smells of sex. And I can't glance at that Queen Anne chair without becoming aroused. Without my core pulsing with need. I can still see him sitting right there, furiously fucking his fist, my pink cami nothing more than a cum rag wrapped around his fat cock to catch every precious drop of seed.

There's not an inch of skin that's not hot and prickly, and I want to dig my fingers into my needy cunt and satisfy the craving, but there's no time. Besides, I promised to save all my pleasure for him. I'm not embarrassed about that, either.

I go downstairs to wait for Antoine. It's been a terrible day. Not to mention costly. Four flat tires, and the hassle of dealing with the tow company, and the police treating me like a flighty woman because I didn't remember leaving the master keys in the car. *I still don't remember leaving them there.*

But maybe I did. I've been so preoccupied with my mother, and with JD, that I've found myself forgetting little things this week. Yesterday, when I went to the pharmacy, I sat in the parking lot, shaken, because I didn't remember anything about the drive there. I could have killed someone. Maybe I did grab the keys by mistake. But I certainly didn't deflate the tires. When did teenage pranks become so destructive? *Now I sound like my mother.*

I let the front desk know I'm leaving for the evening. Tom is on tonight. He's a godsend, especially with Georgina scheduled to be out on maternity leave. Dean recommended him for the job. It's the best thing he ever did for me. That, and taking JD's money and leaving town. The man might very well be the most self-absorbed human being I have ever met. But thankfully, he got in touch with his family and they've stopped haranguing me as though I had something to do with his disappearance.

I make no excuses for Dean. Not a single one. The way he treated me was deplorable, and although there is nothing I did to cause his behavior, I never loved him. Not really. I pretended, not just with him and everyone else, but I kidded myself, too.

After being around JD for a week, just one week, I know my relationship with Dean was ill-fated from the start. Ill-fated because I wasn't done with JD. Ill-fated because no one will ever come close to making me feel the way JD makes me feel. This will always be my cross to bear.

Does this mean I want a relationship with JD that goes beyond our arrangement? Something more than revenge? Something more than discovering the truth about what happened fifteen years ago? Yes, yes, and yes, I do. All of it. There. I said it.

But I won't do it. Even if JD wants a relationship, which I highly doubt, I won't indulge in anything more than mind-numbing sex with him, and closure. I won't risk my heart again. I can't. I'm not a kid anymore. I can't afford to sink into depression, to mope around crying for months when he decides there's someone prettier, or smarter, or better connected. I have responsibilities now. JD has the power to destroy me again, but only if I let him.

I know now what I've always thought. He's my soul mate. As much as I hate to admit it, it's true.

But I'm willing to live out my life alone, or with someone else. While no relationship will ever compare to the unrestrained passion I have with him, or the depth of connection we share, I can still have a full and loving relationship with someone else. I'll learn to be content without the flames. They always seem to singe me anyway. But I can't do any of it until I put JD behind me.

Maybe it's not revenge I need, but closure. I want the answers, *all of them*, so the door between us can close firmly and securely. And forever.

Antoine pulls into the front of the hotel at eight fifteen. It's not like him to be late. "A lot of traffic?"

"Not too bad," he says, shutting the door behind me after I'm settled. The partition is already up between the front and back seats when I get in the car. I guess I ask too many questions.

Sweetgrass isn't far, but there's only one way to get there from here, and Antoine doesn't take the turn that leads away from downtown. I refuse to talk to him through the intercom, so I tap on the partition, until he lowers it.

"Did you miss the turn to Sweetgrass?"

He turns around, puzzled. "We're going to Mr. Wilder's place downtown. I'm sorry. I assumed you knew."

"No." I shake my head. "I didn't. JD must have forgotten to tell me. It's fine." Either he forgot to tell me, or didn't bother. I huff to myself. He's not forgetful. But he is rude.

In less than ten minutes, we arrive in front of a renovated building. It's so close to the hotel, I could have easily walked.

Antoine gets out and leads me into the swanky building to an elevator. "This will take you directly into Mr. Wilder's apartment," he assures me, punching in the code.

On the ride up, I remind myself to ask more questions about the details before agreeing to dinner, or to anything else, if I don't want to be surprised.

JD's waiting when the doors open.

"I realized a few minutes ago that you must have thought you were going to Sweetgrass." He kisses me on the cheek.

To a bystander, the kiss might look chaste, but nothing with JD is ever entirely chaste. This is no exception. I feel the brush of his half-hard erection when he leans in to take my coat.

While he mentioned forgetting to tell me where we were having dinner, he doesn't apologize. That's not his style, and tonight it's not my style to let him entirely off the hook. "I was a bit taken aback. If I didn't trust Antoine so much, I would have demanded he take me back to the hotel."

He rubs his fingers over his chest, right below his neck. "That would have been a mistake."

Maybe. I'm not going to engage. I don't want to fight. "I didn't realize you keep an apartment downtown. It's a nice place." I glance around the cavernous space. It's an open floor plan with a bank of floor-to-ceiling windows. It is nice. But different from Sweetgrass, with its warm, sprawling rooms decorated in traditional fabrics and furnishings. Sweetgrass feels like home. This feels sterile, and modern, and blindingly white. *Designer white.* All the apartments in the building probably have this same stark-white walls and nondescript look about them.

"How's Zack?" I ask, studying his face for more than he's likely to give me. I haven't been able to stop thinking about Zack since last night.

"He's okay."

"JD—when you told me you see him every day...it's all I could think about last night. Your mother—she would—"

He puts two fingers over my mouth to shush me. "Stop."

But I don't. I can't. This is the boy I knew, and it makes my heart swell to see a glimpse of him in the man he's grown into. I need to see if there's more of him there. I just need to. I take the long, roundabout way, but I press on. "An hour is a long time to sit with someone who can't engage. Especially for you. You've never been very patient. And I haven't seen any evidence that's changed."

He's pensive and seems to slip away briefly. "It's funny, but the time goes quickly when I'm with Zack. It's calming and peaceful. At least it became peaceful after I stopped dwelling on how much I wanted things to be different for him. I just—I live in the moment when I'm with him now. Want a drink?" he asks.

"How about a cocktail? Maybe my signature drink that you stole?"

His mouth twitches and curls at the left corner, the dimple appears, and his eyes twinkle madly. Then he laughs.

That's him! That's him! The voice in my head shrieks with delight. I want to launch myself at him. Rub my body against his like a starved animal whose master has just come home after a long trip.

"I don't have any of that cassis here. And I didn't steal it. I only served it to you because I wanted you to feel at home."

"I call bullshit. You wanted me to know you had lots of information about me."

He gazes at me and smirks. "Maybe a little of both."

"Exactly." I look around while he opens a bottle of wine. Stamped concrete counters and floors, with exposed steel beams everywhere. The kitchen is comprised almost entirely of stone and steel. It's sleek and cold. "I can't believe how different this place seems from Sweetgrass."

He lifts a shoulder. "I don't pay much attention to this place. It's not home. It's just somewhere I come to crash now and then."

"A place you bring women."

He glances at me, but doesn't say a word. He doesn't have to.

"Dinner will be here soon. Maybe we can talk about a few things while we're waiting." He hands me a glass of cabernet. "You might want to give it a few minutes to breathe," he says, grabbing a beer from the refrigerator.

I cup the balloon-shaped bowl in two hands, warming the burgundy liquid gently. "Do you have a contract?" I ask dispassionately, sitting back on the stool like I'm a sophisticated player in the world of raunchy sex.

His face twists in confusion. "A contract? *No*."

"I thought these sorts of relationships always had contracts?"

Sparks shimmer in his eyes, and his mouth quirks at the corner. "*Ahhh*, a contract." JD scratches the back of his head. "I don't believe relationships between men and women need contracts." He studies me for a minute, tipping his head to the side. "Do you want a contract?"

I have no idea what I want. I'm just probing to get some sense of what he wants from this relationship. I shrug. "What about a safe word?"

"You don't need a safe word. I'll never let things get that far."

"Really? Weren't you in my apartment yesterday? I'm short one camisole."

"It was never out of control. At least I wasn't."

Right. I pull my shoulders back and hold my head high. "I had a safe word at sixteen, and I want one now. I insist. And—and I fully expect you to respect it."

"Fine. Choose one. Something easy to remember."

I think for a minute. "Wilderness."

He swallows hard, and empties the wine bottle into a swan-shaped decanter. The glass swan is delicate with a graceful neck and outspread wings, like it's about to take flight. It has more movement than JD does right now. His entire body is rigid, and his face is blank. I'd give anything to know what he's thinking.

Wilderness is the stable where we played. Where we first discovered the wondrous, dark side of sex. Where I caught him playing those same games with someone else. It's the perfect word to signify he's gone too far, because that's where he went too far. Too far with Jane—too far with me. *Maybe we both went too far.* The symbolism is scathing, and I know by his demeanor, he thinks so, too.

"I don't plan on giving you anything you can't handle. But use it, if you need to." JD comes over and cradles my face, forcing me to meet his eyes. He blinks a couple of times. His long, dark lashes cast spiky shadows on his cheeks. "Of course I'll respect it. You can trust me, Gabrielle. It might not seem like it, but you can."

More than anything, I want to believe it's true. I want to trust him, again. "I do trust you—to some extent. Probably more than I should. But don't expect me to hand over my complete trust. Again. It's just not possible."

"Because you found me fucking that girl? Fifteen years ago? It meant nothing. She didn't make a goddamn ripple."

"No, not *just* because of what happened in the past." Although the image of you with *her* is imprinted on my soul. It still makes my heart ache. It's not a crushing pain anymore, just an open sore that scabs over, but never fully heals.

I jerk my head away from his grip. "There are the lies you've been telling me, the games you're playing, the secrets you keep. And *that* girl? Jane? Don't you dare say it was nothing. It was *everything*. That, and having your father send me away after I discovered you with her—it nearly destroyed me."

His face twists in agony. The pain and sorrow I see there is breathtaking. But I don't allow it to cow me. "I want the truth about what happened then, and about what's *really* going on now. I know all about the irrevocable trust. You have nothing on me."

He doesn't flinch. And he certainly isn't surprised.

Confusion begins to creep up my spine, followed closely by anxiety, with fury taking up the tail. "You know. You know they told me. You knew it all along." I'm shaking inside, but my voice is oddly calm.

He nods. "I promised to make a donation if your mother is treated well. There's a lot of money at stake for them. The hospital lawyer called me first thing Monday morning after your visit. Told me the caseworker had divulged too much information."

I'm vulnerable. Exposed. Embarrassed—I was sure I had the upper hand—that I knew something he didn't. "When you first came to the hotel, you were prepared to trick me into having sex with you. To rape me."

"*No!*"

"Yes," I whisper. "That's exactly how civilized societies refer to sex with dubious consent. You were trying to blackmail me into having sex with you."

He empties his beer with a long, steady pull. I watch his throat ripple. He drops the empty bottle into a bin under the sink. "It's not that simple. Not anywhere near that simple. But yes, I was prepared to mislead you, or to do anything else I needed to do to keep—" He stops abruptly, without ever finishing the thought. "But you decided to play along, and saved me from my worst instincts. Saved us both."

He always wins. I bury my face in my hands and feel the small fissures lengthening inside me, crisscrossing over one another, until the tiny cracks have spread everywhere. One more assault, no matter how small, and I'll shatter into millions of jagged pieces.

There's no anger inside me. I'm sure it'll come, but right now, I'm just sad and broken. "This entire week I thought—I thought you didn't know the case manager told me about the trust. I thought I had some power over you. Some control over this situation. Over my circumstances. *My* life."

His back is against the counter, his hands gripping the etched lip, watching me cautiously.

I sit in silence, my elbows propped on the cold stone, my mouth resting on my clasped knuckles, trying to understand all of it. Trying to come to grips with my sheer stupidity. "I never had any control. I had nothing. I was just a fool playing right into your hands."

"No." He wraps his arms around me and pulls me into his chest. "You've always had the power. The real power. All of it. *Always,* Gabrielle. That hasn't changed."

He squeezes me tighter, until my cheek is nestled against his beating heart. It's a sound that once soothed me, but not today. Today it's just noise.

I try to pull away, but he holds me tighter still, with one hand on the side of my head, his fingers massaging my scalp gently. "Trust me. You've got to. So much depends on it." He swallows hard. So hard it seems almost painful. "Then I'll tell you everything. I promise."

JD's voice is heavy with emotion. The words emerge thick and uneasy. A strangled plea. A desperate prayer into the wind.

His heart is pounding, a strong and steady gallop. This is as humble as I've ever seen him. As close to begging as JD has ever come with me. I wrestle with the feelings inside, trying to make sense of something that makes no sense. Sorrow, betrayal, and—yes, love—it's there too, stirring the pot.

There's also fear—fear of the unknown. Fear of the fate that awaits me. It's as though I'm swimming in quicksand on a cold, starless night, the baying wolves circling, with no help in sight.

I pull out of his arms and off the stool, cupping my elbows as I contemplate the weight of his words. *Trust me. How can I possibly trust you, JD? How?*

I begin to pace, while he continues to negotiate. "Gabrielle. Trust me. For a little while, and then you can have anything you want. I'll never bother you again."

As I turn over his words, a ray of light peeks through, and my sluggish brain begins to stretch and churn. It starts slow but then whirs faster and faster until the thoughts are pinging off my skull. His pleas are now nothing more than background din. Maybe he took the keys to frighten me into trusting him. Maybe it's a setup.

"I never found my keys last night. And today, when I left a meeting at City Hall, my tires were flat, all four of them."

The blood drains from his face.

"Someone removed the pins from inside, so they deflated without making a sound. When I got into the car to wait for the tow truck, the missing keys were on the passenger seat."

He's deathly calm. "You're just telling me this now?" His voice is icy, and it's shed all pretense of prayer.

I can tell from his reaction that he knows nothing of the missing keys, and I'm relieved. *So relieved*. That would have been the last straw for me.

"Did you call the police?"

"*Mmhm*. They think it's a teenage prank. They also think I misplaced the keys inside the car."

He nods. But he doesn't look convinced.

"Does this have anything to do with the secrets you're keeping from me?"

"I don't know. Flat tires? Probably not." He squeezes the back of his neck. "But I need you under my protection while I figure it out."

"Under your protection?" Any excuse to control me, right, JD? "You must be kidding."

He grabs hold of my upper arms to make his point. "Do I look like I'm fucking kidding?"

I swallow. No. No, he doesn't. He looks furious, and scared. I might have even caught a sliver of terror in his eyes. But JD doesn't get scared, and he's not terrified of anything. That's not how he's built. He grabs danger by the neck and spits in its ugly face, before he slashes its throat. I've watched him do it more times than I can count.

Gooseflesh has taken over every inch of space on my arms,

and the hair at the back of my neck is at attention. It's not the flat tires and mysterious keys that have made me afraid. My body is reacting to his fear. *Maybe you need to listen, Gabrielle. Just listen to what he has to say.*

"What exactly does *under your protection* mean? I'm not leaving the hotel if that's where you're headed with this."

"You can stay for now, unless there are any more bizarre occurrences. But you need security."

"I have security."

"Real security. The kind that will actually keep you safe. They'll disappear into the background. You won't even know they're around. I have it. My brothers have it. It's not a big deal."

It's a big deal to me. I have a hotel to run, and a Christmas brunch to plan. "No."

He holds up his hand to stop me. "It's nonnegotiable. You're getting it with or without your consent."

We'll see about that. "Yes, of course, because you would never let a small matter like consent get in your way." He doesn't flinch. He doesn't react in any discernable way. I try a different approach. "The police weren't all that concerned. Let's not get carried away."

"My father's the president-elect. There are a lot of bad people in the world."

"What does this have to do with me?"

"We're connected."

"Then maybe we should disconnect." It's flippant, and I don't mean it. Not one word.

"Too late."

"I don't get it, JD."

"If someone wanted to hurt me, or wanted to pressure me in some way, they might hurt you."

"It's been less than two weeks. Who could know about us? No one."

"Don't bet on it."

"You clearly believe someone letting the air out of my tires was more than a prank."

"And the keys?" He scratches his temple. "I don't know. Not yet. But you can be damn sure I'll find out."

"If you knew about the potential for trouble—if you knew someone might use me to get to you—why would you drag me into something like this? *Why*?"

He fills his chest with air and blows it out in a resigned *whoosh*. "Had I known, I would have never touched you." His voice is filled with pain. His face. His eyes. All of it, heavy with remorse and sorrow. "I was young and stupid, and you were beautiful and sweet. I never stood a chance."

My heart clenches, and I will away the tears stinging the back of my eyes. "It's someone who knows about the past?"

"I've already said more than I should." His face is lined with worry, his shoulders uncharacteristically slumped. I can almost see the weight on his back.

"The Christmas brunch is the most important thing that's happened to the hotel since it opened. If I increase security, people will notice. They'll ask questions and jump to conclusions. I want everyone to be safe, but I can't have you going off half-cocked."

"No one will notice the uptick in security. It will mainly be your own personal detail, anyway. The changes at the hotel will be subtle." His gaze is hard. "I have a responsibility to protect you, but you have a responsibility to protect your guests and employees."

"Cheap shot, JD."

"Maybe. But it's true."

"Fine. I'll try the security. See what it's like. But if it's too—"

"Good." He nods. "It'll be so much easier on everyone if you cooperate." He hands me a mini iPad. "I need to make a quick call. Why don't you sift through my Spotify playlists, and see what you like." Before he leaves, he slides a thumb across my cheek. "It's going to be fine, Gabrielle. You'll be safe with Smith's team looking after you."

I'm not sure which of us it's meant to reassure.

"I'll be right back," he says, striding out of the kitchen.

"I'm not agreeing to anything," I call after him, as he disappears into a room at the end of the hall. "It's a trial run. That's all."

When the door clicks shut, I turn away, propping a hip against the cool counter. *This is crazy.* I gather my hair into a ponytail at the base of my neck and grip it in my fist, sliding my closed hand over the length to smooth the waves, pulling gently until the end.

JD's paranoid. Overprotective—call it what you want. Possessive and jealous, too, but that's another matter. To some extent, he's always been that way when it comes to me, but after his mama died, he sometimes took the safety concerns to extraordinary lengths. And now, it seems like he's upped his game.

I've always thought the excessive smothering was related to his mother and Sera's deaths. It's a common reaction to that kind of trauma. Some events leave such a deep impression on us, they stunt our ability to react logically under particular circumstances. Instead, we react from somewhere inside us bubbling with primitive emotion. Like Georgie, who worries she'll die after giving birth just like her mother and aunt died. No amount of logical reasoning can put her mind at ease. It's the same way with JD. The security he's insisting on is just another way to keep me safe from the boogiemen he conjures. And to keep any interested men at bay—but that's just a bonus.

I rustle through my purse until I locate my phone. I check for messages, but there's nothing pressing to distract me from the little voice in my head that's hell-bent on being heard.

What are you doing, Gabrielle? Why are you still here?

You want this. That's why. The lies, the secrets, the manipulation. Tell yourself anything you'd like. Justify it in any way you wish, but you want this—every second of it, in all its fucked-up glory. If it involves him, you want it. No matter how much it hurts, or how many scars it leaves. You love him. Admit it. You've always loved him. And you always will.

I scroll through the playlists, looking for something that matches my mood, until I land on Gaga. Yep, this is just right.

I love him. *I do.* All his crazy, and all of mine. Somehow it works—except when it doesn't.

It's all true. Nothing could drag me from here. I'll be careful, I assure myself. I'll be smart this time. I'm older, tougher. My eyes are wide open now. It'll be okay. I know it's all a huge lie, but I swallow it. Every single word.

18

Gabrielle

JD comes back to the kitchen with two bags of food, plops them on the counter, and reaches for the iPad to change the music. "Jesus, Gabrielle. 'Bad Romance,' really?"

"It seemed like a good night for some Gaga. Stop looking at me like that. It was on one of your playlists."

"Yeah, well, I have no idea how it got there."

"Maybe you should stop handing off your iPad to random women," I tell him, putting out dinner. "I noticed that there's nothing on that iPad but music."

"You looked?"

"Of course I looked."

He pins me with a sharp gaze.

"What, you wouldn't have looked? *Please*."

JD tops off my wine and gets himself another beer. We sit at the tall center island, elbow to elbow, Petty playing softly in the background. "Let's start the evening over," he says. "Put the last thirty minutes aside for an hour or two. Can you do that?"

I nod, and he blows out a long breath. "So what else did you learn on the dark web?"

"I'm sorry?"

"Isn't that where you read about contracts and power exchanges?"

I smile, a small wistful smile. "I learned about those things a long, long time ago, in a place not so far away."

I gaze at him. He's sullen and grim. And I can't stand it. "What else did I learn on the dark web?" I ask it in a light, playful voice, that sounds only minimally forced, hoping to coax something resembling a smile from him. "Let's see. Should I call you Sir?"

The corners of his mouth twitch and curl. And the stress slides off his shoulders, at least for a few minutes. He glances sideways at me, and his chest begins to heave with raucous laughter. It's a glorious sound, and I start to laugh, too.

"Sir," he says, his chest still heaving. "That's too damn funny. *No*, don't call me Sir. I can't imagine that word ever rolling off your tongue in a way that would arouse anyone."

"How about Master?" I play along, hoping to keep the sullen look from reappearing.

He shakes his head, grinning. "Just call me Julian."

The room stills eerily before it quakes. *Just call me Julian.* I cling to my fork. His is suspended midair. My heart beats so hard, I can hear it in my ears. He didn't mean to say it. The word slipped out when he was—*being Julian.*

"Julian," I repeat softly. "You want me to call you Julian."

His hand still holds the fork, frozen, inches above the plate.

"Look at me," I demand softly.

He turns his head. Everything is happening in slow motion. At least that's how it's registering inside my brain. There's something in his face. Something I can't read and don't understand.

"Julian," I say again. "I'll call you Julian."

JD—*Julian* nods once. "Only if you want to. During sex. Like you used to." His voice is low and rough. His eyes blazing, so hot, I look away before the fire consumes me.

He begins to eat again, and I shove a small piece of meat into my mouth, too. Chewing and chewing, hoping the repetitive motion will calm me. That it will distract from all the craziness of tonight.

My mind begins to churn again. Our arrangement doesn't need to include sex. I can have control over that part. I speak only when I've fully formed the idea, and have organized the feelings into meaningful sentences. It's imperative that I make my case strongly without hesitancy.

"I want to change the parameters of our arrangement. We sort of did earlier. But I want it to be clear."

"I'm listening."

His voice is firm, and I'm sure he is listening. *But will he hear me? Will he acquiesce?* He won't have a choice.

"I'll play along with your little game, since it's so important to you. I'll o-o—"

"Obey? Is that the word you're looking for?"

I glare at him. "I'll do as you ask regarding the things that involve my safety, and in exchange, when it's over, you will tell me everything I want to know. I mean *everything,* JD. *And* your access to my body is no longer part of the agreement."

"I can live with that. I'll miss tormenting your gorgeous little body, but I can live without the sex."

I adjust my bottom on the stool. "I never said there'd be no sex. Only that it wasn't part of the arrangement."

He shifts toward me, his breath tickling my ear. "I never intended to give up the sex. I was playing you. Your body is mine. Always has been."

I pull back and raise a brow at him.

"I'm teasing," he says. He doesn't even try to make it sound sincere.

"No, you're not."

JD smirks, that knowing, crooked little smirk that makes women's panties wet. "How's the steak?" he asks. "Did they cook it enough for you?"

"Perfectly cooked meat is not getting you out of trouble, JD. The steak's delicious, but the onion rings are addictive." I snatch one off his plate, and he pinches my side, playfully. "Next time, I'm ordering a double batch all for myself." *Next time. Will there be a next time? Who knows?* The words reverberate in my head, until his voice stills them.

"Before we got on the subject of contracts and safe words," he nudges me with his elbow, "I planned on talking to you about birth control. Are you using anything?"

Ahhh, we're back to the nitty-gritty. "I'm on the Pill."

He nods.

"And Dean and I always used condoms."

"I guess you really didn't want to get pregnant."

Condoms and the Pill, Gabrielle—you knew he was cheating, even if you won't admit it. You're always lying to yourself when it comes to men. And you're doing it again, now. "I want babies," I say defensively. "It just wasn't the right time."

"Or the right man."

He's arrogant and smug. So smug. And the worst part is, he's right.

JD drops the last onion ring on my plate and gets up, sauntering over to a column of drawers at the edge of the room. He pulls out a manila envelope from the top drawer and slides it across the stone countertop to me. The return address is a doctor's office downtown. "I'm clean," he announces, leaning over the counter.

I nod. I suppose this is the place where I lay out my lab results. "I haven't been tested since my last appointment, six months ago. And even then, not for everything. I was in a monogamous relationship. At least I—"

JD touches a finger to my mouth to quiet me. I bite down on the pad. It's unexpected, and his eyes are molten. "I'll take my chances. But you really should take a look at what's in the envelope."

He watches me undo the clasp and pull out the papers. My eyes glaze over the small print. This is important to JD, that much is clear. It's an offering of sorts. A small gift. His way of reassuring me that I can trust him. The funny thing about all of it is that I would have taken his word about being clean. It's not the kind of thing he would ever lie about. I would be surprised if that's changed, although there have been so many lies now, who knows anymore?

In many ways, I still understand him so well. His moody eyes, his quirky habits, every ragged breath. My brain interprets the signals as though no time has passed. But in other ways, we're still addressing birth control and HIV status.

Once the appropriate amount of time passes, I slip the paperwork back inside.

He studies me carefully. "Any questions?"

"I'm not sure."

His brow crinkles. "Ask me."

"I can't believe how much you weigh. Where do you put it all?"

The crease at his forehead eases, and he lunges at me. "I'll show you."

I push him away, both hands on his solid chest. "I've seen it. It's not *that* big."

He tickles me until I'm laughing uncontrollably.

"I missed that laugh."

"*Hmmm.*" I don't want to ruminate about the past. Not now. I want more of the light fun. More smiles and tickles. "Now that we got all of the sexy foreplay out of the way, can I have a cookie?"

He shakes his head and grins. "The only reason you're not getting a spanking right now is because I've always loved your sassiness. Still do." His nose touches mine. "It makes the surrender so much sweeter."

He pulls something from his back pocket and lets it brush against my arm. It's soft. I look down. There's a long, silky tie of some kind in his hand. *A blindfold.*

"Let's play a little game," he murmurs, moving behind me and securing the fabric around my eyes. When he's done, he pulls my hair aside and touches his warm lips to the nape of my neck.

I shiver.

"What kind of game?" My voice is breathy. I'm nervous. And excited. As much as I always loved gazing at JD during sex, as arousing and satisfying as it was to watch him wrestle with control—I always loved being blindfolded, too. It meant sensory play. I hope that's what it means now, too. My pussy is throbbing just imagining it.

"Can you see?"

I shake my head. "No."

"We're going to play a guessing game," he whispers near my ear.

I shudder. Now that my sight is gone, the tingling of his warm breath on my skin is magnified.

I hear paper crinkling and sense something under my nose. Lime. And maybe coconut. "What is it?"

"That's what you're going to tell me. I have a half-dozen cookies and you're going to use your mouth and nose to guess what kind."

"What happens if I guess wrong?"

"Nothing."

Oh. I'm a little disappointed, until he nuzzles my throat.

"I'm warming you up for a different kind of guessing game. Tonight is all about pleasure."

I squeeze my legs together, and a small moan escapes. I can't see a thing but I know he's smirking.

JD slides a thin cookie along the seam of my mouth, much like a lover would use his tongue. "Open."

I part my lips slightly.

"Wider. That's it. Now take a bite."

I do everything he asks, and let the small morsel sit on my tongue before I begin to chew.

"What kind of cookie is it?"

"Coconut and lime. It's a buttery shortbread. I think."

"Good girl." He lifts a glass to my mouth. "It's just water. Take a sip. Easy."

I swallow the water, and feel another cookie near my lips.

"This one won't be so easy to guess," he says.

I chew the cookie carefully, focusing on the taste. It reminds me of caramelized sugar. But I'm not sure. "Can I have one more bite?"

He puts the cookie to my lips again, but this time I feel him near my face—it's not just his fingers. At least I think it's not. I lift my hand to check, but he grabs it gently and lowers it, securing both my hands in my lap.

My breathing quickens. The throb between my legs is stronger. I open my mouth and bite down. The crisp cookie crumbles, and pieces fall onto my lap. I feel his breath on my mouth, his lips nearly touching mine. He's feeding me with his mouth. Letting me nibble the treat from his lips, like a little bird.

We repeat the sensual exercise again and again, until I've guessed five different cookies. JD is patient and reassuring. Stroking my skin gently. Letting me feed from him. Rewarding me with unexpected kisses at every opportunity. Every kiss is its own heated event, making me wetter, needier.

"We're done with this," he murmurs, sliding his warm hands under my shirt, and unhooking my bra. He palms my breasts, thumbs circling the hard nipples, until he can't resist giving them a small, sharp pinch.

"*Ahhhhh.*" The pleasure mounts, and I can't sit still for a second longer—but I can't see to move. "I thought there were six cookies?"

He pinches the furled nipples again, twisting until I cry out. Then he laves them with his tongue until I'm gasping for air, begging for more.

"*Julian*," I plead.

But he won't be rushed. And when I squeeze my legs together for a little friction, he pushes them apart with a *tsk tsk*.

"Do you really want the last cookie?" he asks, his hot breath on my neck.

I shake my head.

"I didn't think so."

As soon as I answer, he scoops me off the stool in one easy motion.

"Where are we going?"

"Somewhere you won't fall off a stool and end up in the emergency room."

"But where?"

"No more questions."

It's dark, and I'm not accustomed to being carried. *Breathe, Gabrielle. Breathe.* He lays me on what I'm quite sure is a mattress, and I quickly feel it dip beside me. His hands are on me, undressing me with impatient tugs and pulls. His mouth is everywhere.

Smooth lips.

Wet tongue.

Sharp teeth.

I writhe against the bed, the cool air waltzing over my burning skin. It's been so long since I felt this way—since he made me feel this way. He's the only one who has ever had this effect on me.

"You're mine," he says, grazing the sensitive skin on my inner thigh.

When I'm naked, he takes hold of my wrist. "I'm cuffing you to the bed."

Before I process any of it, I hear a snap, and my left wrist is encased in something wide and soft, like velvet. Within seconds, my ankles are shackled too, my legs spread wide, completely open to him, the charged air teasing my needy cunt. I pull on the restraints to test them. I've been bound before, but it feels new and scary—just a little scary. *You don't need to be afraid. He won't hurt you. You like being tied. Remember?*

I do.

Erotic images from the stable flood my mind. We didn't have a bed, but Julian would tie my hands to a post, or sometimes behind my back, while he ate me from behind, or fucked me until my legs shook.

My pulse is racing out of control.

"I didn't bind you tightly. There's some slack for you to tug on."

His fingers skirt between my ribs, down below my navel. The sensations ripple outward, and I arch off the mattress in response.

"We won't keep the blindfold on too much longer. Too soon for blinding and binding," he tells me. "Too long since we last played like this. But you'll need to be bound for what I have planned."

I whimper in anticipation, and his lips are on mine, quieting me. "*Shhhh.* Just relax until I'm ready for you. It won't be too long." And then he's gone.

Relax? He doesn't want me to relax. He wants me to lay here and wonder what he's doing. Wonder when he'll touch me. Wonder if he's still in the room. Time moves slowly for those who wait, the adage goes. Yes, it does. And as the time ticks away, I begin to work myself into a nervous frenzy, until an inexplicable terror builds and stakes a hold in my chest. I can't breathe. "JD. JD!" I scream. "Don't leave me here alone."

The mattress shifts and a sure hand strokes me, while the

other unties the blindfold. "*Shhh.* Gabrielle. It's okay. I'm right here. I would never leave you alone tied to the bed. Not even for a minute. It's too dangerous, darlin'."

I manage to regain some sense of composure from his soothing. I can feel my breathing steady. I open my eyes and blink. Once. Twice. His shirt is off, and I see the ink on his chest, and more peeking along his left hip. It appears to be a serpent of some kind, that snakes deep into his jeans.

They're new. New since he was nineteen. I want to run my fingers over them, trace the contours, ask him what they each mean. But my hands are bound.

"I'm going over to the dresser. You'll be able to see me the entire time."

I nod. It's such a relief to have the blindfold off—it was too soon to have so much control stripped away.

My eyes track him across the room. He opens the top drawer, and after a few minutes, he comes back with a deep tray, laying it beside me on the bed. I turn my head to peek inside, but I can't make out what's inside.

"Remember how much you liked sensation play?"

"Yes." *Oh God,* yes, I remember. I remember all the little tools —the feathers and puffs. The sharp wheels and the velvet ribbons. Smooth and bristly. Soft and hard. Hot and cold.

"Me too." He smirks. "I'm going to groom you tonight, brush and comb every inch of your skin until it's rosy and glowing. Work out every knot and tangle until you're purring."

I feel the rush of pleasure between my legs, and close my eyes to ride the wave.

"You were straining to see what's on the tray. Open your eyes and I'll show you the brushes. Would you like to see them?"

I open my eyes and nod. Yes, I want to see them—*and feel them, too.* My toes curl, imagining the sweet torment.

He lifts each instrument, each *toy*, one at a time, so I can take a good look, then skims it over my breasts. The powder puff is first. It looks like something a pampered woman might use to spread scented talc over her skin. It's fluffy, with gauzy layers, like a billowy cloud skimming the sky on a spring day. Julian brushes it over my right breast.

"*Mmmm.*"

"It's made of silk," he says. "Soft, isn't it?"

I nod, but I'm not fooled. It's soft now, but soon, even the softest puff will be too much. He lets the silken fibers float over my pebbled nipple, once, twice, and again. It's more sensitive than the breast itself, and I moan.

"Oh, Gabrielle. Baby. It's going to be harder for me to stay in control than it is for you."

He takes each implement from the tray, alternating rough and smooth—a hairbrush with natural boar bristles, a feather duster without the stick, a comb with spiny teeth, and a synthetic pastry brush with a long, wooden handle. When he slaps my breasts with the floppy silicone bristles, they sing.

"Are you wet, Gabrielle?"

I avert my eyes modestly. "Yes." Yes, I'm wet because each time he touches my skin with the brushes and feathers, I feel the sensation rip through my core, as though all my nerve endings share a direct connection that ends there, between my legs.

"This is the last thing," he says, displaying what looks to be an artist's brush.

It's round and about a half inch thick. I know there's something special about it, because he saved it for last.

He twirls the brush directly over my nipple. It's sinister and delicious, just like I knew it would be, and my cunt is pulsing with need.

"I'm not going to blindfold you, but I want you to close your eyes and feel. Just feel."

And I do.

I shutter my eyes as he begins the sensuous assault. He starts with the comb, raking the thorny tines over my scalp and cheeks, moving methodically down my throat, lingering on each breast, before sliding it over my belly and across my freshly waxed mound. I writhe and pull on the restraints, my mind blank to everything but sensation. He combs lower and lower still, down the sensitive skin between my thighs, to the soles of my feet—no splash of skin is spared. I don't think I can withstand too much more—but it's only the beginning.

"Which brush am I using?" he asks each time he picks up a new one. My eyes are closed, and after only a short while, my skin is screaming, and I can't distinguish one from the other.

He eventually has mercy, adjusting the cuffs and flipping me onto my stomach, where he starts with a fresh canvas. The brushes, his mouth, my flesh.

"Julian," I plead, rubbing my body against the sheets. They feel cool and coarse, and I moan and shiver as the sensations swirl into my skin, delving deeper and deeper below the surface.

"This will be cold," he warns, as an icy liquid drips onto the small of my back, pooling in the concave. He dips his fingers into the slippery liquid, dragging it through my slit, to the back entrance, pressing his fingertip against the puckered hole. And like before, there's pressure. So much pressure.

"It's just lube," he assures me. "Lots and lots of lube, darlin'." His voice is low and reassuring, as his fingers slip into my pussy.

I moan and squirm at the welcome intrusion, all while another finger, one that seems longer and thicker, works its way into the pleated bud. The sensation is unfamiliar. My body is confused, and I start to flail as soon as he breaches the first ring of muscle.

"Push out. That's it. Let me in." He strums my clit, and I begin to relax, while his finger works its way inside my ass.

At first, it feels bigger, fatter than it is, but after a few torturous minutes, my body begins to acclimate. I forget all about the dirty, uncomfortable things, when it starts to feel good. Soon, it's so good, I don't even notice his hand leave my pussy.

"I'm going to fuck you here. One day soon," he murmurs, twisting his finger out of my puckered hole.

My mind is blank, my body burning, while he adjusts the cuffs again, and turns me on my back. This time he leaves no slack in the binding. My legs are spread wide. I'm completely open to him. At his mercy. And there is nothing to tug on as he pushes my body to the peak. I'll have to absorb all the sensation. All of it. I'm not sure if I can.

His mouth is on my skin, licking and nipping wherever he chooses. However he wants. Feasting on my body like it's a grand buffet, set out for his pleasure. His tongue flicks my clit, once, twice, and the whimpering begins, and then the prattle of nonsense. I'm going to combust.

"I think it's time to paint," he says, in a sensuous voice that casts anxious tremors, even as it seduces.

"I can't. Julian. It's too much. I need to—I can't."

"Look at me." His eyes are black. There's not a sliver of blue left in them. "You can. And if you're a good girl, I'll let you come soon. You need that, don't you, darlin'? I'm going to make it so good for you. And you're going to come all over my nice clean sheets. Like a dirty slut. Like *my* dirty, filthy slut. Only mine. Only for me."

"Yes," I whimper. *Yes, yes, yes*. "Please. I want to be your dirty slut. Only yours."

I feel the brush slide down my belly and dip between my legs, swirling inside my wet cunt.

He brings the bristles up and paints each nipple, before suckling the hard bead. "Delicious," he murmurs. "*So* delicious."

I tug on the restraints, but there's nothing to pull on. Nothing to help me as he dips the brush into my greedy pussy again and again, spreading the wet slipperiness everywhere. Nothing to pull on while he laps it up.

My body shakes. My mind numbs. And the bristles are between my legs again. But this time he doesn't pull them away.

This time he sweeps them over my clit. Gentle at first. Slow and precise. But soon the assault is faster and harder. Harder and faster. And so delicious.

The angle of the bristles change. *"Oh God! No!"* He's not going to let the little pearl hide. I'm trembling, but he doesn't stop. With a firm hand, he coaxes it from under the hood with the insistent brush.

I scream, thousands of silent screams, while I try to writhe away from the evil bristles, but I'm bound too tight to move.

He tosses the brush aside and clamps his lips over my clit, sucking and licking. Licking and sucking, until I surrender completely.

My head thrashes from side to side when he lets the orgasm come. The tremors, the bucking, and then a free fall through the gossamer shadows. I hear the shattering scream, years of pent-up frustration erupting from a million tiny pinpricks in my flesh.

I taste the tears. But I can't feel them on my cheeks.

JD uncuffs me. Speaking quietly while he massages my stiff limbs. "You're so damned beautiful—tied to my bed—coming apart on my tongue. I've waited a long time to have you." He smooths the hair back off my face. "To taste your sweet pussy. It's so sweet, Gabrielle. So sweet. I'll never get enough of you."

He kneels between my legs and lowers his mouth, kissing away the tears. "You're going to come again, baby. All over my cock this time."

I'm not sure I can come, again—ever. But his cock stands erect, needy, and dark. And when it twitches, I feel the twinge between my legs.

His lips find mine in a scrumptious coupling, and I twine my arms tightly around his neck, not wanting it to ever end.

It's much too soon when he pulls back, to hook my legs over his hips. The short distance between us, almost unbearable.

Then I feel it.

The tremor on my skin.

His hands shaking.

His control gone.

I know what's coming.

He won't ease inside me.

It won't be gentle.

I squeeze my eyes shut, digging my fingers into his back as he fills me with one, long, agonizing thrust. The groan pushes up from my belly, and into my chest, making its way out into the charged air between us. He stills at the sound, still buried deep, and kisses my throat tenderly.

"*Jesus Christ*, Gabrielle. You're so damn tight around my cock." He ruts deeper, bringing his warm mouth back to mine. "I've missed this so much. For so long. Missed you every day." His voice is crushed stone, mined from a fiery quarry deep within the earth.

I'm already starting to climb.

He moves in a steady rhythm—long, punishing lunges interspersed with shallow thrusts that let me catch my breath. My body is awake, every inch of flesh, every muscle, every nerve warbling. He peels the hair off my sweaty face and sinks his teeth into my neck.

I gasp for breath. For sanity.

His hips pound me with long, ruthless strokes. Unyielding. Uncompromising. He wants it. "Now. Give it to me," he growls.

I scream as he takes it. Fast and rough, with no pretense of kindness, he rips the twisting orgasm from my trembling body, leaving nothing behind.

It's brutal.

I'm drowning.

Gasping for air.

Filling my lungs with short, uneven pants, simply to breathe.

The waves swell and surge, pulling me under, finally dragging me to where there is only bliss. Where there is only us.

I feel his muscles tighten in my hands, his frantic pace, his head fall to my breast. There is only the final savage thrust, and the primal roar, when he empties himself into my throbbing cunt.

After a few minutes, he kisses my forehead tenderly, *so tenderly*, and rolls off me. As soon as he's gone, I begin to shiver.

Without a word, he scoops the quilt from the floor and wraps himself around me, the covers pulled up over us. He rains soft kisses on my hair. The kind of gentle drizzle that doesn't disturb the terrain, but makes it lush and fertile. "Every time," he whispers, "every single time with you, it's more than I could ever imagine. *Every time.*"

His arms engulf me in a safe harbor, and I sink into them and surrender to sleep.

When he wakes me, there's no time for a shower before I have to get back to the hotel. No time to process. No time to sort through shaky thoughts and feelings.

"I'm so late. I don't think there's time to wait for Antoine to get here."

"Your security is waiting right outside. They'll get you back to the hotel in time."

"You already arranged security?" *Of course you did.*

"It took one phone call."

I'm too tired to argue. Too sore. And too content to let this spoil my mood. Besides, I told him I'd try.

JD introduces me to Rafe and Gus.

When I turn to say good night, he tells me, "I'm coming too."

Great. I pull him aside, away from where Rafe and Gus can hear. "You can't come to the hotel with me. People will know. My staff will know what we've been doing. People talk. Charleston's a gossip-lover's paradise. You know this."

"You're an adult. You're allowed to have sex. With me,

anyway," he adds. "But no one will know what we were doing. Not unless you tell them." He tips his head toward the big, burly security guards. "I'm sure Rafe and Gus know their business, but I want to get a feel for how they are with you. I won't hang around for long."

"JD." But I don't argue because he's shushing me with his mouth, and his tongue, and his teeth. I even lose sight of Rafe and Gus, who have discreetly turned their backs to us.

"JD." I pull back, panting softly. "I really have to get back."

He tucks a curl behind my ear and nods. His eyes are warm and focused. His face gorgeous and scruffy. The furrows and lines relaxed. I like him like this. Just like this. And it takes everything I have not to launch myself into his arms and beg him to take me back to bed.

19

Julian

I'm on the side lawn at Sweetgrass, stretching before my morning run with Smith. But I can't stop thinking about last night—wondering how many more nights I can squeeze in with Gabrielle before it's over.

It was everything I've ever wanted. Everything I dreamed about in the last fifteen years. *Fifteen fucking years.* But it wasn't just the sex—although, Jesus, that was pretty damn spectacular.

I see Smith winding down the lane. He'll be here in a few minutes. I want to ask him what Rafe and Gus did to piss him off enough to get assigned to Gabrielle's security detail. Poor bastards. She was polite last night, but she bristled whenever she noticed them loitering. And I'm afraid it's only going to get worse for them. But I'll have to talk to him about it later, because we don't discuss business during our morning runs.

Smith's not even breaking a sweat when he reaches me. "You ready?" he asks. It's not a question. It's a challenge.

"I'm ready. Been waitin' for you to drag your sorry ass here."

Smith and I have been good friends since boarding school. We each spent a year there before going on to Harvard, where we were roommates for all four years. We run at five thirty, every weekday morning, and occasionally on the weekend. Rain, sleet, or snow, we never miss our run unless one of us is away.

"I can only do the five-mile route this morning," I tell him. "I have an early meeting."

"We're not even out of the circle yet and you're already bellyaching. You're such a pussy."

"I'm a pussy? You have on those stupid Redskins shorts, and you're all over my shit?"

"My mother sent them to me. Take it up with her."

"How is she?" I ask.

"Fine. Busting my father's balls constantly now that he's retired. But he deserves it, I'm sure. It's her birthday in a couple of weeks. I'm going home for the party. Wanna come?"

"Wish I could." Smith's family is great, and I've spent a lot of time at his house over the years, especially during college, but I haven't been back in a while. "It's been crazy since the election. I'm swamped, trying to get a read on Sayle."

"Too bad. I could use your help. Meredith's bringing a boyfriend home from school with her."

"You're kidding." Smith has four sisters. All younger than him, but Meredith is the baby. "Who said she could date?"

"According to my father, my mother said it. I guess nineteen-year-old college girls are allowed to have boyfriends in some places. It's criminal."

I laugh, but it's bittersweet. My sister Sera never grew old enough to have boyfriends. I rub the cramp in my side. "Your father must be losing it, thinking about her away at school hanging out with some guy."

"He says it's fine. Through gritted teeth." Smith chuckles. "My mother hasn't given him a choice."

Smith's father is a retired four-star general. He served as the head of the Joint Chiefs during the first term of the current administration. "Sorry I'm going to miss the fun. It's been a long time since we laid a beatin' on one of your sister's boyfriends."

"If you change your mind, my parents would love to have you —you're like the son they never had."

I laugh, because nothing could be further from the truth. They couldn't be prouder of Smith. Rightfully so. "What did you end up doing last night?"

"You mean who."

"Let's hear it," I say, rounding the bend near the stable where my mother kept her horses when she was a girl.

"You'd like her. She's your type. I'll text you her number."

"You're done?"

"Oh yeah. As much as I'd like to go a few more rounds with her, she has the potential to be a stage-three clinger."

"So you want to pass her off on me? Thanks."

"I'm telling you, you'd like her. No gag reflex. She's proud of it, too. Likes to show it off."

"I'm all set."

"*Really?* Since when do you pass up a chick who thinks her mission in life is to give good head?"

"I have too much going on."

"Too much going on, my ass. This is about Gabrielle Duval, isn't it?" He shoves my arm when I don't answer. "Huh?"

"Don't be stupid." It doesn't come out convincing, but I don't give a shit. What I do with Gabrielle isn't up for discussion. Not even with Smith.

"Maybe I should tell her she doesn't have to cut off your balls, because you're about to hand them over to her."

"Fuck you."

"We can get her a nice little case for them, and I do mean little, so she can keep them in her purse."

He just played me. He knows I don't say shit about Gabrielle.

So instead of asking me about her directly, he took the sneaky way around. That's what I would have done, too. *But he's still an asshole.* "There was no woman without a gag reflex last night, was there?"

"Only in my dreams."

As I weave through traffic on my way to my meeting, the phone rings. *My father.* I haven't had enough coffee yet to deal with the sonofabitch. "Yeah."

"Good morning, JD. How's my business doing without me at the helm?"

He wants something. I can already tell from his tone.

"It's just fine. Better than ever. I was planning on calling you later. What is it you want so early in the morning?"

"Not only am I your father, but I'm your president, and I expect you to speak to me with a little more respect."

You'll get all the respect you deserve—not a fucking ounce. "It's early. I haven't had enough coffee to be human yet."

"Maybe you should start keeping more reasonable hours and laying off the booze. I've entrusted you with a lot of responsibility."

When it comes to people telling me how to run my life, I don't have a lot of patience. But when it's my father telling me how to be a more productive member of society, I want to murder him. "What was it you said you wanted?" The question comes out as rude as I hoped. He clears his throat, all pissed off. I can practically smell the toxic fumes coming from the other end of the line. Best thing that's happened so far today. I tug on my seat belt a bit and lean back in my seat, waiting to hear the bullshit du jour.

"I have a reporter hounding me," my father says. "Kate McKenna. She wants to do a feature on Zack. A human interest story. She'll need some photos, too."

"What?" I bark, slamming my brakes when the traffic light turns from yellow to red.

"I think it would be a nice thing. Provide some support to families caring for children with brain injuries. She'll be respectful of Zack's privacy. And yours, too."

"There is no fucking way any reporter is coming anywhere near Zack. Not while I'm still breathing."

"He's my son."

A lot of damn good it did him. "You don't have custody. Legal or physical. You don't get to make any decisions."

"Listen—"

"No. I am not having this discussion with you, or with anyone. It's over. And if you don't have anything else to talk about, I've got to go."

"JD, wait. I'm just asking you to consider it. It could be good for everyone."

DW doesn't do a damn thing unless it's good for him. Nothing. "It could be good for you. That's what you mean."

"I would really like it to happen."

"I would really like to have breakfast with my mother on Mother's Day. I would really like to torment Sera's boyfriends. And what I would really, really like, is for you to leave Gabrielle Duval alone. But none of that's going to happen, is it? Not in this lifetime, anyway."

"No one misses your mother and Sera more than me."

He's lucky my fist can't reach his jaw.

"And as for Gabrielle Duval, she's not on my radar. I have a fucking country to run, for Christ's sake."

"So you're not the one who paid someone to steal her keys, or had the air deflated from her tires?"

"I don't play children's games."

Bullshit.

"If I had her in my sights, believe me, you'd know about it."

Stealing keys and letting the air out of tires is bush league, even for him, JD. He prefers messing with brakes and filming underage girls getting off.

"I asked you nicely, because technically you are Zack's temporary custodian, but I would rethink my position on the feature story if I were you."

"You'll have to kill me first. And there's not a fucking thing that's temporary or technical about the custody decree."

"I would also learn to be more respectful, if I were you. And more afraid."

"Afraid you'll have someone kill me? *Nah.* Only so many of your family members can die before people start snooping around and asking questions. And you never know what a tenacious reporter might uncover if she starts digging. You can't afford that kind of scrutiny."

The call ends without a single civilized word. If that asshole thinks he's coming anywhere near Zack, or Gabrielle for that matter—

Get a grip, JD. Sweetgrass is more secure than Fort Knox, and thankfully, Gabrielle's agreed to security.

I let things get out of control with him today. Let him push my buttons like I'm a fucking puppet and he's the puppeteer. I know better than to allow it. It can't happen again. Not if I want to make him pay.

What kind of man commands respect by telling another man, *I'm your father*, or *I'm the president*? If you have to ask for it, you don't deserve it, and you ain't never gettin' it.

I slam my hand on the steering wheel. A fucking human interest story. With pictures. My head is seconds from exploding all over the car. It wouldn't surprise me if he gave the damn woman my address.

I call Smith to give him a heads-up that a reporter might show up with some bullshit story about Zack, and then sit in the parking lot at Sayle Pharmaceuticals, trying to calm the fuck down before I go inside for meetings.

I need Gabrielle. She's the equivalent of a shot of bourbon, only tastier, and more settling. But that'll have to wait until tonight.

The conversation with my father has left me unhinged. I don't trust the bastard, and I don't want to be too far from Sweetgrass this evening. Gabrielle's been hounding me to see Zack. Maybe tonight. *Maybe*.

20

Julian

I'm kicking myself for promising Gabrielle we'd see Zack tonight. I've kept him sheltered for so long now that the idea of bringing in a stranger, even though she's not really a stranger, has been gnawing at my gut all day. Sure, I can still say no, and if it were anyone else, I would say no. But it's her, and I don't want to go back on my promise. Besides, if I can get past the pain in my stomach, I know having someone else, *a good person*, visit him, is a positive thing.

Gabrielle's security team brings her to Sweetgrass at six forty-five. I wave them off at the door. "She's fine here with me. I'll call you when she's ready to leave."

I brush my mouth over hers. It's a quick hello, and I want more. So much more. "It's good to see you haven't chased off the security detail, yet. How did it go today?"

"A whole team, just for me," she says, pinning me with her eyes. "Seems excessive."

"They need to rotate to stay fresh. And you'll be happier if you're with the same people day in and day out."

"I'll be happier when security shadowing me is nothing more than a bad dream."

"You'll get used to it."

"When do we need to leave to see Zack? It's six fifty."

The gnawing in my stomach becomes heartburn. "We're good on time." I take her hand and lead her toward the back of the house.

"JD, isn't the garage on the other side of the house?"

"Yep."

"What are you doing? We don't have time to—"

I squeeze her fingers. "You ask a lot of questions. Now let me ask a couple. Have you showered recently? Put on clean clothes?"

"Excuse me?"

"I'm not asking for me. I like you dirty. But the weather's changing, and it might be hard for Zack to recover if he catches a bug. We're more careful about introducing new people and germs at this time of year." I should have mentioned it earlier, but I'm not used to bringing anyone to see him who doesn't know the drill.

She doesn't say anything, so I keep rambling like an idiot. "You can shower upstairs if you need to, and slip on a paper gown over your clothes."

"JD?"

I stop in my tracks and gaze at her. She's smiling at me. A small, soft smile, with a twinge of melancholy. Her eyes are soft like melted chocolate.

"You're jumpy. If tonight isn't a good night, we can see Zack another time. I'll be disappointed, but I'll understand. Just do what you think is best for him, and don't worry about me."

Right then, I knew what was best for my brother. I wasn't bringing her there to curry favor, or to share an important piece of myself with her, although there was that too, but I want Zack to feel her kindness and sweetness again. If he can find comfort with anyone, it will be with her. He adored her. "Zack will be happy to see you."

She squeezes my arm. "I showered right before I came over, even washed my hair. And these clothes are clean."

"Then let's go." I open the heavy double doors that lead to the back wing of the house. Only a few people, besides my brothers, are allowed in this part of the house. And now, Gabrielle.

Sumter takes one look at her and blocks the doorway. No one's getting in here on his watch, especially not the pain-in-the-ass reporter who phoned me three times today. I run a hand over his head and tell him to go lay down.

"Protecting Zack has become his job. He takes it seriously," I tell her.

When we enter the room, her eyes flit from corner to corner before they land on Zack. It's a spacious room with lots of windows. I had a large sliding door installed so that it would be easier to take him out for walks. But Zack's weak, so we don't do that very often anymore. The room is more functional than beautiful, but it's so much better than where my father had him holed up.

I introduce Gabrielle to Maureen, Zack's nurse, and wash my hands.

She washes her hands too, and peeks up at me while she dries them. "He lives here," she sputters. "With you."

"Yep."

"JD," she whispers, drawing in a breath, and brushing past me on her way to the special chair where my brother's resting. "Zack," she says softly, taking his hand. "It's Gabby." She lowers herself into a chair beside his, never letting go of his hand.

I grab a toy from the basket near the door and play a little tug-of-war with Sumter. I want to give her a little time with him.

She talks sweetly to Zack, as though he can understand every word she says, just like I knew she would.

Gabrielle was the one who forced me to visit Zack when he came home after the accident.

He seemed to recognize us then, but all he did was grunt and flail. Chase dragged his pillow and blanket in every night and slept on the floor beside his twin. Eventually the nurse insisted my father put a bed in there for him. Gray was afraid of Zack. And the truth is, so was I. Well, maybe not exactly afraid, but sickened, and repelled by the thing that had taken over my brother's body. It embarrasses me now to think about how I felt back then.

Gabrielle was never afraid of him. Never sickened or repelled. She's better than that. She'd go in all the time and hold Zack's hand while he pulled at her hair and drooled. She quietly shamed me into finding my balls. Chase, too. There was no way I was letting a little kid and a girl be braver than me. I learned to go in a little at a time, to visit every day, until my father decided it was too inconvenient to have Zack at home. Until my father decided that Zack would be better off dead.

"You should tell him about the Gatehouse. I bet he'd like to hear about it. Wouldn't you, Zack?"

Her voice is cheery as she talks about the hotel. "I bought the building from the city for a dollar. Can you imagine that? It had good bones, but it needed a lot of sprucing up.

"My mom and dad, and Lally, helped with some of the work. And Gray helped too. He didn't actually do any work. You know Gray." She laughs. "But he taught me a lot about restaurants and introduced me to some important people. Gray still knows everyone, and everyone knows him. Do you remember Georgina? She works at the hotel too. It's really special to be able to work with my best friend."

When I close my eyes for a minute, I see a little girl sitting on the piazza steps, chattering incessantly while she blows big soapy bubbles for Zack and Chase to run after. Occasionally one lands on their chubby hands before it pops. They ooh and aah, squealing like she spins gold.

I listen attentively while she tells Zack about jelly candies, and designer sheets, and dozens of other small details I don't know anything about. "The biggest surprise was in the basement," she tells him. "We discovered a half-dozen gates hidden under a pile of rubble. Beautiful iron gates. Philip Simmons' originals. You know, he's the man who made those intricate gates all over Charleston. Even if he didn't make the ones we found in the basement, they're beautiful reproductions. That's why I named the hotel the Gatehouse."

Gabrielle beams while she talks about the hotel. Her voice is light and filled with joy and pride. For a few minutes, I let myself bask in her happiness. I take solace in making her leave Wildwood before my father could get his clutches into her. It was her home, just like it had been my home. It hurt her to be sent away. I hurt her. But he would have destroyed her whole life had she stayed.

I want to ask her some questions about the hotel. I want to know more about the jelly candies, the honor bar, and Frette sheets. But I'm afraid if I speak, I'll spoil the magic, so I keep my mouth shut and my focus on Sumter as I try to catch the bubbles floating in the room.

The hour passes and the nurse returns.

"It's time to say good night," I tell her.

She smiles at me, and it's not just her mouth and her eyes that engage. It's her entire body. At least that's how it seems. Like she used to. Like I'm something more than a huge asshole come to ruin her life.

I smile back at her, holding her gaze for as long as I can. Hoping to capture the moment, the feeling, so when she's gone, I'll have something to keep me warm at night.

I would have gazed at her forever, but she turns to Zack.

"Now that I know how close you are, I'm coming back to see

you," she tells him. "Soon." Gabrielle presses her lips to his forehead. "Good night, Zackie. Love you bunches."

Something squeezes in my chest, reminding me that somewhere inside, my heart still beats. "Give me a minute."

She nods, and says goodbye to Maureen.

I help Maureen get Zack back into his bed for the night. Zack has two full-time nurses who rotate schedules, Maureen and Sue. During the day there's a physical therapist and a male nurse's aide to help, too. Maureen's in her late forties. She's competent as hell and kind. I trust her to be alone with him.

Saying good night to Zack is always bittersweet. He's frail, and I'm never sure when good night will be goodbye. But the prospect of walking out of his room tonight doesn't seem as lonely with Gabrielle here.

Before I go, I smooth the little wisps of hair on his head. "It was nice having Gabby visit, wasn't it? She's a welcome change from my ugly face, that's for sure. Tomorrow we'll finish reading about the dragons on Ponteluna Mountain. I love you." I squeeze his hand and kiss his head much the same way Gabrielle did. "Good night, Zack. Sweet dreams."

It's been years since I overheard the first of many conversations between my father and Olson about the accident. Just bits and pieces, some of it puzzling, and the rest devastating. It was as though he didn't care they were dead. Or maybe, he even had something to do with the car careening off the road.

I eavesdropped on their conversations as often as I could, but that night was the most gut-wrenching of all. That night, a piece of my soul crumbled. That night, I stopped being a kid.

After I left them, I went straight to Zack's room and kicked everyone out. I was too afraid to confront my father. Too afraid he'd kill me too. And I was ashamed. Ashamed for being a coward. More ashamed than I had ever been in life. I sat at the foot of Zack's bed, my knees tucked under my chin, and cried fat, angry tears. Lots of them. I promised DW would pay. That everyone involved would pay.

It was the last time I shed a tear.

It's taken a lot of years and heartache to get to this point. Lots of dead ends, and loose threads that gave me hope but amounted to nothing more than a collection of disappointments. I pulled dozens of those threads, chased every clue that seemed even the slightest bit promising, but nothing ever materialized into anything concrete.

But I have access to Sayle now, and deep down, I've always known the answers to the accident are there.

Sayle is the prize. Always has been. But the only way DW could have gotten his grubby hands on it was if something happened to my mother while my siblings and I were minors. Although there's more to it than just that. Has to be. I just don't know what it is yet.

The answers are there. I'm not sure where they're hidden, but they're there. They have to be, because I've looked everywhere else, and I will not accept failure in this regard. I will avenge my mother's death and Sera's. I will exact retribution for Zack and for Chase, who was in that car with them. And for Gray, too.

I might not live to enjoy it, but that sonofabitch will pay.

21

Gabrielle

I wait outside the room for JD, catching the sweet way he says good night to Zack. *JD, you are the most aggravating man on the planet.* You haven't changed. Not one bit. You have a hard, tough shell on the outside for everyone to see, but all the goodness is on the inside. So much goodness. Don't you dare tell me otherwise, because I just saw your heart.

Before JD comes out, he has a brief conversation with Maureen, something about the change of shifts and additional supplies.

I watch him walk toward me. He's moving slower than usual. There's no swagger in his gait. Letting me visit with Zack was a huge step for him. I realized it right before we went into the room.

I'm bursting with emotion, and I have so many questions. But he's raw. I can see it, and I need to be careful with him. I want to be careful.

He beckons with his head for me to follow, and we walk halfway to the kitchen in silence.

"You take such good care of him," I say. "In just the short time we were there, I can tell. I'm not surprised."

"I don't do anything. Just arrange for caretakers."

I place my hand on his arm. "Don't. Please don't."

"You hungry?" he asks, pulling away from my touch.

"Will you tell me how he came to be here? I can't believe your father allows it."

"My father didn't have a choice."

"How could that be? Zack's his son."

JD shrugs. "It's not that complicated. My father locked him in an inferior facility and didn't authorize the care that might have helped him. By the time I was old enough and strong enough to take a stand against him, it was already too late for Zack, but I intervened to slow the downhill slide. DW's a cold-blooded sonofabitch, but my blood runs just as cold. And at the time, I had nothing to lose from suing for custody." He glances at me, his eyes glazed. "When you've got nothing to lose, you can accomplish almost anything."

I'm having a difficult time following the details. Maybe it's because JD is half mumbling, and half cryptic. Or maybe because it's so much to take in. "You were awarded custody?"

"When it became clear I wasn't backing down, DW signed over custody. He'd been negligent for years. It would have been difficult—maybe impossible—to prove, but he couldn't take the risk of a big, ugly scandal. My guess is he was already eyeing the presidency then. He hated signing over custody to me, but it was his best choice."

My heart is heavy, and I'd like to wring DW's neck myself for what he did to Zack—and to JD. And I'm sure this is only the tip of the iceberg. Lally always said after their mother died, the Wilder boys were left impoverished. I never fully understood what she meant by it until now.

"Does your father come by to see Zack?"

He shakes his head. "He never visited Zack the entire time he was locked away. Not once. He's not welcome at Sweetgrass. If I see him on the property, I'll shoot him."

His voice is mean and dispassionate, and none of it sounds like bluster. Not that JD has ever been much for bluster. My skin is prickly. *He's not kidding.* "If I didn't know better—" I hold onto the wall for support. "You sound like you'd actually kill him."

He doesn't bother to deny it.

"Let's see what Lally left to eat," he says, heading toward the stove.

I don't say anything. But something gnaws at me. If DW finds an unfortunate ending, *God forgive me*, so be it. But I don't want blood on JD's hands—not his father's, not anyone's. I can't let it go. "You wouldn't really kill your father, right? Aside from turning my ass pink, you don't get to dole out punishment. That's what we have laws and courts for. And ultimately, it's God's purview."

"The law and the courts are in his back pocket. Especially now that he's been elected president. I don't think you need me to remind you how I feel about God."

JD pulls a couple of dishes from a warming plate below the oven. "Looks like Lally prepared some pulled pork and macaroni and cheese. The woman's going to give me a heart attack one of these days from all the cholesterol she feeds me." He sniffs the pork and grins at me. "But what a way to go."

He's not going to answer my question. I guess that's its own answer. *We will revisit this before I leave, JD.* Maybe you'll be more forthcoming with your belly full. "Lally's never been big on greens unless they've been rolled around in lard," I tell him. "This note says there's slaw in the fridge."

"You still like your barbeque tangy?" he asks.

"Of course. Who eats that sweet slop?"

———

After dinner, I help JD tidy up the kitchen. "You can have the plane tomorrow night to visit your parents, or Saturday morning, if it's better for you. I don't need it this weekend."

"Thank you. Saturday would be great." He's been true to his word about making the visits easy for me. It wouldn't surprise me if he gave up the plane once or twice when he did want to use it. Nothing about him surprises me anymore. "Then I can be at the hotel tomorrow night. It saves some money, and I don't have to impose too much on Georgina. She never says no, but she's seven months pregnant now."

"I'll have Patrick get in touch with you about the details in the morning. Is Georgina having a boy or a girl? Do they know?"

I wish Georgie could be as comfortable talking about JD as he is talking about her. We've been friends forever, and I hate keeping my life so compartmentalized. "A girl. We have big plans for spoiling her rotten."

"Poor Wade. He'll be outnumbered. It's all downhill from there."

I whack his arm. "What do you know about having daughters?"

"Nothing. Not a damn thing, and I plan on keeping it that way."

Hmmm. He always wanted kids. I wonder what changed. Maybe it's just daughters. "You don't want a family?"

"When I took over this place, I imagined having a family. Most people see that kind of life for themselves." He takes some plates from the dish rack and stacks them on a glass shelf inside the cupboard. Then he shuts the door so cautiously the click is unperceivable. "But I don't see it anymore. I'll call your security detail so you can get home before it gets too late." He glances at me. "What's wrong?"

I realize I'm scowling. "Nothing. I was hoping that maybe—"

"Maybe what?"

"Maybe you'd kiss me." Maybe you'd take me to your bed, here at Sweetgrass, where you don't bring other women.

He stares into my face for a long time. Like he's looking for some excuse not to kiss me. Maybe he's thinking that this is home, not a place for dirty sex. Whatever's bothering him, he eventually relents and kisses me. It doesn't start this way, but it ends with his hands in my hair, his mouth claiming mine, and both of us struggling for breath. "Just a kiss, that's all you want?" he asks.

"*Hmmm*. It's a good place to start. I like it when you cant my hips, so I can feel your cock against my belly when you kiss me."

"Your plan is to tease me?" he asks with mock horror. "I feed you Lally's barbeque and you want to rub yourself against my cock and get me all worked up before you leave?"

I laugh. "Yes. No."

There's a glimmer of mischief in his eyes. "Which is it?"

Definitely no. "How would you like me to make amends, Julian?" Should I get on my knees? I bet you'd love that.

The knob in his throat bobs. "I have a list. A long list. It'll take you a lifetime to get through it."

I rub against him with whatever control I can muster, while I dip my tongue into his mouth. But a little voice keeps intruding. Reminding me we have unfinished business. Reminding me I'm in deeper than I planned. *Your father's not worth it, JD. Do not trade your life—your soul—for revenge. I can't lose you again, not so soon.*

"JD?"

"*Hmmm*?"

"All that talk about your father earlier. It scares me. Really scares me. I need to know you wouldn't kill him, or kill anyone. That you don't have that kind of hate in your heart."

He says nothing.

I have a lump in my throat, because this is serious. Because I'm about to dredge up something that has always been off-limits between us. Something twisted and painful, that made him recoil the last time I mentioned it. I straighten the waistband of my skirt, lining up the darts and seams. When there's nothing left to adjust, I speak. "You always believed your father had something to do with the accident. You still think that?"

He wheels away from me and turns his back to put out the light over the sink. "I never said that."

"You didn't need to." My voice is whisper soft, hoping to soothe some of the sorrow I know he's feeling.

"It's getting late, Gabrielle. I'm going to have them bring the car around for you."

You will not dismiss me, JD. Not on this point. "Not yet," I say firmly.

He turns a piercing eye on me.

Your mean little looks don't frighten me. "Before I go, I want your word that you won't do something so foolish. So awful. Promise me, or this whole thing between us is off. I will not be a party to any of it."

He runs a knuckle along his jaw, back and forth, and for a few seconds, I think he contemplates showing me the door. But he doesn't.

"I have no plans to kill my father, although if he comes anywhere near Zack, I will use his chest for target practice. But I'd prefer to see the bastard suffer." He inches closer to me, until we're almost touching. "This is a ridiculous conversation, don't you think? We could be doing something so much more satisfying with our mouths."

He lowers his head to kiss me, but before he can, I grab hold of his cock, through his jeans, and squeeze. He's smirking but his eyes have a dark, sinful glimmer that makes my pussy flutter.

"'I have no plans' is not a promise, JD."

"This is coercion. No court would ever recognize any promise made under these circumstances."

I squeeze tighter. He pretends to wince. Although he doesn't fool me—in one move, he could easily overtake me. He's that much bigger and stronger. But he's letting me make my point.

"You're going to have to do better than that, darlin', if you want to bring me to my knees. But I'll make you the promise."

I'm not convinced but I let go, and before I can say another word, he spins me around so he's behind me, holding my wrists securely in his right hand. He skates his left palm down my arm, capturing the elbow, his hard cock pressed into my back.

"Give me your panties," he murmurs above my ear. "We've got people in the house. I need something to shove into your mouth, because I'm about to make you scream."

22

Julian

When I get back from my run, there's a message on my phone from Chase: *Sline Slocation*. Secure line, secure location—he must have found out something about SOLO. Or the summit.

Before showering, I go straight to my office, drop my cell phone on my desk, and enter the safe room that acts as my inner sanctum. Outfitted with foil walls, and no windows, it's not much bigger than a generous walk-in-closet. In fact, that's how my brothers and I referred to it when we were kids—the closet. Still do.

My grandfather used the space to take proprietary calls or hold meetings where he discussed classified information. It seems overly paranoid, unless you're acquainted with the level of spying that goes on in the pharmaceutical industry. Smith modernized the security in the closet when he outfitted the security cottage out back that he uses as an office. There are also secure rooms at Sayle, but I don't have the same kind of confidence in them.

I call my brother from a phone inside the windowless room. "Where are you?" is the first thing Chase asks when he picks up.

"The closet. Must be important for you to be up at six o'clock."

"Been up most of the night. GEM is the antidote to a nerve agent. It's a hybrid—viral and chemical agent. The antidote is a vaccine that can be used after an attack."

"Wait a minute. SOLO is working on a vaccine for a nerve agent?" I repeat, trying to wrap my head around nerve agents and antidotes, which I know little about. "Is this a government contract?"

"No. I looked, but I couldn't find any contract. This is SOLO's project."

Sayle's project. And I'm now responsible for anything that happens with the company. "Who has the nerve agent? Do we have it?"

"As far as I can figure out, the US and Russia are the only two countries with the agent—it's leftover from the Cold War. But who knows? Sayle had some—for testing purposes. It should have all been destroyed, but if that were the case, SOLO couldn't be working on a vaccine."

Nerve agents are weapons of war. That's their only purpose. "If we don't have a government contract, then why do we want to manufacture it? Who will be our buyer? It's not like CVS or Walgreens is going to stock it."

"I haven't gotten that far yet."

"Do you think DW would try to sell it to the US government after he becomes president?" I ask. As far as I'm concerned, the answer is yes. But my mind always goes to the darkest places where my father's concerned. I can't afford to chase twisted fantasies. This is serious.

"I don't know. That would be fucked up, but hey, it's possible.

You know he's going to do whatever he can to fill his pockets while he's in office."

"The conflict would be glaring. Congress won't stand for it." But he's doing it for some reason. And Chase is right. It's about money with him. It's always about money.

"How close is that vaccine to prime time?"

"I don't know that either. But it looks to me like they've been running trials."

"Trials? *Jesus Christ.*" Creating an antidote, in and of itself, is not illegal, but testing on humans requires mountains of paperwork, along with rigorous internal and external reviews. "Please tell me they're not conducting human trials?"

"No evidence of that. But JD, that guy Rofler, he was in touch with DW after you met with SOLO."

"I'm not surprised." I ought to rip him a new one and toss him out into the parking lot. But I'm not going to do that. Not yet. I want more information before I kick his ass out of the building.

"One more thing."

Fuck. "There's more?"

"Yeah. That summit you said Gray's going to?"

I massage my eyes to ward off the clusterfuck headache that's creeping up. "Yeah?"

"I didn't find any sign of it anywhere, on anyone's schedule. Including DW's. Nada."

"That sonofabitch is already up to no good."

"He's probably not in it alone," Chase says. "Don't underestimate the number of criminals around him. I don't know if it's every administration, or just the one DW is putting together. They look like the kind of guys who got their lunch money stolen every day, but these are some bad motherfuckers."

23

Julian

"Hey. What's up?" I say to Smith, tucking my phone into the crook of my neck, so I can continue to research nerve agents on the laptop while we talk. It's all I've been doing since my call with Chase this morning.

"Gabrielle Duval ditched her security detail."

My fingers are still on the keyboard. *Gabrielle Duval ditched her security detail.* It takes me a couple of seconds to process the words. "What do you mean, she ditched her security detail? What the fuck does that mean?" I clear the browser, grab my car keys, and head straight for the parking lot. My first instinct is to find her.

"It means she snuck out the back door of a meeting she was supposed to be in, and we have no idea where she is."

My heart is pounding, as I stride right past my assistant without stopping to tell her I'm leaving the premises. "How do you know she wasn't abducted?"

"We saw her on camera. She left City Hall alone—out a back door—and scurried around the corner toward King Street. Never looked back. But that's all the camera caught."

"You're fucking kidding me."

"Who do you think she went to meet that she didn't want security tagging along?" Smith asks.

I don't like the insinuation.

"How the hell do I know?"

"Well, you're pretty chummy with her. I heard she screamed loud enough last week that security entered your apartment because they thought there was a problem. Why am I not surprised she's a screamer?"

"I told Rafe and Gus not to say a fucking thing about that to anyone. I'm going to fire both their asses. And then I'm going to beat the snot out of you."

"This is the problem, JD. The last time I gave you shit about a screamer, you told me you'd give me her number. Said she'd probably scream for me, too. I don't remember you just offering me Gabrielle's number."

"Cut the bullshit and find her."

"We're looking. I'm capable of doing more than one task at a time. But if you just let me handle her security like I handle everyone else's, shit like this wouldn't happen."

"You are handling things. She ditched *your* people," I shout.

"*My* people. But not *my* plan for protecting her. This is all on you, baby."

"I'm getting in my car. I'll see if I can find her."

"You might not want to do that. She left that building of her own accord. She was going somewhere. You might not like what you find. Just sayin'."

I slam the phone against the dashboard twice before I disconnect the call. No, it doesn't make me feel any better.

I call her a few times, but her phone is off. For the next hour, I drive around Charleston. I go to City Hall first, and then to the hotel, scouring the streets for her. My next stop is her parents' house, but someone's staying there while they're away. I doubt she'd go there, but it's worth a try. What if she's in some kind of danger? Someone might have tricked her into leaving the meeting. Or maybe Smith's right—what if I don't like what I find?

I'm still conjuring up all sorts of bad scenarios, one worse than the other, when Smith calls back.

"We found her. She's at Georgina Scott's."

That was my next stop. I release a heavy sigh. This has been the longest fucking hour of my life.

"Took an Uber so we couldn't trace her," Smith continues. "JD, whatever the fuck you have going on with her isn't working. You need to let me manage her security—all of it. I can keep you apprised of what's going on, but she isn't safe this way. And neither are my people. I can't do business like this."

The relief washes over me for about ten seconds, and then it's gone. I'm so pissed off right now, I could smash glass with my bare hands. "I'll have a word or two with her. You've met her. She's stubborn. And she doesn't want security."

"We can stage something to convince her she needs it."

"There have already been a couple unstaged incidences that haven't seemed to sway her."

"Like what?"

"Someone took the hotel master keys out of her office. And the next day, all four of her tires were deflated while she was at a meeting. The missing keys were on the passenger seat."

"You didn't think it was important for me to know about this?"

"The police downplayed it." Even as I make the excuse, it sounds ridiculous. Smith won't buy it for a second.

"This is exactly what I mean, JD. You didn't tell me because you knew I'd insist on making a security plan that she wouldn't like. One that included tracking her phone—at the very least."

"We press too hard, too fast, and she's going to push back."

"She's already pushing back," he says. "Any ex-boyfriends who might not like that she's hanging around with you?"

"No."

"You answered that way too quickly."

"There's an ex-fiancé, but he's in prison."

"You sure about that? They move people through the system quickly these days."

"I'm sure."

"The keys and the tires as separate incidents don't bother me so much. But deflating the tires and leaving the missing keys on the seat? Sounds like someone might be gaslighting her. If that's the case, it's a whole other breed of bad. You have any idea who might want to do something like that to her?"

"I don't know," I mutter.

"You sound like you might know. Don't be such an obtuse prick. My people. Her life. Spit it out."

"My father."

"DW?" Smith asks, like he might have misunderstood me.

"Do I have another father?"

"I have no fucking clue what you rich people do. You could have a dozen fathers. But that one's the president-elect. Of the United States, for fuck's sake. You think he's gaslighting some woman you're chasing. Why?"

"Keep me out of his business."

There's only quiet breathing on the other end of the line. It's like he's weighing what I just told him, and trying to come up with a response. It does sound preposterous, but I know it's true.

"Listen," Smith says, softly. "I know DW's a huge asshole, and having Gabrielle running around without security today got to you. But she's fine, and she wasn't doing anyone, unless she's into pregnant chicks. So, pour yourself a whiskey, or get Zack's nurse to give you some anti-anxiety meds or something, because this stuff about your father is crazy talk. And it's one thing to say shit like that to me. It's another to repeat it in polite company. You do know that, right?"

"I'm well aware." Which is why the fucker is still walking the streets instead of in jail where he belongs.

"Let me up the ante. Help Ms. Duval come to the conclusion that she needs some big scary dudes hanging around to protect her."

"Not yet. Let me try one other thing first."

"You're too involved with her to be in charge of her protection detail."

"No."

"JD—"

"Not yet, Smith."

24

Julian

I haven't spoken with Gabrielle since she eluded security yesterday. I've picked up the phone a dozen times since then, but I've been too pissed off to even speak with her. Don't trust what I might say. Probably better to deal with her in person anyway.

I have some semblance of control tonight. The urge to beat her ass has receded into the background, although it's still lurking.

I thought sex was the way to control her. To make her soft and compliant. I'd done it before, although last time, I had no ulterior motive. But I've gotten so caught up in her, so caught up in how good she feels in my arms, how good she smells, and the amazing way her pussy clenches around my cock, that I slacked off. I let it become the kind of relationship my heart wants, not the kind it needs to be to keep her safe. That ends today.

When I get to my apartment, she's already there, making a

mess in the kitchen. Pots and pans everywhere. *God help me.* The woman can't boil water without destroying the kettle.

"You're early. I was hoping to surprise you with supper," she says, with a big, beautiful smile.

"Is that your way of making nice after ditching your security detail and having everyone frantic with worry?"

"I didn't mean to cause any worry. I thought I'd be back before anyone realized I was gone."

"Really?"

"I went to visit Georgina. She wasn't feeling well, so I brought her a quart of soup from Millie's. She and Wade are having some trouble, and she needed me."

"None of that explains why you left Rafe and Gus holding their dicks outside City Hall."

"I didn't want to bring an army with me to her house."

"Two men is not an army. This is bullshit, Gabrielle. Your detail is professional."

"They make Georgina anxious."

"Well, that's just too fucking bad."

"JD—" She places her hand on my cheek, brushing her lips against mine, but I'm not in the mood for sweet kisses.

"Is that chicken?" I ask, pulling away from her.

"Yes. Lemon chicken and rice pilaf."

"Is that how you're planning on killing me?"

She swats me on the arm playfully, and my dick jumps. *Find your balls, JD.*

"The only thing I'm hungry for right now is you," I murmur, yanking her toward me.

She plays along, jutting her hips forward, her belly rubbing against my lengthening cock.

"After supper," she says, in a seductive little voice, "you can have whatever you want."

Whatever I want? Oh, Gabrielle you have no idea.

"Forget the food," I urge, digging my fingers into her ass. "I want my dick in your sassy little mouth. Right now." It's coarser than I've been lately, and her eyes widen.

"Take off your clothes, Gabrielle. All of them."

She hesitates for a few seconds, and then begins to undress, quietly. My dick's hard, but I'm not feeling the sexy. When I start to have second thoughts about punishing her, I think about her being abducted, or worse.

"Get on your knees and take out my cock. You were a bad girl yesterday, and I'm still not myself. I need you to help me relax, to make it up to me for all that time I spent worrying about you."

When she doesn't immediately obey, I haul her to me and bury my hands in her hair, claiming her mouth, until she moans.

"Julian," she whimpers, but I don't want to hear it.

My hand slides to her pussy, and I finger her hard, until she's gasping and shaking. But I pull my fingers away before she comes. "On your knees, Gabrielle. I won't ask again."

She wets her lips and kneels at my feet, unbuckling my belt, hands trembling.

My cock leaks while her clever fingers work the zipper. I wind her hair around my hand, aroused by every move she makes.

She doesn't free my cock. Instead, she tugs at my trousers to pull them down.

"No. I said take it out. The only bare-ass person here will be you."

Gabrielle sits back on her haunches and gazes up at me, her stained lips rubbing against each other. "No."

I wrap her hair more tightly. "No?"

She shakes her head. "I will not suck you off on my knees while you're fully dressed and I don't have on a stitch of clothing. Not when you're in this kind of mood. It feels—it feels—"

"Like a punishment?"

She blinks. "Degrading."

"No more degrading than if someone kidnaps you and rapes you, leaving you for dead. Take out my cock."

She doesn't budge, but I can't let this go. Not after yesterday. Let's do it your way, Gabrielle—the hard way. "Fine. You want me to take my clothes off? I can do that. You want to play like that? Let's play in the bedroom."

I drag her down the hall. She's tense and guarded, and she should be, because what I'm about to do won't be pleasant.

"Are you going to spank me?"

"Not tonight." I strip down bare. "Is this what you wanted?" I ask, tossing her on the bed and covering her body with mine before she can answer. I suck a dusky nipple between my teeth and bite down until she cries out, and then I tweak the other roughly.

While she whimpers, I take both her wrists in my hand and cuff her to the bed. There's no play in the restraints tonight. I do the same with her ankles, spreading her legs wide so I can have unfettered access to her pussy. When she's secure, I shove a pillow under her hips.

"What are you doing?" she asks breathlessly.

"Giving you exactly what you deserve. Maybe I should keep you here, bound like this all the time. Then I wouldn't have to worry about you running around the streets of Charleston alone —an easy mark for anyone who wants to hurt you."

"I don't believe anyone wants to hurt me. The security is your way of controlling me," she says softly. "And to ensure there are no other men in my life."

"I don't need Rafe and Gus to *handle* any other men in your life. I'm quite capable in that regard. But I'm jealous and possessive. You're right about that. And don't test my patience," I warn, checking one more time that there's no movement in the restraints.

"Please don't leave me here like this. *Please*."

I don't say anything to reassure her.

"Will you respect the safe word?" she asks, with the twinge of anxiety in her voice.

I want to say no. That I won't respect it because I want to teach her a lesson. Because I want her to submit fully to me. Because I want her to do every fucking thing I tell her to do. Because I'm sick and tired of her rebelliousness.

I wrestle with all these feelings while she watches me with wide eyes that are growing more and more apprehensive as the seconds tick on.

"JD?"

"Of course I'll respect your safe word. Always." I slide my hand between her legs and stroke her hard little clit. "But I'm going to make you very uncomfortable. You're going to pull on your chains and beg me for mercy. You'll sweat and whimper. Your pussy will weep all over the sheets. But there will be no mercy for you. Not tonight."

She shivers, and I feel the gush of arousal on my fingers.

"I think the better question is, will *you* respect the safe word? Will you use it only if it's absolutely necessary? Or will you safe out the minute things aren't going your way?" It's a total dick thing to say. But I don't give a shit.

She nods, and I lean over to kiss her cheek. "Good girl."

I cross the room, and when I pull the artist's brush and a blindfold from the dresser, I hear a gasp from the bed.

25

Gabrielle

JD places the brush and blindfold beside my head, so every time I turn my neck, I see them. He lays on his stomach, between my bound legs, and licks my pussy, avoiding the clit like it's iced with deadly poison. He laves and bites, small nips—not hard, but not gentle, either. The moans form deep in my belly and bounce free, one after the other, while his tongue teases.

He's in a mood tonight. I shouldn't have ditched security yesterday. I knew he'd be upset. I knew it violated the terms of our agreement, but— "*Ahhh.*"

He holds my clit between his teeth, then pulls away, scraping the swollen flesh.

My stomach does little flips when he reaches for the blindfold, his eyes smoldering. Is it passion? Anger? I don't know. But they're the last thing I see before the silky fabric blinds me.

Before I adjust to the darkness, the brush is on my mouth, painting my lips.

Then he works the evil bristles inside my mouth. "Suck," he demands.

And I do.

Until he's satisfied.

Until he runs the brush down my chin, between my ribs... down, down, down, until it hovers over my clit. Grazing the swollen bead.

I grab for the sheets. I'll need fistfuls to help withstand the torment he surely has planned for me. My fingertips dance on the soft fabric, but I can't grip even a tiny piece. The binding is too tight.

He lowers the brush.

My muscles tighten. Every one. The bristles prick the sensitive flesh. It feels as though it's made up of millions of pointed fibers. My legs shake uncontrollably, and as I arch my back in a final surrender, he pulls the brush away.

I whimper. "JD. Please." It's such a desperate, pathetic whimper.

"Remember this feeling. Remember it well the next time you're tempted to put yourself in danger."

His voice is tightly controlled, but I hear the anger bubbling beneath the surface. My heart pounds—*boom, boom, boom*—and I instinctively pull on the restraints. But there is no slack.

JD pushes the blindfold up.

It takes me a minute before my eyes adjust. His cock is in his hand. He's stroking and squeezing. His eyes never leave mine.

"Do you want this, Gabrielle? Do you want to milk my cock with your pussy? Do you?"

I don't say anything. I'm afraid of him right now. *Just a little.* I should use my safe word, but I don't.

His pulls are shorter, harder now, his breath coarse and uneven. Without warning, he comes all over my belly and tits. I gasp loudly. JD stares into my eyes as long ropes of cum sail over my skin.

He will mark me like this, twice more, before the night is over.

I lose count of how many orgasms he deprives me of. How many he ruins. He's vicious, without an ounce of compassion, masking my eyes whenever he chooses and forcing me to watch when it suits him. And as he promised, I'm a sweaty, blubbering mess, floating in blissful darkness, among the gauzy shadows, where nothing touches me.

Wilderness. It was on the tip of my tongue, during those brutal seconds, before I began to float. But I never said it. And I'm not sure why.

He eventually lets me sleep.

When I wake, the cuffs are off, and I'm piled with soft quilts. He has juice for me, and salty crackers.

"How are you feeling?" he asks, sitting on the bed next to me, in a pair of well-worn jeans.

I test my legs, stretching them along the mattress. My muscles are stiff and sore. "Wrung out. That was brutal." I begin to wonder why I let him do that to me. But I'm still too foggy to think clearly.

He nods. "Don't ever ditch your security again. Don't ever put yourself in danger like that."

He pulls me to his chest, but my exhausted body finds no comfort there. And a small part of me wonders if I'll ever find comfort in his arms again.

"How about a shower before you go home?" he asks, smoothing my hair.

Yes, a shower, my muscles beg. I would love nothing more than to huddle under a warm spray. I nod and pull away, slowly lift my torso out of bed.

JD guides me to the bathroom and turns on the water in the shower.

I catch sight of myself in the mirror as the room begins to fog.

I'm washed out, like someone coming down from a prolonged drug high. My drug was sex. The mirror is steamy, but I stare at my pale complexion and sunken eyes until the reflection disappears in the haze.

We get in the shower, and JD washes my hair and carefully soaps every inch of my skin with sandalwood soap that smells like him. When I seem unsteady, he props me against his body and secures me with a strong arm. I feel his erection growing while he attends to me, but he doesn't touch me in a sexual way. The shower is purely utilitarian.

After long minutes under the warm water, I begin to awaken, my body humming with desire. The feeling is no longer urgent, but it's gnawing for release.

I sway into his thickening cock, but JD shifts away. When I do it again, he slaps my ass. Not hard. But it's sharp. Like his words.

"Not for you. There's no relief for you tonight. And when I see you tomorrow, you're going to look me right in the eye and tell me if you touched yourself when you went home. If you lie, if I even think you're lying, we're going to do this all over again."

I gaze up at him. The light flickers in his steely eyes, not like fireflies on a warm summer evening, but like bullets during target practice. *Why did you allow it to get this far, Gabrielle?* I wanted to placate him. I thought we could work out our feelings with sex. His anger. My regret. It was foolish of me to think sex was the answer.

"Wilderness," I mouth. "Wilderness." This time the word is loud and clear, echoing off the cold, white tile.

He freezes, his eyes all over mine. He doesn't understand.

"The safe word isn't just for when you've pushed my physical limits too hard," I say. "It's about pushing my emotional ones, too. You went too far. And I don't feel like you're done."

There's a ripple when he swallows, but otherwise, he doesn't move.

"I didn't use it earlier—I thought about it, but I could see how worried you were when you came in. How much you needed to punish me. I wanted to give that to you. And deprivation is brutal, but it brings its own kind of toe-curling pleasure. Eventually." I stop for a breath. "I didn't safe out while you were edging me, but I probably should have, because you demanded things of my body, in a way that I'm not sure was playful, or even arousing for you. I was confused at the time by all the sensation. But I can see things more clearly now. Everything you did in there, it was angry and threatening—you're still threatening me. None of this feels right to me, JD—it feels almost abusive."

"I'm sorry," he says quietly. "I'm sorry."

I wait for more, for some kind of explanation or meaningful remorse, but there's nothing. "That's it? That's all you have to say for yourself?"

JD turns off the water and grabs two towels from a hook outside the shower. He starts to dry me, but I grab the towel and finish drying myself.

Right now, I don't want him touching me.

"Yesterday," he says in a heavy voice, "all day, even after I knew you were safe, I was apparently the biggest asshole on the planet. At least according to my brothers. Lally threw a spoon at me and kicked me out of my own kitchen. Patrick went home early with a migraine. And Smith offered to go a few rounds with me. I should have taken him up on it." His eyelashes flutter gently. "After I knew you were safe, I was so angry with you. All day, and all night. Furious. I wanted to see you. But I didn't trust myself to respect the boundaries. The safe word. Human decency. I was raging, Gabrielle. I couldn't even talk to you on the phone, I was so pissed."

He tips his head, gazing at me with those blue, blue eyes. "I thought I was in better control today. I should have canceled tonight."

His confession is staggering. I should be afraid of a man

capable of that much anger. I should run out the door as far and as fast as I can.

But I don't.

I know the difference between an abusive, out-of-control man with no respect for boundaries, like Dean, and a man who spins out of control, but who understands his impulses. Who respects boundaries. Should he have engaged in this little game tonight while he was still on edge? No. And while I'm not responsible for his actions, I shouldn't have played, either.

"I think we both learned something today. When I was with Dean and things got out of hand, I couldn't stop it. There were no safe words. We didn't have that kind of relationship. And even if we had, no safe word would have stopped him from hurting me that night. You stopped bullying me when I asked."

JD winces when I use the word bullying, but that's how it felt to me.

"When we play these games, the lines between reality and fantasy blur," I say quietly. "It's what makes them so seductive. We bump against the edges, so there are bound to be blips. You stopped the second I asked you to stop."

"Gabrielle. I'm just agitated today. It wasn't hard to stop. But I was furious yesterday. With you. Out of my fucking mind. It wasn't a game. I don't think there was a single boundary I wouldn't have crossed. You should know that."

I nod. "You understood that about yourself. You had enough control to think about it."

"Don't give me more credit than I deserve. I might have hurt you." The pain in his face is overwhelming.

"I'll take my chances."

He steps toward me. "You're a fool." It's a halfhearted warning, delivered in a strangled voice.

"We'll see."

I step into the mirror and slide a wide-toothed comb through my wavy wet hair, occasionally glancing at his reflection as he watches me. The woman in the mirror isn't a fool. She's strong and smart. She knows what she wants. And the man standing behind her? The one she's loved all her life? She wants him. With all his broken pieces. The nicked and dented fragments, and the twisted shards, beyond repair. Every one of them.

"Is there any chance I can get something to eat before you send me home?" I ask.

"I'll fix something while you get dressed," he says, slinging the towel around his neck.

When I get to the kitchen, JD's barefoot, in worn jeans and a long-sleeved Gamecock T-shirt. His hair is damp. He doesn't look dangerous. He looks young. And delicious.

I climb onto a kitchen stool and JD brings a tray of food over to me—chunks of cheese and smoked ham, and cubes of sweet pineapple.

"What happened to the chicken I made?"

"I tasted it. I think we've both been punished enough for today."

I smile, and then laugh. A silly, out-of-control, exhausted-to-the-bone laugh.

He laughs too.

"Gabrielle?" he says, wearily, even before our laughter fades.

"Hmmm?" I ask, biting into a bit of salty ham.

I'm still savoring the salt on my tongue, when he swivels both stools so we're facing one another. He drags mine closer to his, until our knees touch. "The security isn't there to put a crimp in your life. I would never do that to you. They're there for your protection. That's all. I don't want to lose you."

His voice is grave. The raw intensity in his face winds its way to my heart, and I reach up and brush the hair from his eyes. "I know."

I know you believe it's all about my safety. Even tonight. I know that. I just wish I could ease your worry.

26

Gabrielle

I'm in an abandoned corner of the hotel kitchen, polishing silver serving pieces I borrowed for the brunch tomorrow, when my phone rings. *JD.*

It's been nearly a month since the night I used my safe word. I haven't had to use it since, although he's still bossy and controlling. That'll never change.

"Hi," I say, happy to talk to him, even though there's so much going on in the hotel. "You're on speakerphone, so behave yourself."

"Lally cut her finger," he says. "It sounds bad. She needs stitches, but won't go to the emergency room."

"Damn pig-headed woman. I'll call her."

"Gabrielle. I'm not in town. I need you to go over there and take her to the emergency room. I know the timing sucks, but there's no one else."

I look around the kitchen. There's so much to do before

tomorrow. I gave Georgie a few days off so they could spend the holiday with Wade's sister, and two people I was counting on for help have called in sick. The very last thing I need right now is to go to Sweetgrass. "I'll head over right now."

"Thanks. Call me from the ER when you know something."

As Rafe pulls into the circle at Sweetgrass, I'm surprised to see white lights strung around the porch and trees, and luminaires lining the walkways. None of it was here last week. Lally must insist on decorating for Christmas.

"Just keep it running," I tell Gus when he opens the car door for me. "I'll have her out in five minutes." Even if I have to drag her by her bleached-blonde hair.

I run up the porch steps and ring the bell. JD answers the door. "What are you doing here? I thought you were away? I don't have time for games today."

"Are you finished?"

"No. Is Lally even hurt?"

He shakes his head and motions me inside, but I turn around to go back toward the car.

JD's not having it. He grabs my arm and pulls me inside. "I have guests. Find some manners before I take you to meet them." With a squeeze, he lets go of my arm.

"Guests?" I hiss. "You brought me here under false pretenses to meet your guests?" I stammer. "You know how busy I am today. How short-handed." For the most part, I know what to expect from JD—at least out of bed. Although he still surprises me, and not always in a good way. But this is too much. "It better be the fucking Queen of England you want me to meet."

"Sweet pea, you givin' this man a hard time?"

I glance at JD, and then at the man ambling into the foyer. "Daddy." My voice is muted, almost a whisper.

What's he doing here? I just spoke to my parents yesterday. "Is everything all right? Where's Mama?"

He holds me in his arms and pats my back, reassuring me like he did when I was a child. "Everything's fine. And if you're done dressing down JD, you can go say hello to your mama."

I catch JD's eye, my mouth still hanging open.

He's smirking. "Your mother's in the living room, visiting with Lally," he says. "We waited on you for lunch."

I'm having a hard time processing everything. Surprise parties are like that. It's why I've always hated them.

JD helps me with my coat and nudges me in the direction of the living room. I follow the laughter. My mother's laughter. Lally's laughter. I feel JD's hand on the small of my back, steadying me. He presses his lips to the top of my head. "Merry Christmas, Elle."

Elle. I stop and gaze up at him.

He opens his mouth as if to speak, but he doesn't, and when he finally does, I'm certain it's not what had been on his lips a moment before. "Your mom's been anxious to see you. Go."

My mother looks great, dressed in deep-red velour pants and a beautiful white top with a beaded neckline.

"Oh my God!" I run to hug her. "It's wonderful to see you. I was planning on visiting the day after Christmas, but I'm so happy we'll be together on the holiday."

"Me, too, baby. Me too."

"When did you plan this?" I ask, pulling back. "The doctors let you come home? How did you get here? And you, Miss Lally, your fingers look just fine. Were you in on this too?"

"So many questions, Gabrielle. My goodness." Mama laughs.

"And still no answers. I'm sure you had something to do with this, too, JD." I crane my neck over my shoulder, but he's gone.

"JD thought it would make a nice Christmas surprise for you," my father says.

"The doctors said it's okay?"

"I've been in the treatment for seven weeks, and they weren't going to do anything over Christmas. I have a three-day reprieve. JD worked out the logistics. Brought his plane and a nurse with him to bring us home."

"Said he wasn't leaving anything to chance," my father pipes in. "Said you'd whip his backside if anything went wrong."

My father seems so happy. And my mother. It must be a relief to be back in Charleston, even for a few days.

"I know Lally's nephew is living at your house until you get back, and the hotel is full, but you can stay in my room. I'll have a cot made up in my office. It'll be perfect."

"That's not necessary," Lally says. "I prepared a room upstairs for your parents. There's a nurse on duty here all the time. This is the best place for your mother."

I turn to my mother. "Are you sure you want to stay here? I have to be at the hotel. I won't be around much."

"You sleep in your own bed. We're fine here. More than fine. You do what you need to do. I'm hoping Lally will let me help with Christmas Eve supper."

"Help with supper? You're crazy, woman," Lally says flippantly, dismissing my mother's offer to help. "You need to rest."

Mama's face drops, and Lally doesn't miss it. "You know how I am about people in my kitchen. Even you, Vivien." She wraps her arm around Mama's shoulders. "But I'm sure I can use the help. We'll be feeding more people than I'm used to."

I catch Lally's eye and wink. "Where did JD go?"

"He's getting lunch."

This I have to see. "Maybe I should help him. That man shouldn't be anywhere near a kitchen."

"Same goes for you, missy," Lally says, and everyone laughs.

"I'm better in the kitchen than he is."

"I'll be right there. Don't even think of turning the stove on while you're in my kitchen."

I roll my eyes. "I'm not that bad of a cook."

"You are that bad. I've eaten your food. Almost killed me."

"I'm just going to help JD carry things in. Surely I can do that without causing an outbreak of food poisoning."

What I really want is a few minutes alone with JD.

"It took some effort to do this," I say, when I get to the kitchen.

JD is rummaging through a cupboard and doesn't respond.

My chest grows heavy in the silence. And my mind wanders aimlessly. Flitting in and out of the dark shadows—I begin to wonder if this is in some way about the secrets. If this is a manipulation of some sort. I walk over to him and place my hand on his back. "Why, JD? Please tell me this isn't connected in any way to the secrets. Please tell me it's as my father said, just a Christmas surprise."

He recoils from my touch.

"Talk to me, JD."

"It's not like you're a normal woman. I couldn't just send Patrick out to buy you a pair of diamond earrings. You would have been all pissed off."

It's a Christmas present. I feel the stress slip away. "If Patrick had picked out my Christmas present for you? Yeah, I would have been annoyed."

"Even if I picked out a pair of diamond earrings myself—it's just not something you would have loved. It's not something I would have been comfortable with either," he mutters. "When you've got money, diamond earrings are the kind of thing you give a woman when you don't know what to give. When you don't want to give too much of yourself. I wanted your Christmas present to be special. I wanted you to know that I put thought and effort into it."

I rake my fingers through his hair, lingering near his temple. God help me, I love this man. "Like the frame you made me in shop class when you were a senior."

He shrugs a shoulder.

"Thank you. Thank you from the bottom of my suspicious heart." I try not to cry, but a tear slips out, and then another.

"I want you to be happy, Gabrielle. And safe. That's all I want."

JD pulls me to him, molding my hips to his, and cups my face while he kisses away the tears. I could stay with him, like this, forever.

I don't hear the approaching footsteps, and I don't think JD does, either.

"Have some respect, JD," Lally admonishes, "before I take a broom to you. Her father's in the house." And then she mumbles something to me about cows and milk that I don't entirely catch, but I get the drift.

She begins pulling food out of the refrigerator and dishes from the cupboards, chastising and poking at us while she works, but she's biting back a smile. I can hear it in her voice, and the twinkling in her eyes is unmistakable when she hands me a platter to take to the living room.

As we sit and have lunch, my mind keeps going back to the hotel. There's so much to do there. I peek at my watch. Twenty minutes, and then I have to leave.

I watch JD with my parents, and with Lally. For the first time, I feel ridiculous for thinking he sent me away when he was tired of being my boyfriend. I'd held onto the childish self-centered idea because it was easy. And because I needed to believe *something*. I needed answers when there were none. My parents never would have allowed such a thing. And Lally. She would have pitched a fit the size of Texas. I'd like to say it doesn't matter anymore, but it's not true. In some ways, it's never mattered more. I still need closure—I need to close the door on the past, not so I can start fresh with someone else, but so we can start again. So we have a real chance to build something.

I glance at the clock on the mantel. "I have to get back to the hotel. I'm so sorry. I didn't plan very well for this."

"Do what you need to do. We're just fine here," my mother assures me.

"What time will you be back for supper?" Lally asks.

"I—uh—"

"Wildflower is closed today and tomorrow," JD says, looking at me. "Gray sent some staff over to the Gatehouse. A few extra sets of hands so you can have dinner with us tonight. They should be there by now." He nods reassuringly. "Don't worry. They've all had experience with difficult clientele."

"It's Christmas. I don't know how he managed that," I blurt out much too abruptly. The words sound frazzled and ungrateful.

"Not everyone likes to spend the holidays with their family," he explains patiently. "We'll make it a late supper. And then you can go back to the hotel before Santa comes."

JD always thinks of everything. He pretends he doesn't like to get into the weeds, but he cares about the details.

I turn to my parents. "We're doing a brunch in the morning with Santa, and we have all sorts of fun planned for guests, but I'm off the hook after brunch. We can spend the rest of the day together."

"After church," Lally says, "maybe your parents can go to your fancy *brunch*. And I'll make a late Christmas dinner, here. How about four o'clock? Does that work for everybody?"

"Perfectly," JD answers for all of us.

"Aren't you going to your cousin's?" I ask Lally.

"Good excuse to break that tradition. I can't stand her husband's side of the family. Sloppy drunks. Besides, your mom can't do everything, and who are we putting in charge of the kitchen, you?"

Everyone laughs, including JD.

"Why don't you come by for brunch, too, Lally? I'm not cooking." The thought of having everyone at the hotel for brunch, especially this brunch, makes me happy. And I love the idea of feeding Lally. Fussing over her the way she always fusses over us. "It's Christmas, Lally."

"I'll be spending the day with my stove. I don't want it to be alone on Christmas," she says, waving me off.

But I'm stubborn. I go over to her and clasp both her hands in mine. "I would love for you to be with us, even for a short while."

"Maybe for a very short while," she says, squeezing my fingertips.

I glance at JD. "You don't mind us taking over your house when you're not here?"

"Where am I going?"

I realize I've been so wrapped up in my own Christmas plans that we never talked about his. "I—I just assumed you'd be going to Wildwood to be with your father and Shelby, and your brothers."

"Shelby and my father spend the holiday in Palm Beach. Her family joins them. I never go, and it's hit or miss with my brothers."

JD is the one speaking, but I can feel all eyes on me.

"Gray and Chase are coming here for Christmas dinner tomorrow—or supper, or whatever it ends up being. If there's food, they'll come. They'll be by tonight, too."

"That sounds wonderful." I try to sound sincere, because spending Christmas with my family and JD's brothers is wonderful. Almost too wonderful.

Will I always feel this hesitancy? The need to protect my heart? Will I always be looking over my shoulder, wondering when my happiness will go up in smoke?

27

Gabrielle

When I arrive at Sweetgrass on Christmas Eve, my parents are resting, and Lally is in the kitchen.

"Do you need some help?"

"It's all done. Gray sent a couple girls over here, too. They set the tables and will be back later to clean up. I don't know why he had to do that."

I smile. Lally doesn't know how to let anyone take care of her. She and JD have a lot in common in that regard. Come to think of it, they're both bossy and controlling too. "Gray loves you and wants you to enjoy Christmas, too." I glance at the time. "Is JD with Zack?"

"Mmhm."

"I have something for them. I'll be right back."

"Take your time."

I make my way to the back of the house and through the big doors, toward Zack's room. A nurse I haven't met is seated in an alcove, eating a sandwich, with her nose in a book. She looks up when I approach, and I smile and nod hello as I pass.

I've visited Zack several times now, and Sumter is used to me, so he doesn't bother to get up, although he does have one eye trained on me. "Hi," I say when I walk in. "Let me wash my hands and then I have a Christmas present for Zack."

"Everything ready for tomorrow?" JD asks.

"More than ready. The extra staff is a game changer. Thank you."

"Thank Gray," he says.

"I will. But your hand is all over it, too. Here." I hand JD two packages. "This one is for tonight, and this one is for tomorrow. I thought you would both enjoy these."

He fiddles clumsily with the paper for a few seconds, before impatiently ripping it off. The smile spreads slow and warm, melting over his face and seeping into his heart.

I know that smile. I haven't seen it in years, but I recognize it.

"*The Night Before Christmas*," he says. "Look, Zack." He lifts the book, so his brother can see.

My heart breaks for him. For them.

"I wasn't sure if you had a copy for tonight." My voice is thick with emotion. And I blink back the tears threatening to spill all over the buffed wood floor.

"No. We don't."

"Why don't you read it to Zack and me," I say, softly. "Do you mind me horning in on your time together?"

JD shakes his head. "We would love you to stay."

I lean back against the night table and close my eyes, lulled by his smooth baritone, visions of sugarplums dancing in my head.

After supper, we sing some off-tune Christmas carols, and mostly relax in the living room. JD feeds the fire all night, and it's toasty and warm in here, and everything I could ever want on Christmas Eve.

Gray is enthralled by something his friend Mae, the hostess at Wildflower, is whispering in his ear. When he walked in with her earlier, he said she didn't have anywhere to go.

"Yeah, sure," JD murmured, when Gray turned his back. "Have you ever known him to bring home a stray?"

"*Shhhh*," I whispered. "She's nice. I'm happy to see him with someone nice."

Ten thirty comes quick, and I need to get back. "I'm sad to say it, but it's getting late. I need to be at the hotel by the change of shift."

"I'll drive you," JD says, getting up.

Drive me? That's new. "No security?"

"Going anywhere without security isn't *ever* an option for you. I thought we were past that." He pins me with a gaze, shaking his head disapprovingly. "They'll follow us."

I kiss everyone good night, and wrap my coat around me, but I don't leave before inviting everyone to brunch the next day, even Mae, who has Gray wrapped around her finger. I think I have a girl crush on her, too.

JD and I chatter on the way to the Gatehouse. Well, mostly I chatter and JD grunts or nods.

"Would you like to come in for a drink?"

"It's still early for me. But you have to be up before dawn. You sure you want me to come in?"

"One drink. It's Christmas Eve."

I make myself a Gatehouse special, and mix JD a classic whiskey sour with a single giant cube of ice. When I rub some orange peel around the rim of the glass and then lay it on the ice, he whistles softly. "If you can mix a cocktail like that," he says, "who cares if you can't cook?"

"You might want to taste it first."

He sips the drink, savoring slowly. "It tastes as good as it looks. Maybe better." His eyes are molten and I'm not sure we're still talking about cocktails.

"Why don't we go upstairs?" I say. "I have something for you."

"Do you?" There's mischief in his eyes.

"It's a gift."

"It's always a gift. The best damn gift. Every time." He smirks and motions with his hand for me to go first. "I'll follow you."

We haven't had sex here since that first time. I've been reluctant to bring him here, to entangle the two parts of my life. I've made every effort to keep JD out of hotel business. This is mine. It's my future, the place I'll seek refuge if things don't work between us. I don't want his face, his smell, his memory, all over the place when it happens.

Besides, JD makes Georgie uncomfortable. Really uncomfortable, which makes me uncomfortable. So far I've managed not to have them run into each other, but it hasn't been easy. I'm never sure when JD's going to make an appearance. But so far I've been lucky. "Stairs or elevator?" I ask.

"Love that back stairwell," he murmurs in a lecherous voice.

"Me too." I grin.

When we get to the top, he takes my drink and places it on the step, with his right beside it, and flicks off the overhead lights. He puts his hands on either side of my face, and teases my lips with his tongue until they part for him. "I know you don't like me up here. That this is some kind of Christmas concession, so I should warn you, if you invite me to your room, I won't be fucking my fist tonight. But I will be fucking you."

I stare into his eyes, trying to find the courage to crack open my chest and lay my heart at his feet. "Does it always have to be about dirty sex? Will you ever—" I lower my head.

"Hey." He tucks a tendril of hair behind my ear. "Ever what?"

I shrug. "Make love to me? Or let me make love to you. It's Christmas."

JD slides a thumb under my chin and forces me to look at him. "You like dirty sex. Making love is just an old-fashioned way to pretty up a good fuck. No one uses it anymore. We're all enlightened now." He's smiling, and I force a small smile, but it's fake and he knows it. "Should I go? Your decision."

My decision. My choice. "I do have something for you. But now I'm not sure if tonight is the right time to give it to you." I feel silly. My plan seems so foolish now. I don't know what I was thinking.

"If we go to your bedroom, we will have sex. I won't take it from you, but it'll happen. Don't kid yourself." He gives me a minute to kick him out. When I don't, he picks up our glasses and hands me mine. "Let's go get that present you keep talking about."

Except for one smoldering kiss that lasts about ten minutes, we manage to get through the rest of the stairwell and into my suite without too much distraction.

I flip on the gas fireplace, and the room is warm and glowing. We sit on the loveseat in front of the fire and sip our drinks in silence while the shadows dance in the flames.

JD squeezes my hand. "What is it, Gabrielle?"

"I was just thinking about tonight at Sweetgrass. You were quiet. Quieter than usual. Not your usual bossy self. Like you were soaking it all in."

"I was." He rubs his thumb along his bottom lip, still staring into the fire. "I wanted to make sure I remember it. All of it. Christmas hasn't been special for me in a long, long time."

"We can do it again next year—if—we're still—"

"Don't." He pulls me into his side and brushes his mouth over my hair. Not really kissing, just feeling the soft strands on his lips. "Where's my present?" he asks.

I put my hand over my heart and feel the steady beat. *Right here.* Please don't return it. And don't betray it, or stomp on it when you don't want it anymore. I pull a big breath through my nose, fill my lungs, and blow it out quietly.

"When I agreed to—the arrangement," I start, just above a whisper. "I didn't agree to save my mother. Well, initially I did. But after I talked to the case manager, I knew I didn't need to agree to anything that made me uncomfortable."

He's stroking my head, and I let my eyelids flutter closed.

"At first, I wanted revenge for the past. I wanted your heart to be broken this time. And I wanted to understand all the secrets and lies. I wanted something that would allow me to close the door firmly behind you, for good." He stiffens, and I rub my palm up and down his forearm. "That's what I told myself. But really, what I wanted was you. I knew the night you came back that I never stopped loving you."

He combs his fingers through my hair. "You sure didn't act like it."

I smile. No, I didn't. I was confused. And angry. *Angry that you waltzed in and in five minutes, the wall I'd carefully constructed around my heart was crumbling.* "The minute I saw you, all I could think about was your warm mouth, your rough hands on my skin. That, and a thousand other feelings swamped me. It had never—not since you—been like that. I wanted it again, JD. Deep down, I wanted it again. Not just the sex part, but all of it. I was so sure I could handle you, handle my feelings."

"And now?"

"Now I think I'm fucked."

He throws his head back and laughs. It rings clear with a pure joy that I rarely feel from him. "It's a small, elite club," he says. "Welcome."

Should I ask him? Do you want to ruin the intimacy, Gabrielle? The joy. I can't wait anymore for answers. Not to this question.

"Why did you send me away?"

I feel him take two breaths before he says anything.

"To keep you safe. I would do it again, Gabrielle. I will do it again if it becomes necessary. I can't promise I won't. This," he squeezes me, "what we have right now, is a hundred times, a thousand, more than I ever thought we'd have when I walked into your office election night. I want to enjoy every single second we're together, because I don't know how long it'll last."

When he says things like this—it feels as though our relationship is out of his control. Like someone else is pulling the strings. Me? Does he think I'll send him away?

He drains his drink, places the glass on the side table, and pulls me into his lap. He's a big, sexy man, with strong hands that hold me against him. It's intimate. So intimate. More intimate than sex.

I rest against him, lifting my head to nuzzle his neck. "When you talk about sending me away again, it scares me. It makes me think that maybe I can't do this with you."

"If I send you away this time, I promise it won't be like last time. I promise I won't send you off without an explanation. Last time I had to. I kept you safe in the only way the nineteen-year-old me knew how to keep you safe. But I've sifted through it thousands of times since, and even as I look back on it right now, I'm not sure there was another way. I was too young. You were too young."

"Can't you tell me more?"

"I can't—not yet. Part of keeping you safe is not telling you too much."

"Safe from what?" When he doesn't answer, I crane my neck to look at him. "You don't trust me?"

"That's not it." He pushes my hair back and kisses my forehead.

It's Christmas and I don't want a fight. It feels like he wants to tell me—and for the first time, I believe, really believe, that he will tell me why he had me sent away. Someday. *You've waited this long for answers. You can wait a little longer*. I can.

I scoot around and straddle him, my knees digging into the sofa, my fingers raking his hair, tracing the contour of his jaw, letting the stubble prick them.

His lips graze my throat. "You want to play?"

I shake my head. "No. No games tonight. No toys, nothing but my hands and mouth, pleasuring you. My body loving yours."

He pulls the curls off my face. "You want to own me."

I nod. "You'll struggle, because you don't like to give up control. You're already sweating and we're just talking about it." I cup his jaw. "I want you to let me have it. I want your surrender. I don't want you to take me tonight. Let me take. Let me give myself to you tonight. Everything. It's my gift to you."

28

Julian

I nod and swallow hard. Her skin is silky and warm. Her voice is husky, like she's been enjoying cigars and whiskey all her life. "Gabrielle, you've always owned me." The admission doesn't sting as much as I thought it would, so I confess fully. "If it seems like I'm the one in charge, it's because I'm a damned good actor. But I'm not sure I can do what you're asking." I stop to kiss her finger. "I like the control. I don't need toys or props, but I still need the control. That's how I'm built."

She begins unbuttoning my shirt, like she didn't hear a word I said. One button at a time. Caressing the skin that's revealed as each button is freed from its tether. By the time she reaches the last one, my dick is throbbing, and my fingers are twitching on her ass, lightly cupping, itching to crawl all over her.

"Gabrielle." I breathe her name. "I don't know how to give up control. I'm not sure I can. If someone wants it, they have to pry it from my clenched fists."

She grinds her pussy into my cock.

I groan. "You're a tease, woman."

"I learned from the best."

Her words are like a dull ache in my chest, but she's unbuckling my belt, and I can't think about anything else right now.

"It looks like you might need a little more room in here," she murmurs, pulling my zipper down.

My hands dive into her hair, and I lower my head to reach her mouth. I'm desperate for a taste. But she doesn't let me feed off her.

"If you try to wrestle control away from me, again, I'll send you home. Hard and wanting. I hear blue balls are a real thing. A sixteen-year-old boy once told me that."

I chuckle. Maybe I should go. I can't give her what she's looking for tonight. But before I can move her off my lap, she sinks her teeth into my neck like a little vixen, and I know I'm not going anywhere. "You are wicked," I say, grabbing hold of her hair. "And it's Christmas."

There's a sultry gleam in her eyes. "Unzip my dress." She climbs off my lap. Her hair is mussed. The waves have become corkscrews. Her lips are glistening with promise.

She sits at the edge of the sofa, facing away from me. I pull her hair over one shoulder and lower the zipper, one tooth at a time. Planting my mouth at the nape of her neck, I let two fingers follow the line of the zipper down her back.

She trembles. "You're cheating," she warns.

"You love it."

My control is completely frayed by the time she stands and lets her dress glide to the floor. There's not a shred left to surrender.

Within seconds, we're both naked, and she's spreading the drops of precum over my cock, running her nails over my inner thighs, and cradling my aching balls.

When she pulls me into her hungry little mouth, I growl. She laughs softly, and the vibrations around my cock are mind-blowing. My balls are tightening against my body. My hands are in her hair. She slides her hand into her panties and rubs her pussy, squirming into her fingers. I'm not sure if it's for my pleasure or hers.

"Let me taste you," I murmur, tugging her arm up and sucking her fingers into my mouth. It's nowhere near enough, but it'll do for now. "You're a dirty, filthy girl. And I am one lucky sonofabitch."

She takes me deeper. The tingle in my spine is beginning. She tips her head back and swallows me. My toes curl into the rug, when I feel her gag reflex kick in. "Gabrielle. *Oh, baby.*"

I squeeze her shoulders, and she swallows my cock again, fucking me with her mouth, her hands, hard and fast until I twitch and unload in her throat, with long, hot spurts that seem to go on forever.

"Get up here." I don't have much strength, but I manage to pull her from her knees and find her mouth. I suck on her tongue. I taste myself there. Salty and musky, mixed with her honey taste. I'm ready to go again. My balls ache, and right now, I can't ever remember not being hard.

My fingers shove aside her panties and I stroke her pussy, paying special attention to her clit. She sways into me and mewls. And I'm fresh out of control.

I toss her over my shoulder and lay her on the bed. With one move, her panties are off and balled into her mouth. "You're a noisy little wench, and we don't want to alarm the guests." I pull her legs over my shoulders and lick her pussy, sliding my fingers into both her tight little holes, until I hear nothing but muffled cries of pleasure.

I pull the panties from her mouth and kiss her, long and hard. "Bite into my shoulder if you need to scream." I lower myself onto her, wrap her legs around my waist, and fuck her like Adam fucked Eve. No toys, no props, no little games. Just my throbbing cock sliding in and out of her hot pussy. It's paradise. That's all I think about as her walls clench around my shaft. All I think about as she milks me with her tight little cunt. All I think about as she takes everything from me. *It's paradise.*

I catch my breath and roll over, bringing her with me. "You really don't give up control easily," she says into my chest. "Although you did better than I expected."

"We'll have to practice more," I say to her, wrapping her tighter.

I feel her smile, on my skin. "Stay with me," she whispers. "All night."

It's a mistake to wake up next to her in the morning. I know it, but I'm going to do it anyway. "You sure?"

"*Mmhm.*" She snuggles deeper. "Merry Christmas. I hope you liked your present."

"Best gift anyone's ever given me. Except for that birthday present when I turned seventeen." It's the last thing I utter before falling into a deep, dreamless sleep, wound around her luscious body.

29

Julian

The alarm wakes us at the crack of dawn Christmas morning, and Gabrielle reaches over me to turn it off. "It's freezing," she says.

I don't know if it's because I've been wrapped around her hot little body all night, but I'm damn cold, too. "Get back here, and I'll warm you up."

"I have too much to do. But you don't need to get up. Sleep for a while longer."

"I don't want to stay in bed without you. Let's get in the shower. We'll kill two birds with one stone." I drag her into the bathroom and turn on the shower. We huddle in the corner of the stall, waiting for the water to heat up. I pin her ass against the tile wall, running my mouth over her neck and shoulders.

She wriggles out of my grasp. "Later. I need to get downstairs," she says, backing into the spray.

"Oh my God! The water is ice cold!" she squeals, jumping

away from the water. "The furnace must be out. But I don't understand why the generator didn't kick in. Hopefully it's just this furnace."

I stick my shoulder under the water. "No one's showering in this." I turn the faucet off and grab towels. "How many furnaces in this place?" I ask, wrapping a fluffy white towel around her.

"Four units. But I don't get it. The systems are all new. I replaced every one of them. The generator's new, too. My guests. *Oh my God!* They're going to have cold showers, too. It's Christmas morning."

"Hey." I cup her face with both hands, forcing her to meet my eyes. "I'm sure it's just the unit that heats this part of the building. We'll get it taken care of before your guests are even out of bed. Are the units in the cellar?"

She nods. "They're still under warranty."

"Get dressed. I'll go down." Because there's nothing I'd like better than to trade shower sex with a hot woman for a trip to the dusty basement. "If the furnaces are new, there will be a sticker from the company that services them on at least one of the units. I'll make the call. You have service contracts?"

"Yes. But it's Christmas. I'm not sure they'll come out."

"They will," I assure her, pulling on my pants. "Don't worry. This is nothing. I promise, it'll be okay. All my problems should be this easy to fix."

She doesn't look like she believes me.

On my way down the stairs, I stick my head onto each floor. It's cold everywhere. I grab a young man with a nametag—Kevin—and instruct him to light the fireplaces on the first floor where the brunch will be served. He tells me most of the guestrooms have gas fireplaces that throw enough heat to warm the room. That's all good, but it doesn't solve the problem of the ice-cold water.

After calling the service company, I look around the basement. My present for Gabrielle is on the concrete floor, the tarp kicked aside, the ribbon torn to shreds. This is not how I left it yesterday afternoon. I lift the gate, dust it off and cover it with the tarp, again.

I poke around a bit more, and while I don't know much about furnaces, it doesn't seem like any of them are working. *Don't jump to conclusions, JD—not yet.* I don't, but I know we have a fucking problem on our hands. My blood pressure soars while I wait for the repairman.

Within thirty minutes, he's here. "The furnaces are all down," the repairman explains. "The rotors have been disabled in all four of them. I have some extras on the van. Not sure if I have four, though."

"Do the first floor first, then let's concentrate on the guestrooms. Maybe we can get some space heaters from somewhere if you don't have enough to get them all running."

"It's Christmas morning," he says, unscrewing a panel. "I don't think anywhere is open."

I already know the answer, but I ask anyway. "What are the chances these furnaces all had this same problem? Today?"

He shakes his head. "Zero. I serviced these myself for the winter a few months ago. They were fine. These are good units. I'd say somebody is up to no good."

Gabrielle is on her way down. I hear her talking to someone at the top of the stairs.

"Merry Christmas," she says to the repairman. "Thank you for coming out."

"It's the rotors," I tell her, like I know what they are.

"In all four systems?" she asks.

I nod.

"JD," she whispers.

"Why don't you go back upstairs? Do whatever needs to be done for the brunch. I'll stay down here." I squeeze her arm. "Don't worry. I called Smith, and he's on his way over. I'm sure some of the other hotels downtown are jealous that you're doing the Christmas brunch. Someone's tweaking you."

"I thought about that, too. The industry is a small, tight community and people talk. I know some of the hoteliers don't feel we've been around long enough to deserve the honor."

If only it were that simple. "We'll figure it out," I tell her. "Once the furnaces are up and running, I'm going to sneak home and change, and then I'll be back."

She chews on her lip and nods.

I watch her climb the stairs, and wonder if there's some other problem waiting to rear its ugly head. Because this is no coincidence. And while it's possible there's a crazy hotel owner orchestrating this malicious prank, my money is elsewhere.

I don't have one foot in my own damn kitchen before Lally starts busting my balls. "Going to join us at St. Cecilia's this morning? Is that why you're up so early?"

"It's been some time since I darkened the doorway of a church." My mother's funeral, to be exact. "Don't want to shock God on Christmas morning. You never know what might happen if he's surprised. The earth might start to wobble."

"It's been some time since you spent the night with a lady, too, but I see that didn't stop you. First time for everything."

"How do you know who I spend the night with? For all you know, I have a different woman holed up here every night and send her away before you show up in the morning. That's what a smart man would do, given that you're such a busybody."

"I said spent the night with a lady. Those floozies you chase are not ladies. And you best not be bringing them here."

"Some people might say you're much too familiar given that you work for me."

"People say a lot of things. Much of it isn't true. And when did you start caring what people say? When you find the love of a good woman to keep you on the straight and narrow, I'll hold my tongue. But not a second before."

"There's about as much chance of you holding your tongue as me finding the love of a good woman. I won't be holding my breath on either account." I hug her. "Merry Christmas, Lally. I'm happy you're not at your cousin's this year."

"Merry Christmas, JD. Grab yourself some fresh coffee and a little something to go with it. Then you better go change before Gabrielle's daddy wakes up and sees you skulking around in the clothes you were wearing yesterday."

"Yes, ma'am," I say, taking the stairs two at a time.

I shut the door to my bedroom and call Chase. "Hey, Merry Christmas."

"JD?"

"Did I wake you?"

"It's Christmas morning, not even seven o'clock," he grunts. "It's not like I wake up at the butt crack of dawn to find out what Santa brought."

"Sorry. I waited until a semi-decent hour to call. This is important. I need you to do something for me."

He groans. "Does this have to do with Gabby again?"

"Someone disabled all four furnaces in the hotel during the night. Nobody saw anything."

"Jesus."

"I need—"

"I know what you need, but I'm not convinced we're going to find anything on the film this time either."

"Try. And if there's nothing there, see if the film's been altered."

"Have you talked to Smith about this?"

"Had to. Smith will want to put the cavalry on this, and Gabrielle's going to balk. But we need to try to get to the bottom of it."

"I'm on it. I'll call you when I know something."

"I appreciate it."

"Yeah, well, you can explain it all to Gabby when she wants to kick my ass for hacking into her security system."

"Pussy."

"JD?"

"Yeah?"

"Why not go to the police?"

"Not sure they can be of any help in this situation. The culprits might be too big for the local police to reel in."

"Who do you think is behind this?"

"I don't know. But I'm hoping you'll turn up something that will help us figure it out."

I'm back at the Gatehouse before eight. I see Gabrielle huddled across the dining room with—Georgina. Their backs are to me, but I'm pretty sure that's Georgie.

Hmmm, she was supposed to be away until after Christmas.

I've known Georgie as long as I've known Gabrielle. Never cared for her. Always thought she was skittish, like she was hiding something, especially as we got older. She was always a huge flirt, but I never had any interest in what she was offering.

The last time we spoke more than a sentence or two was the afternoon she tried to kiss me when we were teenagers. Gabrielle was in the shower, and Georgie plopped herself on my lap and tried to put her lips on mine. I tossed her on her ass, called her a slut, and left.

I never said a word about it to Gabrielle. It would have hurt her too much.

"Merry Christmas, ladies."

They're both startled. Gabrielle practically jumps out of her skin when she hears my voice, and Georgie looks like she's being force-fed lemon wedges.

"Hi, JD. Georgie just stopped by to see if I need help. They got back early from Wade's sister's place. It's supposed to snow in Georgia. Wade doesn't like to drive in the snow."

Gabrielle can't stop blabbering. She says about ten more things. Each one more random than the last. And Georgie's still sucking on lemons.

"Congratulations," I say to Georgina. It seems like the polite thing to do, and although she's still not my favorite person, I've softened considerably toward her over the years. "I hear you're expecting a girl."

"Yes. We just found out—we're having a daughter. Thank you," she answers, turning to Gabrielle. "It looks like you have everything under control here. I should get home to check on Wade. He was still sleeping when I left."

"I'll walk out with you," Gabrielle says.

"Anything I can do while you're gone?" I ask.

Gabrielle shakes her head and smiles. "Believe it or not, we're done with the setup. Now we just wait for the guests to show up."

Georgina hasn't met my eyes once since I walked in. But she doesn't look as sour now that she's about to leave.

"Merry Christmas, Georgie. Give my best to Wade, too."

She nods. "Merry Christmas."

"I'll be right back," Gabrielle mouths to me before they walk away.

I take a quick look around the first floor while she's gone. It's plenty warm, and everything seems under control. I'm about to go back down to the basement when Gabrielle sneaks up behind me.

"Thank you for taking care of things this morning. You were a lifesaver." She slips her arm through mine and pulls me into an empty room off the kitchen. When we get there, she twines her arms around my neck.

"We always made a good team." I dip my head to kiss her. But she pulls back. "What?"

"Nothing," she answers, looking like there's definitely something eating her.

"Nothing, my ass. Is this about Georgie? I thought she was gone until after Christmas?"

"It's not about Georgie," she says defensively. "She and Wade had a fight, so they came home late last night. The snow was just an excuse."

"If it's not about her, what were you about to say?"

"Sometimes—when you say things like we always made a good team. After you say it—your face twists into something painful. I don't know. It makes me feel—I don't know."

"Sad?"

"Sad is too mild of a descriptor for how much it makes my heart hurt."

I cinch her waist and pull her closer, until I can reach her mouth. When all the loose ends are tied up. When the evidence against my father is so strong that he can't wiggle out, it'll be over. She'll be safe. And I'll tell her everything. She'll hate me, but she'll be able to get on with her life, and fall in love with a nice guy from a respectable family, and they can raise a bunch of kids together. My gut's burning just thinking about it. "You got a cup of coffee around here you can spare?"

She nods. "Yes. Anything for you. How about a chocolate croissant to go with that coffee?"

"Anything for me? Is that the same as *anything* I want?"

She nods. "*Anything.* But it'll have to wait a few hours. I only have about twenty minutes before guests start filtering in."

"You won't believe what I can accomplish in twenty minutes," I say, pinning her into a corner. "But you're about to find out," I murmur, sliding a hand under her skirt.

"JD," she pants, while I stroke her pussy over the silky panties.

Her breathless voice makes my cock harder. "I don't have—I can't—someone might see."

"My body blocks you from view. Even if someone walks in, they'll have no idea what we're doing." I lower my head to her ear. "It's much more likely they'll hear you. If you don't want that, you'll need to be really quiet. Can you do that?"

She whimpers something that sounds like *mm*.

"Now be a good girl and spread your legs for me, so I can give you something I've wanted to give you since I opened my eyes this morning."

"Brunch," she squeals. "I have the brunch."

"This will only take a few minutes, darlin'. Trust me. Just think of how nice and relaxed you're going to be for your brunch. How pretty you'll look with a little color in your cheeks."

"*Oh*, JD."

"That's it, baby. Squeeze my fingers with that sweet pussy."

I'm standing near the entrance to the room, nursing a coffee, waiting for Smith to come up from the basement. And I'm watching Gabrielle, who's floating around the room, chatting easily with guests. Anticipating their needs before they have them. She's a natural. And I was right. Her flushed cheeks are gorgeous.

"Hey," Smith says, approaching me from behind. "Step out for a minute."

"Find anything?"

"No." He shakes his head. "Not a goddamn thing."

I blow out a loud breath. I'm disappointed, but not surprised. "Chase came in a few minutes ago. He said he couldn't find anything either. He doesn't think anyone hacked into the system. Said it looked more like someone turned off the cameras from inside the building. Sounds like it's someone who has inside access."

"Maybe. This whole thing feels like amateur hour," Smith says. I hear the frustration and annoyance in his voice. "Any one of these incidents—the tires, the furnaces—could have been perpetrated by any idiot with internet access. I'm starting to think someone has a score to settle with her."

"What about the security cameras?" I nod at a waiter wheeling a cart of cups and saucers past us. "Whoever turned them off knew where to find the cameras."

"They could have flipped the circuit breaker. The cameras are on their own circuit. Everything's marked. We dusted for prints, but I'm not hopeful." Smith leans against the wall and folds his arms across his chest. "This feels personal and petty."

"It wouldn't have been petty if the brunch had been sabotaged or if guests had woken up to cold showers. It would have ruined Gabrielle's opportunity to showcase this place and take it to another level. And it would have been a long time before she got another opportunity like this."

"That's just what I mean. Who does this kind of shit? Someone who's jealous or has a score to settle. And it takes a special kind of perpetrator."

"What does that mean?"

"Think about it." He glances at his feet, and then at me. "If you were pissed at someone, would you steal their keys and slash their tires? Disable their furnace?"

"*Pfft.* No." I don't need a second to think about it.

"Of course not. You would either kick his ass, fuck his woman, or do some real damage to his business. It would be big and splashy. Decisive. Not conniving and sneaky. This is bush league."

"You think it's kids?"

"*Nah.*" He buries his hands in his pockets. "Maybe a woman. Or a guy who doesn't think like a guy."

"A guy who doesn't think like a guy? What the fuck does that mean? Like he's gay?"

"No, asshole. Like he lives with his mother, or he hasn't spent enough time around other guys—bonding and shit. It's a prototype for this kind of behavior."

I pause for a minute before raising the possibility. Smith won't want to hear it, but I can't let it go. "Don't discount my father in any of this. He's got a long reach."

Smith glares at me. He doesn't turn his head. Only his eyes move to meet mine. "I'm going to pretend you didn't just say that."

"Then you're an even dumber bastard than I peg you for." I take a couple of steps forward, until I'm in his face. "I'm telling you, it's in the realm of real possibilities."

Smith sidesteps me and brings his hands to his face, scrubbing the weariness away. "Why don't you go check on Gabrielle. I'll handle things on this end." He starts to leave, but turns before he gets five feet away. "JD?"

I'm sure this is more shit about how my father is the president-elect, and how I need to resolve my daddy issues in therapy. "What?" I challenge.

He glances at me for a second and shakes his head. "Nothing."

30

Gabrielle

"Okay, just one more thingy to glue on," I say proudly to Georgie while I hunt for a glittery pink heart. We're sitting at Georgie's dining room table, making a growth chart for the baby's room, one of those long sticks that hangs on the wall. The one we're making has a ballerina at the top, pirouetting on a unicorn.

"It's gorgeous," Georgie gushes. "I can't believe how crafty you are."

"I hope she loves it," I muse, adding the final heart.

"She will. She'll love all the things we made. Especially the part where her mama and her godmother spent hours planning and painting. I want her to grow up to be the kind of girl who appreciates that part of a gift most of all."

"She will. How could she not with you and Wade as her parents?"

"I'm putting all of it in my pregnancy journal. Every detail, so she can know how excited we were while we waited for her."

"One day you need to let those journals inspire you to write a book."

"One day," she says wistfully. "It's on my bucket list, but I'm not sure I want that kind of inspiration. I wish you had brought the quarterly reports with you. I don't sleep well when Wade's gone. I could have worked on them."

"I'll drop them by tomorrow."

"Maybe I'll follow you back to the hotel when we're done here. It won't be that late."

"Georgie, the baby will be here any time now. You are not driving around alone at night to get some stupid reports that aren't due for another month. What if your water breaks or something?"

"First babies aren't born that quickly," she says, peering out the window again. "I keep thinking that car out there is someone lurking."

"It is."

"Besides your security. I've felt that way all afternoon. I guess it's Wade being gone. This is his last overnight trip until after the baby's born."

"I'm glad. Everything good between you two?"

"Better since I talked to him about it, but I don't think things will get back to normal until after the baby comes. It's not that unusual for expectant fathers to have anxiety before the baby's born. That's what all the books say."

"Imagine if they actually had to push it out?" I roll my eyes. "They'd need to be on anti-anxiety meds for the entire pregnancy."

We laugh, but Georgie's looking out the window again. "Have you gotten used to them following you around everywhere?"

"Rafe and Gus? Pretty much. They really do melt into the background unless I think about them. Then I get prickly at JD, even though he means well. Have you watched any of the inauguration coverage today?"

"No."

"I haven't seen much either. Although I did catch JD scowling on national television. Do you mind if I turn on the news?"

"Go ahead. The remote's above the TV."

Georgie gets quiet and tense when the news comes on. The reporters are talking about President Wilder. She still hasn't warmed up to the idea of JD and me together. And after that day in the hotel when they met by accident, I'm beginning to think she never will.

There's a split screen on the television. The politicians preening in their fancy clothes on one side, and the warehouse fires burning out of control, a few miles away from here, on the other side. "Wow. I can't believe they haven't gotten that fire under control. It's been burning most of the day."

"It keeps spreading," she says. "There have been multiple explosions. Thankfully those buildings weren't occupied."

I hear Georgie, but my eyes and my mind are on JD, whose handsome face is on the screen now. It's a shot from earlier. He's with Gray and Chase. They're watching as their father takes the oath of office. Their faces reveal nothing. Not a trace of emotion. Certainly no pride or joy.

"You still love him," Georgie says, when she catches me red-handed, sneaking a peek at him. "I see it every time you bring up his name. Even if you're cursing him while you do it."

"I'll always love him, Georgie. I've told you, it's my cross to bear. Even if we don't end up together, I'll always love him. When he walked into the hotel after all that time, I knew. I knew that night, even through all the rage, even as I chucked a vase at him and got water all over his fancy suit, I knew I would always love him. No matter what he did. No matter how awful it is. I'm such a wuss when it comes to him. It makes me so mad sometimes."

"*Hmmm*. That's a powerful kind of attraction. I'm not sure I feel that way about Wade, and I love him with all my heart and soul. But JD was your first love."

I nod. "That's part of it. Another part is that we had sex kind of young."

"I know, but lots of people have sex kind of young and they don't feel it forever."

"Dirty sex."

Georgina's lips twitch. "Dirty sex?" She giggles. "Is that like kinky sex?"

"Just like that."

"Oh my God." She puts her hand over her mouth to stifle the laugh, but her chest is heaving. "How come you never told me that part?"

"It was embarrassing to think about in the light of day, let alone say the words out loud. And I don't know, I guess it was private. It seemed like it would be more special if we just kept it to ourselves."

"You could make up for it by spilling the beans about what you're doing now. A pregnant beluga who can barely move her body during sex could use hearing how the fit and fabulous are doing the deed."

I swat her away. "It's not about first love, or sex. There's something about JD that—completes my soul. Sounds so stupid, doesn't it?"

She shrugs, but a building on the screen implodes in flames before she can respond. "Sweet Jesus. Look at that." She clutches her belly. "It's awful. I pray to God they're right and no one's stuck inside those buildings. What an awful way to die." She shudders.

"I'm turning it off. It's not good for a pregnant woman, or for me, to watch this kind of thing before bed. It'll bring on nightmares."

31

Julian

Today has been the clusterfuck of all clusterfucks. If I had to listen to any more bullshit about the new president and his handsome family, I was going to puke or punch someone, or maybe both. I almost hauled the Speaker of the House off the dais during lunch to tell him to stop lying to the American people about how impressive and wonderful the Wilders are. *Fuck that.* We're just a bunch of dysfunctional assholes posing as a family. We clean up pretty well, but that's just for show.

I settle into the backseat of the limo and call Gabrielle. "Hey, gorgeous."

"Hey yourself," she says. "Are you at one of the inaugural balls?"

"Hell no. I'm in a car on my way to the airport."

"You didn't look very happy today."

"Not a lot to be happy about here. I showed up for Gray and

Chase, that's it. This is all bullshit. I want to be home—wrapped around your naked body. Or maybe making you crawl across the floor to me. Or tying you to the bed and licking your pussy until you scream. The possibilities are endless."

"Promises, promises."

"All of which I intend to keep. What did you do tonight while the ass-kissers were out in full force all over our nation's capital?"

"I had dinner with Georgina. Wade's away for a couple nights. We made a list of the last-minute things she needs before the baby and put the finishing touches on the nursery. Tom covered at the hotel. He's really stepping up into the manager role."

"Sounds so much nicer than how I spent my evening. I'm glad Tom's working out. Don't demote him when Georgina gets back from maternity leave. If you keep him as a manager, it'll free you up for me more often."

"I can't afford another big salary. Not if I want to buy that building behind me when it comes up for sale at the end of the year."

"I can afford it."

"No. And don't bring it up again, or the only person crawling will be you to beg my forgiveness."

"*Pfft.* I'll crawl when pigs fly. Maybe not even then."

"Have you seen what's happening on the Port of Charleston?"

I hear anxiety in her voice.

"I caught bits and pieces, but the national news has been covering the inauguration pretty much nonstop all day."

"It's a multi-alarm fire. They can't seem to get it under control. There's a black cloud of smoke over the city—I can see the flames from my room. It's scary. I turned off the news because it's too awful to watch."

"Gabrielle, we're approaching the tarmac. I need to get off the phone in a minute."

"Safe travels. And say hello to Smith for me."

"I left Smith behind. He didn't want to stay in DC either. But my brothers are still here, and they don't have Secret Service protection, either. I want him to keep an eye on them. Gabrielle?"

"*Hmmm?*"

"The only fire I want you thinking about is the one between your legs."

"It lit as soon as I heard your voice."

She says it so seductively, I want to take out my cock and stroke it.

"Don't you dare touch *my* pussy," I warn her, in a low voice. "Be a good girl and go to sleep. I'll ease that burn for you tomorrow. Sweet dreams, darlin'."

32

Gabrielle

I shoot up out of bed when the smoke alarm blares. Before my eyes have adjusted to the dark, Rafe is in my room.

"There's a fire downstairs!" he yells over the screeching alarm.

"A fire!?" I scream. For a second, I wonder if it's a dream. If this is a nightmare about the warehouse fires. But Rafe's hand is on my arm. It's not a dream. "Where? Where is the fire?" I shout, trying to be heard over the alarm, as he drags me toward the stairs.

"Back offices. I'll find out for sure as soon as you're out of the building."

"No. No!" I yank my arm away. "We have a security plan in case of fire. I need to make sure everyone's out first." I grab a small knapsack from the corner of the room. "Where's Gus?" I shout, closing the door behind us. I can smell the smoke now that we're in the hall.

"He went home sick about an hour ago."

When we get to the third floor, guests in pajamas are on their way down the stairs. Everyone is moving in an orderly fashion. I stand to the side and take out two hand towels, and soak them with water from the knapsack. I hand one to Rafe. "Cover your mouth and nose." I also hand him a fat piece of white chalk. "Check all the rooms on the second floor, and place a large white mark on the outside of each door after you've cleared the room. I'll check the third floor. Amy at the desk is responsible for the first floor."

"I'll do the third," he says. "You get out of the building."

"No. We don't have time to argue."

"Fine, do the second," he says, "and then get the hell out of the building."

"Meet us in the parking lot across the street when you're done," I yell, running down the stairs.

The smoke is thicker as I make my way to the first floor. We've practiced this drill countless times, and it looks like everything has gone according to plan.

When I step onto the sidewalk, I don't hear any sirens approaching. I run across the street to Amy, who is gathered with hotel guests, checking names off.

"Everyone's accounted for," she says.

I don't see Rafe, yet.

"Did you check the first floor?" I ask.

"Tom did," she says. "He told me to come outside and start moving guests away from the building."

"Where is he?"

"He went around the building to make sure no one's in the parking lot."

I finally hear sirens. I scan the area for any sign of Rafe or Tom. When I look down the street, I see it. *Georgina.* That's Georgie's car!

"Amy," I shriek. "Have you seen Georgie?"

"No."

"That's her car."

The back office. Oh my God.

I grab the wet towel and run back inside, covering my mouth and nose. The smoke is thick as I feel my way to the back of the hotel. By the time I reach the office, I can't see more than six inches in front of me. I put my hand on the knob. It's red-hot. I scream and take in a mouthful of smoke.

"Georgie!" I shout. "Georgie!" She doesn't answer. I get down to try to find something to smash the door with. I'm crawling, one hand keeping the towel over my mouth. But it's not working well anymore. I can't keep the smoke out. My eyes sting. I can't see anything. I can't breathe.

33

Julian

The plane stops taxiing, and I look out the window to see Antoine running across the tarmac toward us.

Zack. Something happened to Zack.

I call Antoine's cell phone while the flight crew is unlatching the door, but he doesn't pick up.

"Gabby's hotel—the Gatehouse," he yells from the bottom of the steps as soon as the door opens. "It's on fire."

"What do you mean, it's on fire?" I race down the stairs and grab him by the shirt. "What do you mean?"

"They're saying on the radio, the Gatehouse is in flames. I can't get service out here on my phone. That's all I know."

"Let's go!"

Smoke permeates every molecule of air, and even with the windows up, the ghastly odor wheedles its way into the car. It's all I smell as Antoine weaves through downtown toward the Gatehouse.

I have no information about Gabrielle.

The fire marshal isn't taking calls, and neither the police chief nor the mayor has anything useful to offer. Not a fucking thing.

I try her again, but my call goes directly to voicemail. Rafe and Gus don't answer either.

"Antoine, turn up the volume."

The news accounts are sketchy, and the reporters at the scene keep repeating the same bullshit: The fire department has been working overtime today. They're spread so thin that reinforcements from the surrounding areas have been called in to assist. Everyone was evacuated from the hotel immediately after the fire started, but those reports are unconfirmed. *Blah, blah, blah.* Nothing. They've got nothing.

I scroll through my phone, searching for answers. Hoping there's been some mistake. Hoping it's another building with a similar name, or a structure nearby that's engulfed in flames. But the internet is too wrapped up with the inaugural crap to care much about the Charleston fires. What the first lady wore. What a handsome couple the president and his wife make. How the country is embarking on an exciting new path.

Right. A new path—straight to hell. And this road is not paved with a single good intention.

My father. He's behind this. Somehow, he's behind it. *Not on Inauguration Day, JD.* No, he wouldn't want the focus off him today. And he wouldn't burn an entire section of the city to get back at me—would he? Gabrielle's hotel, yes. He'd have it torched without a second thought. But the warehouses are too important to him.

My brain wars with itself, the logical versus the illogical. But my gut knows it's him.

Fuckfuckfuckfuckfuck. I pound on the car roof in a desperate attempt to blow off steam, but all it does is punish my hands.

The ride from the airport to downtown normally takes Antoine twenty minutes, but tonight we make it in ten. The longest ten minutes of my life.

We're still several blocks away, but the smoke is getting thicker. I can't tell if it's coming from the Port of Charleston where the warehouse fires are still burning, or the French Quarter, where the Gatehouse is located.

Hundreds of images of Gabrielle tick through my brain. Some old, and others, brand-new. She's smiling. Laughing. Crying. Reaching for me.

I'm shaking inside, ready to jump out of my skin.

As we turn the corner onto Broad Street, a sea of flashing lights illuminates the crowd gathered in the road ahead, their eyes glued to the orange flames licking the night sky. "Pull over. Right here. You won't get any closer."

I don't wait for him to pull over. Before he brakes, my feet are on the cobblestones, racing toward the flames as fast as I have ever run.

Dozens of onlookers watch the blaze from across the road. A few are barefoot, using scraps of cardboard as makeshift rugs to protect their feet from the cold ground. Others are in flimsy pajamas with their arms wrapped around one another to stay warm. The scene is chaotic as people push their way into the crowd to get a better look. I glance at the burning building, and my heart drops into my stomach. Please no. Please.

Panic fuels me as I scour the growing crowd for Gabrielle. For her security detail. For anyone who can tell me a fucking thing.

I search frantically. Person to person. Every dark-haired woman gives me a fresh sliver of hope. But it's dashed again and again.

Only a couple minutes have passed, but it feels like an eternity. I can't find her anywhere.

Gabrielle, where are you?

I slide both hands into my hair and pull. *Dammit, where is she?*

Inside. She has to be inside. As I make a beeline for the building, I spot Rafe in the parking lot across the street. He's getting oxygen.

I reach him in seconds and pull the mask away from his face. "Where is she?" I scream.

"Hey!" The paramedic tears the mask from my hand.

"Don't know," Rafe chokes out. "Can't find her."

A roar erupts from somewhere deep inside my chest. It's raw and primal, reminiscent of the chilling howl that comes right before an animal surrenders to its predator.

THANK you for reading DEPRAVED! I hope you loved JD and Gabrielle, and the dangerous, delicious world of Charleston. Find out what happens next in DELIVERED **HERE**

FOR SNEAK PEEKS and treats sign-up for my newsletter **HERE**

JOIN me in my group, JD'S CLOSET for all sorts of shenanigans **HERE**

If you enjoyed Depraved, please consider leaving a short review. Thank you!

ACKNOWLEDGMENTS

Writing a book is always a huge endeavor with lots of ups and downs, but writing this book was particularly daunting. It was loads of fun, but it was also hard at times, and there was a lot of internal strife. I often worried that I'd bitten off more than I could chew. Fortunately, I had a ton of love and support along the way, much more than I deserve.

I am blessed, and I don't say that lightly, to have so many wonderful people in my corner. I will be forever grateful for your kindness, generosity, and support. Thank you to everyone who helped breathe life into J.D. and Gabrielle's story!

A huge thank you and a big hug to Veronica Adams of L. Woods PR. Depraved wouldn't exist without your initial nudge and ongoing encouragement. You have helped me grow in ways that still amaze me. And that voodoo magic with the ghost links? I bow to you, woman!

A very big thank you to Dawn Alexander of Evident Ink, who provided content editing. Although content editing doesn't begin to describe everything you did to whip me into shape. Your input, and those pesky thought bubbles I see in my sleep, brought the characters to life. But more, I thank you for all your time and good humor as you guided me through the process.

To Nancy Smay of Evident Ink, who edited the manuscript. First, thank you for accepting me as a client! I wasn't joking about holding my breath while awaiting your response. Second, your attention to detail, big and small, made the story shine. Third, I hope you know you're stuck with me forever. I'll camp on your doorstep if necessary.

Thank you to Lisa LaPaglia of Evident Ink for your careful proofreading, and insight. Every author needs someone like you in her life. But I'm still not telling whether Georgie set the fire.

A heartfelt thank you to Virginia Carey who I trust to be the very last set of eyes on my books before release. Your eagle eye during the final proofread always catches the little things no one else does. When you say a manuscript is ready to go out into the world, it is. More, I cherish your support and friendship.

A colossal thank you to Letitia Hasser of RBA Designs, who perfectly captured the broody J.D. on the original lickable cover. And thank you to Wander Aguiar who shot that amazing photograph, and to the very sweet Zack Salaun for being the perfect JD, albeit in looks alone.

A giant thank you to Murphy Rae who created the gorgeous "object" covers! You took my simple, primitive idea and turned it into something dazzling. I hope that my story does your stunning cover art justice.

A big thank you hug to Michelle Rodriquez, secret keeper extraordinaire, who read the first draft of the manuscript and gave J.D. the thumbs up for being just the right amount of *a**hole!* Your experience in these matters is unparalleled. Thank you for all your support and friendship, Wonder Woman.

Thank you to L. Woods PR, Enticing Journey, Give Me Books, and RRR Promotion. You are highly organized, wonderful to work with, and just plain amazing.

I don't even know how to begin to thank the bloggers who

have given Depraved so much love. *Gahhh!!!* I appreciate your generosity, and your willingness to take a chance on an author who was dipping her toes into the dark for the first time. *Eva who?* I'm keenly aware that despite your professionalism, you are not paid for your time. I will always be grateful for everything you did to help launch The Devil's Duet.

To the readers, my New American Royals' readers who followed me into the shadows, and to all the new readers who found me through Depraved, a big, big heartfelt thank-you for reading my dirty little story, telling friends about it, leaving a review, or contacting me with kind words. Thank you for taking this journey with me. I'm truly humbled by your generous spirit and support. I don't deserve it, but I'm gobbling it all up anyway. My heart is full.

Andy, there really are no words to thank you for supporting everything I do, always—even when it means everyone you work with will now know I have a kinky imagination and a potty mouth. (It should make the next gala interesting.) You are the love of my life. There's no one I'd rather spend forever with.

ABOUT THE AUTHOR

After being a confirmed city-girl for most of her life, Eva moved to beautiful Western Massachusetts in 2014. There, she found herself living in the woods with no job, no friends (unless you count the turkey, deer, and coyote roaming the backyard), and no children underfoot, wondering what on earth she'd been thinking. But as it turned out, it was the perfect setting to take all those yarns spinning in her head and weave them into sexy stories.

When she's not writing, trying to squeeze information out of her tight-lipped sons, or playing with the two cutest dogs you've ever seen, Eva's creating chapters in her own love story.

Sign-up for my monthly newsletter for special treats and all the Eva news! VIP Reader Newsletter

I'd love to keep in touch!!
eva@evacharles.com

Check out my website!
evacharles.com

MORE STEAMY ROMANTIC SUSPENSE BY EVA CHARLES

THE DEVIL'S DUE

DEPRAVED

DELIVERED

BOUND

DECADENT

A SINFUL EMPIRE TRILOGY

A SINFUL EMPIRE (A Prologue Novella)

GREED

LUST

ENVY

CONTEMPORARY ROMANCE

THE NEW AMERICAN ROYALS SERIES

SHELTERED HEART

NOBLE PURSUIT

DOUBLE PLAY

UNFORGETTABLE

LOYAL SUBJECTS

SEXY SINNER

Made in the USA
Monee, IL
17 June 2024